HEROES

ARTHUR MAYOR

ONE

As soon as I reached the alley Feral was done being carried and nipped my fingers until I let him down.

"Just ask." I sucked my finger. Again, just a playful bite.

Raptor's protocols always told me to never take the same route from nest to home. It was so drilled into me, that I forgot it didn't matter anymore.

It was now eleven-thirty. There would be no pretending that I'd rushed home as soon as Mom had told me to come. I was putting off the inevitable. At this point she was probably already in bed.

Tomorrow, if she had time before getting to work, there would be hell to pay.

What was I doing? What did I want to do?

Two weeks ago it had seemed so clear. No, not even two weeks. It was thirteen days ago when Raptor fired me. I'd wanted to be a full member of the Guard. But now I didn't even know what that would mean. And would I still want it if I could have it?

I'd been in situations where people had died, a lot of people. The poor axe guy was just the latest. I'd only avoided death myself by chance more than once in the last week.

If Raptor dropped from the sky right now and asked me to start fresh, would I do it?

I wasn't paying attention to my surroundings, but before I knew it, I was standing in front of my house. The house I had lived in all my life. In the dark it didn't look as neglected as it did in daylight. You couldn't tell the concrete in the front step was disintegrating, or that the siding needed paint. The lawn was mowed, but that was just because I was trying hard last week. Usually it was a week or two overdue.

Why would I give up all this, just to be a hero?

I gave one last look around to make sure no one had followed me. I don't know who would want to.

The neighborhood looked just like it always did, although someone had gotten a nice car. Probably a rental. It looked like a rental.

Feral bowled into me and arched his back into my legs. He looked at me, then the house.

"Sure, she's not going to be mad at you. You she'll feed."

The mention of food was good enough to get Feral going, and he was scratching at the door before I caught up to him.

The door opened at the scratching. She must have been right at the door waiting for me.

She'd been crying, her eyes red and puffy. "Ryan." Her voice was scratchy, but firm. "It's late." She backed away from the door and I entered.

My excuse died on my lips. Don't know why. You'd think the sheer weight of habit would have carried it out of my mouth.

"Hi, Ryan," my dad said.

"Dad?" That was a legitimate question. I hadn't seen my dad in over a year. It was a cognitive dissonance, like walking into a football stadium and seeing your third period teacher ready for class.

"We have to talk. Sit," Mom said.

Well, now I knew why she'd been crying. Dad had that effect on her. She took a seat and so did Dad. The chair pulled out for me put them directly across from me.

"What's---"

"Just sit, Ryan," Mom snapped. She was hanging on by a thread to be that jumpy.

I sat.

They exchanged a look. Maybe at some point they could have communicated with just a look. When I was nine, they would scold me like this. Or Mindy. Gosh, I hadn't thought of Mindy for a while, but seeing my parents together brought everything back. I was nine again, and the cops were at the door.

Mom's "We have some-" was crossed with Dad's "Your mother and I--"

He waved her to start, but she couldn't. More tears, and she looked away.

Dad looked at me, then away. Was he embarrassed, or ashamed of me? "Your mother and I have been talking."

"I can tell." I didn't mean to sound that angry. Must be because I was that angry. "What are you doing here?"

He wiped his hands across his face, then gazed at me. "I'm moving into the city for work."

"Marrying rich means you need to relocate to the city?" By the look in his eyes, Dad thought that was a cheap shot, but I thought it was a valid question.

"My father-in-law's company is opening a branch in

Darhaven. I'll be transferring to that branch." He said it like I hadn't just pointed at the elephant in the room.

What did old Not-Grandpa do? I couldn't remember. I could ask, but I got the feeling that wasn't the point of this little sit down. And I didn't care.

"Well, if you guys need to rent out the basement for offices, I guess I'm cool with that. Good chat."

He stopped my standing with a hand. "Let me finish, then you can start the disrespectful jokes."

"Okay, one, you don't get to tell me when I can start with the disrespectful jokes. By the nature of them being disrespectful, I really can't wait on your timing. Otherwise that would be respectful jokes and that's not my vibe. Two, YOU get to tell me exactly Jack and Crap. You don't have a dad card to play. You tossed that in the discard pile seven years ago." See what I did, extending the metaphor? Nice to see even when I'm filled with righteous indignation, I've still got it.

"Stop!" And my righteous indignation took it to the chin. "Just stop," Mom said. "Sit down and let him speak."

I sank back in my chair.

"You're right." Dad said it twice, but it was in such a small voice I didn't really hear him the first time. "I did... make a mistake."

I inhaled to examine that phrase,

"I made a lot of mistakes." He cut me off. "And those mistakes impacted you and your mother most of all. I can't make up for that. I can't undo it. But I can help now."

"I don't want your help." The words were out of my mouth before I knew I was going to respond.

"You're not going to graduate!" Mom said.

I blinked. "What?"

She turned to the kitchen table without getting up,

picked up a piece of paper, and handed it to me. "You're not going to graduate."

The embossed logo of my school's seal was centered on the top of the stationery. Made it look official. My credit report showed a different date of graduation than next June.

"I'll make it up."

"That would have been in summer school, this summer. This summer that is almost over," she said.

The guidance counselor had called me to her office more than once, but I'd just used it as an excuse to skip class. I'm sure they'd tried to call home, but we don't have an answering machine. Just makes it easier to avoid collection agencies.

"It'll just be an additional quarter, less if I can get some classes taken care of next summer," I said.

"It's not just graduation." She was exhausted and frustrated. Her tears weren't because of Dad, they were because of *me*. "It's all of it. You're out all hours of the night, you only give me excuses. You drift in and out of this house like a ghost."

"I'm trying, This week--"

"This week ended the same way every week ends. It's midnight, and I don't know where my son is!" Desperation now.

"I--"

"No! I don't want to hear it, not unless you're finally going to tell me the truth!"

This would have been a good time to say something, but I didn't. I couldn't lie anymore, or at least right now. And I couldn't tell her the truth.

"Your mother and I think it would be a good idea for you to come live with me and Shar," Dad said.

Mom looked slapped, but didn't disagree. She didn't say anything. She sat back and her shoulders sunk in on herself.

"It wouldn't be like before. You would still be in the city, but have access to better schools." Dad kept talking, getting out his sales pitch while everyone else was too stunned to interject. "You can get to know your brother and sister."

"Half," I said, again pure instinct. "I knew my sister. You might remember her if you think hard, back to your crappy life."

He slouched in his chair. "That's not fair. Not a day goes by that I don't think about Mindy."

"No, you don't get to sit in this house and say that!" I stood so fast the chair hit the floor. "You ran! You ran away from all of this as soon as you could. You left us!"

"I didn't leave--"

"What is that supposed to mean?" Mom was ramrod straight again. "Are you saying it was my fault?"

"No." He put up his hands. "I'm just saying it wasn't my choice to leave."

"I kicked your worthless butt out, but you left inside a bottle a long time before that," she screamed. "And you come back here glad that I screwed up and couldn't raise Ryan without you!"

"I want to help," Dad started.

"You can't help!" I said. "You had an opportunity to help, seven years ago. Instead you left, and never looked back. Now you come here in your expensive suits, fancy rental cars, and apartments on the Island and think that you can rub your good fortune in our faces? Sorry Dad, unlike you, Mindy getting shot down by gang bangers wasn't the best thing that ever happened to us."

I knew I'd gone too far. About a mile back was too far.

But I couldn't take it back. I wouldn't. I'd just go farther because when you're on a roll... "He said I wasn't worth his time and I guess you think that, too!" They would have no context for that statement. It might sound weird, but I couldn't slow down, never mind stop. "Sorry I'm such a disappointment to you both." I'm not going to say it, I'm not going to say it. "It's too bad that I didn't eat the bullet and Mindy would be here so you could have your perfect life." And I said it. That was three states over from too far, but I couldn't stop myself.

Dad stood up, his face turning red.

Mom just sat there, her mouth opening and shutting.

"Screw this." I left through the door I'd entered.

TWO

I just got a phone call from a dead man.

Let me explain. It's complicated.

I say "just," but in reality it was about two hours ago. I had to catch three busses and a delivery truck to get across town. And I do mean "catch." I can't just hail a cab or use my bus card when in uniform. For one thing it would be awkward, like going to a party in a costume that isn't a costume party. For a second thing, I'm wanted by six or seven federal and state agencies for illegal vigilante activity.

Everybody freaks out when those of us with superpowers try to help out.

Yes, I have superpowers, but they are not that super. I can't fly or run super fast or even skip real well. So if I want to get around town I either run and hop rooftops, or I hop onto a big vehicle going my way.

Don't try this at home kids, because who would want a city bus in their home?

I say phone call, but I mean text. I got an address. That's it. No, "Hey, good job saving the world or at least a couple of city blocks. I was wrong about that whole 'you don't have what it takes' thing. Drinks on me." What I got instead was an address in an area of town that was crap.

It was crap for two reasons. One, it was in Darhaven, the city that snatched corruption and decay from the jaws of the American Dream. Reason two, it was by the Docks. I didn't know the Dockyard area. I mean, I knew it in the broad strokes, but not enough to have memorized routes I could parkour my way around. I didn't have a GPS in my gear. My mentor was paranoid about that kind of technology.

And when I say "dead" what I mean is, I think he's dead. Raptor was my mentor for a year plus. He was a jerk, but he never missed a day of work. Then all of a sudden when everything went sideways, he was nowhere to be found. Also, a crazy guy who was crazy on crazy wrapped in crazy with a generous sprinkling of plain nuts told me he killed him.

It's been ten days, and it still hurts. Raptor is gone.

Or is he? There was no body. It's probably buried under a building that collapsed on him. So I just got a text from a dead man.

This isn't the first time Raptor gave me little missions like this. It was part of the training. I never had to take two hours out of my day before, but I would get cryptic messages like this, go to the address, get an encoded message, decode it and follow the directions.

It was a pain in the ass.

Figures that Raptor had found a way to be a pain in the ass from beyond the grave.

So here I was, in the rain...did I say it started raining? And in the dark. Every part of this city was dark, every third street light was still working in the less crappy parts of town. This part of town had no such luxury.

I managed to get to a warehouse that overlooked my target, only a narrow alley separating the two buildings.

Did I mention it was raining? Nothing like a good climb in the dark on wet surfaces. Best Day Ever!

And this was probably for nothing! Why was I here? Even if Raptor set this little training course up for me, he fired me before he died. Probably died.

I checked the heads up display. I will say this about Raptor, he did have some fun toys. My mom's calls had capped out at seventeen.

Why was I here?

I had spent a few days healing from some bruises. I can't fly but I heal on the quick side. I'd also been building trust with Mom. I'd been trying to get some closure, a little ceremony with my fellow apprentices, the only surviving members of the Guard. I'd promised I would be home twelve refused messages ago.

But Raptor had sent me a text, and I'd dropped everything to go across town.

The message ticker clicked over to eighteen.

She had never called me this much. I answered.

"Hi, Mom. Sorry--"

"You need to come home right now! Where are you?" I could hear the broken heart in her voice.

"I just lost track of time." I always said that.

"Things have--" She paused. "You just need to come home." Translation: "You always lose track of time and I'm sick of fighting about it."

"Yea, I'll be home soon." Hopefully I could shave some time off how long it took me to get here, and I could get to my nest, take off my uniform, and get home in like two or three hours. "I..." What? Was sorry? At some point that doesn't work. I'd crossed that point over a year ago. "I'll come home."

"Ryan." It was weird hearing my real name when I was in uniform. It always gave me a little panic flutter. "Just come home." She didn't believe me, an unfortunate side effect of not being believable.

"Heading home right now." Just after I do a meaningless task for someone who won't know I did it. "I love you, Mom. Bye."

She tried to say goodbye, but she sobbed instead.

Nice, Ryan, keep up the good work.

She hung up first.

My insides warred for a second. Angel: get back home now! You've caused enough pain to your mother, and it isn't like there are lives on the line. You're out. You can't keep playing superhero without Raptor's support. Start trying to make up for the last...forever...to your mom and stop being a tool.

Devil: Sure, but you're already here, and the ten minutes it will take to check the place out isn't going to matter to her one way or the other. And besides, if you don't at least check it out then pissing her off will really be for nothing.

As God is my witness, I was going to follow the Angel.

THREE

I was so going to follow the Angel.

Go home.

Walk the strait and narrow.

Start a rewarding career in the food service industry. I mean, I really do want to know if you would like fries with that. I do.

A van pulled up to the warehouse.

As a rule, I don't have anything against vans. It showed up at ten-thirty, not really all that suspicious. It's late, but this is the Docks. There's all kinds of activity in this area.

But it caught my eye.

A side door opened, and a man came out. This guy looked like a card-carrying member of a reputable motorcycle gang. He had a beard that could support an ecosystem, a jean jacket with arms ripped off, and let's just say that the man worked out and loved his ink.

Also, on a big patch on his back he had two crossed axes over a skull, the logo of the Headsmen. The Headsmen are the elite henchmen of one Jack Midas. Now that Caesar's dead, Midas is the heir apparent to take over the city. There will be gallons and gallons of blood spilt before he gets the crown, but there isn't anyone close to Midas right now.

The bearded man also had an eye patch. I saw it when he crossed the headlights of the van.

He talked briefly to the van driver, and the van drove in.

Two weeks ago if I'd been on patrol and seen this, I would have called in Raptor and let the adults handle it from there. I might have hung around the perimeter and made sure no civilians got hurt, or let Raptor know if evil reinforcements arrived before the Guard was done busting heads.

This week, I am the Guard. The five full members were all dead, and the four other apprentices all retired as of two hours ago. There was no Raptor, no support, no one else.

Angel: According to all the protocols that Raptor taught you -- back away.

Devil: But it was Raptor who brought you here. There might be something that he wants you to see.

Angel: And what are you going to do if you see something?

Devil: Yeah, that's a point. I mean, you walked away from that whole thing with Clockwork, but you needed and had a lot of help.

Angel: But what if it's human trafficking? A lot of that kind of stuff happens at the Docks.

Devil: There could be a baby sausage factory, but what are you going to do about it?

Angel: Well, you should at least see if there's anything to be done about it. Raptor wouldn't send you some place that wasn't important.

Devil: You're a poopy face.

Shut up the both of you.

Okay, I'd have to check this out. And if it didn't register at least an eight on the horrible-o-meter, I'd sneak away.

Yeah, that should work. Seriously, it should work. I wasn't being sarcastic. This will work.

I leapt from my vantage to the corner of the building. I didn't dare land on the roof. That might have been noticed, but I grabbed onto the edge of the building.

I know what you're thinking. Didn't I say it was raining? What if the ledge was too slippery to gain purchase?

To that I would say, "Where were you ten seconds ago!"

I had that moment where I thought I was going to slip, then the relief that I was not going to fall.

Then I fell.

Twist, scramble, scramble, and I stopped my momentum on a window ledge.

Okay, not a great start. Get your head in the game Raven. You have to leave the mom stuff and deal with this stuff.

I hung there, making sure I had a good grip, but also listening for signs that I'd been heard.

The rain must have been making enough noise to hide my scramble down the wall. At least no one came to check it out.

Just in case, I used a small decorative ledge to make my way to another window. The lock was easy to jimmy, and I was in.

The warehouse wasn't one of the abandoned buildings that blighted the city. It was actually being used for whatever business still happened on the Docks. I could have started opening crates to make sure there wasn't any obvious crime happening, but if I'd found anything, what would I have done about it? Leave a strongly worded letter? It wasn't like l had any kind of police powers. If the cops showed up, they would be more interested in arresting a vigilante over the Headsmen.

I walked around a little more, listening for anything.

This was stupid. Right now the only thing I knew was that a member of the Headsmen let a van park here. I may have just uncovered an illegal valet service. This could go all the way to the school board.

If I didn't find some sign of evil soon, I was bugging out. I had an apology to compose.

A woman screamed. Not the scream of joy one might use when presented with the brand new van of their dreams. The other kind of scream. The torture kind of scream.

Angel: You have to help her!

Devil: Yeah, what he said.

If there was any backup I would have called, but even if the other apprentices had still been monitoring the line, it would have taken them the better part of an hour to get there.

The women screamed, "No!"

No time.

I kept low, but gave speed more focus than stealth as I moved from crate to crate in the direction of the scream.

I was on the second floor. The center looked like it was open spaces.

I saw the flare of a cigarette butt and pulled back before the smoker saw me. I peered around the corner. His back was against the wall by the loading elevators. He had an actual axe over his shoulder. A ridiculously huge axe. A styrofoam axe that big would be unwieldy for a normal human. This guy had it one-handed and was smoking a cigarette with the other. He was what we in the industry refer to as a brute. A parahuman level 1, with superhuman strength. Para level 1s don't have any kind of powers that vanilla humans don't have, they just had more of it than normal humans.

I'm a Para level 1 kinist. Think photographic memory for your muscles. I could learn to do any physical activity eighty millions times faster than normal. Came in handy when learning martial arts, acrobatics, and parkour.

A Brute was similar, but they put on muscle mass ten to twenty times faster than a normal. This one had that Nordic god of thunder thing going. His blond hair was in a ponytail, and he wore a leather jacket with the crossed axes and skull of the Headsmen.

When you've been in the industry for as long as I have, you can put these clues together and infer that man was a member of the Headsmen.

He was not in the running for Headsmen of the year, however. If he was supposed to be guarding, his heart wasn't in it.

I snuck around him.

The center of the building had a couple of large crates, and stacks of crates that reached my level. Might as well have been an elevator to a guy like me.

In the center was some kind of medical set up.

A woman was bound to a gurney. Several electrodes connected her to an EKG. The person monitoring the device wore red robes and a hood. He had black gloves except for his thumbs.

The combination sounded familiar, like I'd read about it in one of the files Raptor continually forced me to study. All the known supers were on my reading list, especially ones known to use their powers for evil.

But except for the Darhaven residents, I could never keep all the names straight.

Standing to the side was another Headsmen. This guy was sporting a man bun and glowing. His body type was the exact opposite of Nordic the Barbarian. He was a hundred and ninety pounds soaking wet, and over six feet. His name was Arc.

His file I remembered. He was a Para level 2.8 who had control of this blue electricity, and was a member of the Twelve, the ruling body and elite warriors of the Headsmen.

"Confessor, how much longer is this going to take?" Arc asked.

The Confessor! That's it! I remember. He... can... I don't remember.

A shudder went through the robbed figure. "I only just arrived. You will have to be patient."

"We've been waiting in this hole for two hours for you to arrive. You're a mind reader. Can't you just read her mind already?"

"If you would have given me any kind of warning, I would have been prepared when you called," the Confessor hissed.

"She was on your list, and she left her security building on her own. We weren't going to get that opportunity again." Arc shrugged.

"And I see you questioned her already." He motioned to burn marks on the woman's thigh and shoulder.

She looked catatonic, staring off into space.

"She didn't say nothing." Arc shrugged again. "I was a little rough with her and she just went all space cadet." He waved his hand over her blank face.

"That's an act," the Confessor said. "I assure you she's very alert. Aren't you, Julia?"

The blank stare transformed immediately. "I hate

egoists." The woman's expression was now aware, intelligent, and not filled with blinding terror.

Arc jumped back as if she'd just sprung horns. "But..."

"But I had to pretend to be catatonic while you beat me. Got you to stop, didn't it?" She spat some blood. "So what do you want? I'm worth millions. I'll give you the number of Marcus Yaltin and we can get the ball rolling."

The Confessor chuckled. "We're not interested in ransom."

Arc disagreed. "I'm very interested in ransom."

"If I go back damaged, there won't be any money," she warned. "I'll double it though if you kill this asshole." She indicated the Confessor.

He reached out and put a hand on her exposed arm. A burst of light emitted from where the Confessor's finger touched her bare skin. Her jaw slammed shut. "That will be enough of that, Mrs. Valtire."

Mrs. Valtire? Valtire was the name of that rich guy in the news. The CEO or something of BioGlobe who blew himself up working late at his laboratory or something. It had happened just after my epic battle of epic epicness, and totally stole my news cycle.

If she was any relation to that Valtire, she would be worth millions. That Valtire's company, BioGlobe, had the only one-hundred percent accurate blood test for parahuman ability. It couldn't indicate what you could do, but it could tell if you were a parahuman or not. At ten thousand dollars per test, she was worth mad bank!

"Let me first offer my condolences for the loss of your husband. He was a public treasure." The Confessor kept one hand on her arm, a yellow crackle of energy passing between his thumb and her skin. With his other hand he removed a thin blade from her fingers. "I see you were almost through your binding."

Her jaw clenched, and she seemed unable to move, but she deflated.

"Please return this blade to whoever she stole it from."

Arc had to cross to the Confessor because the Confessor did not release her arm. He took the blade and gave her another appraising look.

"I think we're all done underestimating you," the Confessor said. "Do you promise to behave?"

She suddenly had enough control over her neck to nod. Then she gained control of her mouth. "I hate egoists." Still not an ounce of fear.

At this point, I wasn't sure who in the building was the most scary. The god of thunder, god of lightning, king of creepy, or the damsel in distress. It sure wasn't me. And I had to ask myself, what had made her scream?

"You're rather more than the trophy wife we were led to believe." The Confessor seemed delighted with this new information.

"If it's not ransom, what do you want?" She had enough control of her neck to tilt her head toward the Confessor.

"We want to know everything you know about the Phoenix."

"The city? I have an aunt there. I guess pollen is a problem now--" Her jaw slammed shut.

"It's something Archibald Valtire had. Now I need to know where it is. Where is the Phoenix?" He slowly placed his thumb at the center of her forehead.

I hadn't noticed it before, but there was a thumb-sized burn mark. For the first time, she looked nervous as his thumb covered the burn.

Another yellow light, this time like a flash bulb.

"Where is the Phoenix?" the Confessor yelled.

She twisted, trying to keep her mouth shut.

The glow intensified and she let go with a scream. "I DON'T KNOW, HE MOVED IT. DIDN'T TELL ME WHERE. I DIDN'T WANT TO KNOW."

The glow stopped. Both she and the Confessor were panting.

"Where did you learn to resist mental probes?"

She didn't answer.

"Who knows about the Phoenix?" This time the light was more intense.

Arc, and another guy I hadn't seen before, grunted at the sudden flash.

I wasn't going to get a better distraction.

"Edward Bosin!" she yelled. "Frank Kause!" She thrashed and thrashed. "Mr. Y!"

I rolled, jumped and flipped down the crates, and double somersaulted.

The Confessor was so focused on his task he didn't notice me. "Who trained you?" More light.

"Section Five," came out easier. She shook her head, trying to dislodge the thumb, but she didn't have the range of motion.

I finished my somersault into Arc's head. We both collapsed. I followed up with a roll, chop to his neck, back up, and dive roll.

The second guy was pulling a gun. He was the ZZ Top fan who had let the van in.

I know ZZ Top. My dad was a fan before he left when we needed him most. To be fair, he could still be a ZZ Top fan. I just don't care anymore.

ZZ's gun cleared the holster, but I was fast enough to kick it out of his hand, and it slammed against a crate.

ZZ didn't let that slow him down. He swung at me and made a good solid strike to my ribs, but the suit isn't just to look cool -- and it does look cool. I also have impact plates for armor. I didn't really feel it.

He blocked my first strike, pretty impressive for a vanilla human. Then I followed up with strikes two through five and he collapsed.

"Raven, behind you." The woman -- I will call her Julia until I know different -- yelled out.

I ducked and rolled.

The Confessor swiped his glowing yellow hand where I had been standing.

Double front kick to the chest knocked him on his butt. I followed up with another kick to the stomach, but the bugger was fast. He got out of the way of my attack and put a hand on my leg.

Pain burst through my calf like a sun, but I didn't experience the total locking of muscles that Julia had gone through. Maybe he wasn't trying, or maybe he needed direct skin to skin contact.

I did lose use of my leg though, and toppled like the kids on the playground had tied my shoelaces together.

I rolled, avoiding another slap of his hand of pain, spun on my back, caught his chin, and sent him reeling.

I didn't trust my leg yet, so I didn't bother getting up. I rolled again and back fisted him in the crotch, then brought up my fist as he buckled over.

I hopped up. My leg was still a little unsteady, but pins and needles now, not devastating pain.

I half-limped to Julia and started pulling off her straps.

"We have to get out of here. I counted seven more Headsmen."

"Seven?" I unstrapped her faster.

"Down!" She was free enough to roll off the gurney and I went the other way.

A blue streak of electricity fried the bed and sent the EKG sparking.

Arc was up on his elbow. The hand not supporting him was glowing again.

I jumped. The crate behind me exploded.

Another arc of electricity. Hey, you don't think that's how he got his name?

This left a chunk of concrete and a smoking hole.

I grabbed a new chunk of concrete -- hot hot hot -- and threw it at him.

He was still woozy because he got his shield up a second too late and the block of concrete bounced off his head.

Crap, I could have killed him.

He made a half-hearted attempt to sit up, then dropped.

Pain flashed again, this time on my shoulder and down my spine.

I'd lost track of the Confessor.

Somehow I was able to spin with my elbow, catch him in the nose.

The pain stopped, and it wasn't as bad as when he'd thrown the whammy on my leg. Maybe he was tiring out.

I trapped his arm, trying not to touch his glowing hand, and twisted.

The Confessor grunted in pain and swiped at me with his other hand.

Snap, I broke his arm.

That made him howl. See how he likes it.

"Gurrah!" yelled my favorite Viking god. I looked up to see the axe-wielding Brute launch himself at me from the second floor, axe back over his head as if about to chop me in half.

Overreact much?

Bang! A gunshot rang out and the Brute's head exploded.

Julia had ZZ Top's gun, and she'd just shot a man through the head in the air.

Good news: I am not facing imminent bifurcation. Bad news: Three-hundred-fifty pounds of muscle is still heading my way.

I let go of happy hands and just missed death by Swede.

The Confessor spun away as well and missed the impact. I told you that guy was fast.

He looked at me over the dead Headsman and ran. "Over here! They're over here. The Guard."

All this happened in seconds, The Headsmen posted throughout the warehouse were just starting to converge on the location. Arc's lightning wasn't quiet, and everyone knew what a gunshot sounded like.

I looked over at Julia. "Hey, no way."

She was walking over to a stunned Arc, gun in hand.

She looked at me. "Do you think he would treat you any differently?"

I closed the gap and got in front of her. "Not an argument. We're good guys. We don't do this."

"And we get killed for what?" Tears rolled down her cheeks. It was such a burst of emotion I wasn't ready for it.

"We have to go now." I moved to take the weapon.

Whatever moment she was having was over. "Fine, we let them hurt and kill other people. As long as we're the good guys."

"That's what good guys do." And the sky is blue.

"That's what Raptor told you?"

It just dawned on me that she'd yelled out my name --

my code name or handle or whatever -- and she knew I worked with Raptor. "It's what he taught me."

She laughed, wiping her nose with her gun hand. "That's rich, Archie preaching non-lethal doctrine. Don't eat honey, says the bear."

"Archie?" Did she just say Raptor was a killer and also Archie Valtire?

"Yes. Oh, God. He didn't tell you?" She started walking with purpose.

"Nope." No telling here.

While we were talking, I was kind of just following dumbstruck.

A guy with tattoos and a Headmen shirt jumped out at us. I hit him in the neck and she kicked him in his manhood and we didn't break our stride.

"Are you telling me that Raptor was the CEO of BioGlobe?" We will just put a pin in the murder allegations for a second.

"Can you drive this?" She pointed at a motorcycle.

"In theory." I mean, how hard can it be?

"Of course. He probably had you dead jumping buildings, but didn't show you how to drive a car, did he?"

I shrugged. "I think jumping rooftops is cool."

"Get on." She hitched up her tasteful skirt and straddled the bike.

And I would like to draw everyone's attention to the fact that I rescued a damsel in distress against impossible odds. Not the fact that I was out-cooled by said damsel and escaped with my life trying to hold onto her without holding onto her.

FOUR

I tried looking back to see if anyone was chasing us, but that was scary. Julia drove like a psycho.

"You're holding on too tight," she warned.

Like hell I was. I was hanging on just enough.

And then she took a turn, threading us between two stopped cabs.

I jump from rooftops as a hobby, but this was scary.

The second the bike stopped I hopped off like it was on fire. Just in case she started driving again.

Every inch of legal street parking was taken. So she didn't worry about legality. She stopped the bike in front of a fire hydrant.

Take that Headsmen! You're going to get towed. Ha!

"Are you okay?" She hit the kick stand.

"I'm fine."

She shrugged. "I thought I heard you scream."

Oh, you heard me scream. "It was probably every motorist and pedestrian we passed."

She didn't lose any of her urgency and started walking

down the line of parked cars as if shopping for her next purchase.

"What are you going to do?" she asked.

"I... What?"

She stopped and looked at me. "Listen, thanks for the assist."

"Sure."

She started looking at cars again.

"Nothing says thanks like explaining what the hell that was all about." I had to run a little to catch up with her.

"They grabbed me. I was doing one more stupid mission for Archie before I disappear."

Wow, bitter much?

"Mission?"

She put her hand in her pocket and gave me a letter. "All the ridiculous scavenger hunts he put you on? That was me. Well, I delivered the letters and sent the address. He wrote the actual instructions. I just had to run all over town."

I took the letter. It looked like all the other letters, wrapped in a plain white envelope. "He sent a letter to me?"

"It was in a file, to be delivered if he died." The d word was tough for her to get out. "Died," she said firmly. "I had a file of a few things I had to do. That was one of them." She held up her watch. "It has a GPS. I hit the crown," she pointed at the watch's button, "and it sends a text message to the apprentice of choice with the address." The crown is the windy thing on the side of a watch. I had to look that up.

She unstrapped the watch. "Archie was so paranoid he couldn't just give me a number to text. I had to have some spy vs spy crap." She dropped the watch and stomped it.

"Good thing," I pointed out.

She looked like she was about to say something, but didn't. She gave the area a quick look around, broke off an antenna from a car, and kept walking as she bent it into a hook. "I know there isn't any reason for you to do whatever training exercise is in there. It isn't like he's going to be training you anymore." She rounded on me so fast I took a defensive stance. "Do you know if he's dead?"

"What?"

"Do you know for sure?"

What to say? I'm just going to go with the truth. I think she could bend me into a pretzel if she caught me in a lie. "No, not for sure."

She deflated a little, but a different kind of stress crossed her face.

"Silhouette told me he killed him. We got a voicemail from Cat saying they were all dead, right before Silhouette killed Cat, too."

"All of them..." She repeated the words in a daze. "All of them." Then back to herself. "If Silhouette said it, then it's probably true. He's too far gone to bother with lying. He also has the ability. Where is Silhouette now?"

"SSA have him." I hoped.

"Fine."

"And if Raptor was still alive...." *I'd know?* "He would have made contact. It's been almost a week." I don't know if he would have contacted me, but his golden boy Peregrine would know.

"Fine," she said again. She turned back to the car she was working on and popped open the door with one motion.

"You're good at that," I observed, no judgement. "Did 'section 5' show you how to do that?"

That got a sharp look. "How long was I being tortured before you did something?"

"I was getting into position." *You can't rush this kind of thing.*

"Don't repeat that name. Don't repeat anything. Just go home, Raven. Archie told me a little about you."

Danger! Danger! "How much?"

"Oh, relax. After Shadowhawk, or Silhouette as you know him, did... what he did to Osprey's family... Well, Raptor became obsessed with security. He wouldn't have told anyone your real identity."

"What did Silhouette do?"

"It doesn't matter." She shrugged. "It was like dominoes played in Hell." *I don't know if I was supposed to hear that part.* "He loved you like a son."

Um, no. Also, subject change much?

"He loved all his apprentices like his children," she continued.

Okay, in a vague 'I love you man" kind of way.

"Maybe he would still be alive if he would have just had children of his own." And if bitterness could kill, I and the building behind me would be a smoking hole. "Just stop, Raven. Stop all this." She took in my dream of making a difference and being someone who mattered with a wave at my uniform. "It isn't just your life you're risking. Burn that letter, burn your nest. Get out of this damned town. It will consume and kill you just like it did him."

"I... don't really have a choice." I meant that I had to drop the hero biz because I didn't have the resources to continue. Eventually I would run out of material to repair my suit.

She took it wrong. "That's what he thought, too. But he did have a choice." Enough bitterness to blaze a path to the river. "He made it. I hated Raptor for killing Archie. We had a minute there when we could have been..."

Whatever they could have been, she didn't say.

"Well, I have choices too, and now I'm making mine. I'm gone. I will never see you again. Don't be an idiot. You don't owe Raptor anything, you don't owe this sick town anything. The people you care about are who you owe." The engine started up. "Move." She shut the door and pulled away from the curb.

I had to jump out of the way. She didn't wait for me to get on the sidewalk.

But my point is, if I hadn't been suited up and doing the hero thing, you would be a drooling puddle for the Confessor right now! I didn't yell it at her. But I wanted to.

The car was on the road and she gunned it.

"You're welcome." I gave her the two finger wave.

Standing on the street was making my back itch, so I headed for the shadows. And home.

FIVE

Home sweet not home. My nest.

In an abandoned factory, Raptor had set me up with my own efficiency apartment, emphasis on the efficiency and not on the apartment. I had a workspace, a cot, a shower, a microwave, a toilet, a mini-fridge, and tools and materials to make small repairs to my uniform.

It was the most awesome treehouse ever. Today, I had company.

"Feral, how did you get in here?"

The cat had made a bed in my cot. He looked up at me with a lazy eye and rolled over on his back.

I gave him a quick rubdown and started taking off my gear. The letter landed on my desk.

Feral wasn't just any cat, he was way weirder. When I asked him *how did you get in here*, I really wanted to know. I either go in through a secret entrance on the roof, or crawl through a back alley access, then up through an abandoned elevator shaft in pitch black.

So how did a cat get in here?

Feral wasn't my cat. Well, maybe he was now. I met

Feral when I was learning parkour from his previous owner, Cat. Cat was one of the full members of the Guard. Feral was his focus, meaning he could communicate and see through the animal. Since Cat's death, Feral had adopted me. He'd even managed to convince my mom to let him stay.

In a way, we were keeping each other company through our grief. We'd both lost people we cared about. And we were both a little lost ourselves.

But, seriously. "How did you get in here?"

Feral answered with a yawn.

I showered and put on the uniform of normal life: beat-up jeans, t-shirt, hoodie, and a pair of chuckies.

Feral was no longer on the cot. He was lounging on the desk, but the letter was in his mouth.

"Yeah, my last homework assignment from Raptor." I took it from Feral's mouth.

The big black cat batted playfully at my hand. I know it was playful because the scratch he left didn't bleed.

The letter was crumpled, like all the letters he'd left for me. I looked for the subtle watermark of a bird of prey. You wouldn't see it if you didn't know what you were looking for.

It looked legit.

On the front of the letter, covering my name, was a small post it note with an address that didn't mean anything to me. Probably the random place Raptor wanted it delivered. Julia had been on her way to deliver it before she was grabbed.

I opened the letter.

The code Raptor used was, of course, a complete pain in the ass. I don't know the technical name for it, but the letter would correspond to a book Raptor and I shared, with page numbers and counted words. It took forever to decode a long one.

Good, this one was pretty short.

Probably translated to, "You're fired! Why are you still running around following my directions?"

I checked the chain of numbers that identified the book. And rechecked. It went by ISBN, but not the complete ISBN. The ISBN did not match any of the books he'd coded for me. I had about ten of them on a shelf above my work space.

So my last letter from Raptor wasn't even for me. It was probably meant for a different apprentice and he'd written Raven by accident. Didn't sound like Raptor, but he might have had a lot on his mind. He probably wrote it on his way out to meet his destiny. I checked the time code, but couldn't read it because it was coded.

Of course.

I put the letter in my uniform's belt pouch. I'd give it to Cameron, AKA Peregrine, the apprentice golden boy. It was probably meant for him.

But now I had a date with the maternal firing squad. I gave myself a salute in the full-length mirror on the door. "For those about to die..." I turned to Feral. "I assume you can see yourself out?"

No, he couldn't. He hopped onto the floor then up into my arms. "Sure, I'll carry you down a ladder for three floors. No problem."

SIX

So what does a moody teen who has superpowers do when life sucks? He makes lemonade.

Actually, it was some kind of energy drink, but I slammed two. And started pacing. My nest doesn't have any room to pace in, but that was where I was. The only safe place I had left.

Damn it, I wish I had better snacks. I'd raided my own cupboards a week ago when I thought I was never coming back. Now all my energy bars were at home. It was a kind of middle finger at Raptor, but guess who was feeling like a chump now.

Damn it! What the hell was Dad doing at my house? If he wasn't there, I could have just ate my crow, found out I wasn't going to graduate, and come up with a plan. But all I could do was look at his expensive haircut, the complete opposite of the crazy curls he had when we were a family.

I dropped on the beanbag, a personal touch to the furniture. "What am I going to do?" I looked around to see if Feral was there to talk to. Nope.

Fine, I would cool off and go home. Maybe Dad had

figured he'd done enough damage and gone to kick some other family in the crotch.

I would just talk to mom one on one and we could get things back pointed in the right direction. I knew she had a lot to forgive, but if I stopped the extracurricular activities, I could be... what? Less disappointing.

And then I could get in the family business and marry rich or clean office buildings.

I banged my head against the wall in time with how much this sucked.

Screw it. If I was going to give up the hero gig, I might as well do one more patrol. It would calm me down more than sitting here and stewing. I had a favorite route that was a fun parkour run.

Just to clear my head. Then I'd go back home and try to patch things up with Mom.

I was out and running in record time. Could have been the doubling up on caffeine and sugar, but I was running hard.

I finally started to untense. I'd done this run so often that I could do it with my eyes closed. It was like finally getting back into your own skin.

I got a good running start and bounced from one wall to another until I reached the roof.

If I had been actually patrolling, I wouldn't have stopped there, but I wasn't patrolling. I wouldn't be patrolling again.

Whatever relaxation I had been feeling cracked, and I was stressed again.

From the rooftops I could see the city in a way that I would miss. All the tar paper, spider webs, and rancid rain pools. This was where I was free. This was where I was king.

It was hard for a king to give up his crown even if it was inevitable.

Well, I'm still king for now.

I turned on my helmet's police scanner and started running.

There were plenty of police calls, some out of my effective range, some I would have had to run to, and some that I would not have been a value add. The last thing a domestic needed was a guy with a bird on his chest showing up and really stirring things up.

I was only half listening when a nine-four-seven code came over the line that caught my attention. That was the code for multiple parahuman activity. The call didn't have much to go on, but it sounded like two rival gangs had bumped into each other. Things were flying, people were jumping, and there were flashing lights aplenty. Sounded like supers to me.

So it was on. Cops don't show up to para-on-para slugfests, and if they do, they never do it twice. This was the kind of thing Raptor and the rest of the Guard dealt with, the kind of thing I was training to deal with. The Police Chief or the Mayor condemned vigilantes every other week, but they depended on them to deal with these situations. Thirteen days since every full member of the Guard had died. The Feds might show up, but I wouldn't bet a civilian's life on it.

Soon, everyone was going to realize the Guard were gone. Then this city was going to explode.

Not my problem, city. I'm retired.

Retiring.

I'm going to go be normal and go... nowhere.

Keep your mind on the here and now. The future is not your problem.

More reports came in. It was an even bigger incident than I'd thought. I got close enough to hear the fight.

Something crashed into a car. It has a very distinctive sound -- the crush of metal and shatter of safety glass.

A bang-crack occurred, nothing I recognized.

I got to an overlooking building.

I'd seen worse. I'd seen worse last Thursday. That isn't to say I wasn't way over my head here. I was way over my head Thursday, too.

I counted five supers. One brick, a brute that could add superhuman toughness to his resume. This guy had thick chunks of some coal-looking substance all over him. Each chunk of coal had hard edges.

An energy caster was holding off the Coal Golem. When she spun her arms, a blue whirl of energy the size of a plate spiraled from her and into Coal.

Smoke was pooling around another guy who was making a snow angel in the hood of a Buick. I'm no detective, but I'd blame the Coal Golem. I knew the Smoke guy was a super because he was getting up.

Coming up on Smoke guy, who I will now think of as Marlboro man, was a thick beefy guy that was running on all fours. He was obviously feral, parahuman's that tap into some animal nature. Until otherwise informed, I will call him Badger. Badger was going to run Marlboro man down before he could get up.

And then we find number five. He looked like a college dude in the wrong part of town, but he let loose with a heat distortion thing that separated Badger from Marlboro.

Badger didn't stop, he just jumped into a ball and rolled over the top of the heat shimmer effect.

Let the record show I will call that guy Shimmer.

Shimmer shimmered -- okay having second thoughts about the name. Maybe Glimmer or Distortion?

Anyway Shimmer -- nope, now he's Shimmer in my head -- let loose with another shimmer. Badger dodged that one, too. But the shimmer kept going and cut through another parked car and connected with a civilian trying to run for cover.

The energy, mostly dispersed, ripping the car apart and still smashed her into the wall of a shop.

There were other normals running around, too. Or they might be something else. I wouldn't have picked out Shimmer or the Blue Whirl if I hadn't seen what they did. Regardless, there were some lives that needed saving.

I ran to the edge of the building and spotted a lower roof in jumping distance, if I rolled when I landed.

Piece of cake.

From there I landed, rolled, and stood at ground level.

The woman was trying to stand, but she was too dazed.

"Are you all right?" I asked. Okay, dumb question. "Sorry, dumb question."

She looked at me blankly, then fearfully.

"No, I'm with the Guard." I reached for her. You know, reassuringly.

And she wasn't scared of me.

Badger collided into me.

He probably assumed that he knew all his friends. I wasn't a friend, so I was going down. Or he was so battle-crazed it wouldn't have mattered because the dude was gone.

I twisted, got my feet underneath him, and kicked him over me and up in the air.

A column of shimmer caught him midair and spun him off into the building with a thud.

I kicked up and dodged a shimmer strike of my own. I scooped up the woman, who was still pretty dazed.

I didn't know where else to put her, so I bounced between two walls back and forth and got her to the roof.

I told her to stay. She didn't look like she understood me. If her eardrums were ruptured, it wasn't like she could read my lips through a full face mask.

Back to the fight. A couple teenagers were cowering as the Blue Whirl's disks bounced off Coal Golem and ricocheted over their heads.

I plotted a way there right before a black streak landed and took off with one of them.

I knew that streak! I turned on the Guard's channel. "Peregrine, are you at the nine-four-seven?"

"Raven, are you active?" That was Butterfly.

"I'm going to say yes, and what the hell?" It wasn't like they were cheating on me, but they were getting their vigilante on and no one had even tried to ask me. I was hurt.

"We're trying to save lives," Peregrine said. He landed, grabbed another civilian, and lifted them away. "Stop feeling all hurt and ignored, and help."

"I'm not hurt." Silly, silly man. But he also had a point. "What assets do we have on the site?" I scanned the area for anyone in trouble.

The Smoke guy stood up and a wall of smoke sprayed from his fingers. Soon the quadrant that included Coal Golem was hidden from view.

That engulfed a number of the rest of the students that Peregrine was trying to save. "Can you see through that fog stuff?"

"No," Peregrine admitted after a beat.

"The only assets we have are you and Peregrine," Butterfly responded. "I'm just support."

Fair enough. Last time Butterfly got in combat she did not like the person she became. She'd pressed more and more into her power and went from a computer with a human soul to a computer without a human soul. A problem with the cognit power class, I'm told.

"I've got the fog. You get everyone else out," I told Peregrine.

"Affirmative." Peregrine didn't argue.

"You didn't argue?" I dropped, stopped my momentum on a decorative ledge, spun, and rolled. "What did you do with the real Peregrine?"

He flew by me, middle finger extended, and scooped up another civilian.

I went into the smoke and instantly regretted it. It was so much worse than just something that cut down on visibility. But it did that really well. I was in complete darkness. I couldn't see my hands.

That was okay, I knew where I was going. Just so long as no one moved.

Someone moved.

I bounced off the Coal Golem. Easy to identify with his sharp-edged exterior. For some reason he hadn't left the fog.

I dodged on a guess, and didn't feel the Golem crush my skull, so win!.

I headed toward the three students I'd spotted before being engulfed by the fog. They were still huddled on the floor.

At first I was relieved. I'd half-expected them to be running around in this stuff. They had the good sense to stay down and stay put.

Then I put a hand on one. No reaction. The smoke

swirled enough for me to see a face. A pretty girl, maybe old enough to buy beer. Her eyes were bugging out of her head as she sucked air.

This stuff was poisonous! It was killing them.

My helmet had a bit of a gas mask -- must have been enough to protect me.

Then the world started to spin.

Protect me for a little while.

"Peregrine, drop Marlboro man, now! He's killing these people." And me, too.

"Damn it," was the only response.

In good health, I would have tried for two, but I wasn't sure my feet were steady enough to get me out of there. I heaved the girl over my shoulder, one hand on the wall, and started running alongside it.

The cloud must have doubled since I'd entered it. It couldn't have been this thick or this long when I entered.

"Raven, report!" Butterfly had been talking, but I'd just realized it had something to do with me.

"I'm almost out." I had to be almost out. I staggered a little, but got my hand back on the wall. It was pitch black in the fog. If I lost the wall, I wouldn't know which way was out.

"Peregrine's in trouble, he needs assistance." Butterfly was not panicked. A sure sign she was pushing into her power, trying to find the best solution to the problem. Hopeful she wouldn't go all soulless and write us off as a waste of her time.

And fresh air.

I gasped. I'd been holding my breath because I figured it was better than inhaling the smoke.

The freshman I was carrying also gasped and started breathing. Still dead weight, but much better.

I kept running just on the off chance Shimmer or Whirl were looking for targets.

And they were.

A plate-sized disk spun at me, and would have connected if I hadn't hit the clear at a sprint.

I was still wobbly and lost my balance as the sidewalk turned into a curb. I controlled my fall, turning it into a slide and rolling for cover. Yea, I meant to do that.

I think I banged up the woman more in my rescue attempt than she'd been before, but she was breathing normally.

"Who are you?" Whirl yelled. "You don't work for Bullet." Another energy plate hit the car I had taken cover behind.

I didn't want to leave the coed here, but there was nothing more I could do. I couldn't run around with her on my back, and after I moved, she'd be less likely to take friendly fire.

"I'm Santa Claus," I yelled back. "Guess who's on my naughty list." Times like these I don't know what is coming out of my mouth. It takes too much of my energy to stop my lips from flapping. "Fly, where's Peregrine?"

I ran along a few parked cars, but had to show myself enough to draw fire away from the civilian I was trying to rescue.

"I do not have real time information," Butterfly said. "He is not responding."

I ran as far as I could, the effects of the fog clearing out of my system. "How long on SSA?"

"There is no indication they have taken this case," she reported.

Two weeks ago, a fight with five supers, collateral damage, and a number of affected civilians would have been front page news. But after the battle that destroyed the Carlton hotel, this would be in the local section under pictures of squirrels trying to keep cool in the August heat.

My head was clear now, and I risked a better look around.

Whirl walked towards me, her hand spinning in the air. The disk she made wasn't as bright as before.

I used the car as cover.

Peregrine was pinned to the wall by a column of whatever Shimmer does. He was still in the fight, trying to push himself off the wall, but he was losing.

The smoke was larger now. Marlboro man was standing on the car that still bore his indentation, and he had this crazy grin on his face. Like he knew he was killing people and was loving it.

Maybe that was just his concentration face.

"Die! Die! All who oppose me, die!"

Nope, totally his crazy crazy face.

I didn't see Badger anywhere, but I couldn't see half the area now that the fog had really started going. Badger could have run for it or he could be fixating in the fog.

Whirl spotted me. I ducked, and an energy plate skimmed by me. Definitely not as bright as the ones she was kicking into the Coal Golem

"Whirlly, you feeling okay?" Didn't have time to do anything else. I jumped onto the car I was hiding behind then fired myself at her.

She managed to get out of my way, but didn't send a whirl of blue death at me.

"It's just that you seem to be losing your pep."

She brought up her hand to spin, but I batted it down.

"Just saying, if you want to make the big leagues..." I knocked her other hand and before it could form a circle, gave her a right cross.

She dropped like a bad habit.

"Cardio."

I didn't have much time to celebrate my success.

"Die!" Marlboro man yelled and a thick column of smoke landed right on me.

I was ready for it, so I held my breath, but I was in the dark again.

For a second before it hit me, I saw Blue Whirl start to thrash. Then I was blind.

Damn it.

SEVEN

I put her over my shoulder, and this time I started running towards the Marlboro man. If he was immune to this stuff and just encased himself in it, this was going to be a quick fight.

I broke the fog, coming out a little to the left of where I'd intended. I got my bearings and inhaled deeply.

Another cloud covered me.

This time I ran faster, using his fog as cover.

I broke cloud cover, this time exactly where I wanted to be. "Can't catch me!" I yelled.

He hit me with another smoke plume.

Which was kind of the point since I was now standing right next to Shimmer.

"Wilcox, you moron!" I heard a gasp and Shimmer dropping to his knees.

I kept running, looking for fresh air, and found it.

My plan worked. We'll call it a plan.

Peregrine was now free from the crushing power of Shimmer and turned all his attention to the Marlboro man, AKA Wilcox.

Peregrine was a first-class jerk, but he could lay the smack if he was so disposed. Imagine a first-rate martial artist able to attack you from every direction and build up speed for his kicks just by thinking of it.

I've sparred with him enough to feel sorry for smoke guy.

The Marlboro man seemed to be a one trick wonder. He blocked a couple of strikes then was just taken apart and dropped back into the same car that he'd been standing on.

One second the cloud was all around, clinging to the ground and the walls, then it was a thin mist and gone.

"And that is how the Guard does it!" I shouted.

"Guard!" It was a deep, deep voice filled with hate. "I will kill you!" Coal Golem was standing now, shaking off the effects of the fog.

"No, I mean, that's how the Guard would do it if they were here," I clarified. "There are no Guard here. I hate those guys."

Badger, who had been caught in the cloud, was getting up, too. He didn't look as solid as before, or as wild and out of control. That's pretty common with ferals. But the second he locked eyes on me, he started to get in touch with his animal side and howled.

"Come on, we just saved you guys," I said.

Didn't seem to matter. Badger charged.

Here we go. I started running at him, too. If that's the way he wanted it.

It was good to see that Whirl wasn't permanently injured, either. She'd shaken off my punch and the fog, and was now mixing it up and using a different power in her tool box. Curling light rays wrapped around my arms and legs and she pulled me right on my back.

So glad I wear a helmet.

Now that I was on my back, Badger leapt, colliding with my stomach. I felt that.

My armor took the shot, or I would have been wrecked. Then he leapt off me and took some of my uniform with him. He had claws on his feet. That would have gutted me if I wasn't armored.

"You're welcome on the whole able to breathe thing," I tried to yell, but it was more of a wheeze.

"Get up, Raven," Butterfly said. "You need to get up."

I thought she didn't have eyes on us? Maybe she was just playing the odds. I got up.

Badger was caught mid-jump with a wall of shimmer and bounded off it.

Whirl was getting her second wind back and kicking up a good one. Not aimed at me, finally some luck.

She was aiming at the Coal Golem charging my way.

Yep, that sounds like my luck.

I got up and ran, right into a shimmer wall. It had all the joy of running into a brick wall, but with the added benefit of an electric charge.

Awesome.

I bounced right back into the path of the coming Coal avalanche.

Whirl let her disk fly.

I tried to jump out of the way of that, but it expanded as it left her fingers and caught my feet.

Flashes of pain ran up my leg to my pelvis and spun me until I impacted pavement.Peregrine flashed by and clotheslined Shimmer.

I got up, then didn't, then got up again.

Whirl was aiming for Coal Golem and hit him square. The brick's momentum was stopped, but he didn't look nearly as impressed as I was.

What to do? What to do?

There were still civilians. The fog had hit them a lot harder than any of the parahumans. Most were moving at this point, but not everyone.

Whirl laced more blue lights around Coal, but I could see it in her face that she was terrified and didn't have many more tricks up her sleeve or gas in the tank.

Badger rebounded, jumped, and caught Peregrine as he flew by. They went spinning into the shop front.

"There is nothing else to be done. Make extraction of the team." Butterfly had just enough emotion in her voice to prove she meant it. But she was looking at things strategically.

I wanted to tell her no, but I didn't see what else I could do, either. A week ago I went head to head with guys that would make this bunch soil their drawers, but I'd had a lot of help and something that changed the rules of the game.

"Just as soon as I get these people out of here." I worked up a good head of steam and dove right into Badger as he was pulling back his hand for another strike.

The collision sent Badger and me to the ground struggling for a hand hold.

"Get off me, Guard!" Badger growled.

"Love to. Stop trying to kill my friend... my associate." I got a grip on him, flipped him, and pinned him.

He was strong. I had the leverage, but he was breaking my grip.

"Listen, we aren't your enemies." I forced him back into shape and he gave up that contest, but started another.

"You raided our base."

"No." Probably. I didn't really know what Peregrine and BF were doing here. "That was those guys. Smokey and his bandits."

He stopped fighting me.

"We just want to get the civilians out of harm's way. You guys can beat the living crap out of each other if you want." I didn't dare let up.

Peregrine got up. His suit had a gash that ripped through the leather and scored a gash through his plate. No blood.

"Get those people out of here." I pointed at the students who still were not moving.

He hesitated, like he wasn't sure if he was going to leave me with the feral, but after a heart beat he took to the air and scooped up the nearest comatose civilian.

"Let's have a truce. You let me get the civilians out of the way. You don't want vanilla deaths on your hands, anyway. SSA will take an interest in you for sure if you're at this kind of massacre."

He grunted. "Fine. Don't get in my way and you can pick up the mess."

"That's all I want." Okay, time to show a little faith. I let go and stood back.

He turned, and we shared an appreciating nod, two professionals doing a job with respect for each other as warriors.

No, not really.

He turned on me the second I stepped back. Crying out loud, what is wrong with these people?

I was ready for his sudden charge -- I guess I don't have that much faith in humanity -- and used his momentum to flip him. He landed on his feet, and came right back at me.

I grabbed both of his wrists and stopped them from ripping out my stomach. I say stopped, but it was more just slowing him down.

At this point, Badger went full on rabid. A lather was

forming around his lips, and his eyes were bugged out and darting all over the place. "I hate the Guard! My mother and father are in prison because of the Guard!"

"And their crimes probably had something to do with it." Just trying to give perspective. I caught his chin as I flipped up and dodged some of his pointy bits.

He didn't really know how to fight -- he was all ferocity and brawn. I bet that combination had served him well. It was serving him well now.

On a long enough timeline, I think I could have gotten the better end of the fight. I was already picking up on how he fought and where I should not be so he couldn't get a good slice with those claws.

Ordinarily, my endurance gives me an edge in these fights. It takes a lot to get me winded. But ferals, as a rule, kick my ass in the endurance game. They don't seem to use energy like the rest of us. The more beat up they get, the faster they get.

It's kind of unfair. The one edge I have is I use adrenaline like a beast, but they do it better.

I caught a flicker of light and a thunder clap as something happened with the main event fight to my left. But I didn't dare take my focus from the task at hand.

Badger did.

I delivered a crack to his chin and followed it up with a double front kick to his face. That dazed him and I kept up the pressure. He tried to get his hands up, but he was swinging blind. Score one for training and my kinist's ability. I learn quickly so I don't have to worry about all the hours of discipline stuff.

And score three for just having big, big friends.

I had a second to realize that the situation suddenly sucked as Coal grabbed me and flipped me over his shoulder in an offhand way. I tried to ball up and get control of the fall, but it happened too fast. I hit the pavement on my side and did a header into an SUV.

Not sure what happened at that point. Everyone else could have taken a smoke break for all I knew. But then I was in the air again, this time suspended by the same black Coal Golem. Coal had me right in his face and was screaming at me.

That guy has some pipes.

That's when I noticed the crumpled form of Whirl. Smoke and Shimmer were nowhere to be seen. Badger was almost fully recovered and heading my way.

It's times like this that I review my "just focus on the problem in front of me" policy.

I headbutted Coal right in his eye, or at least his eyeish spot on his blocky black scary head.

He tossed me to the pavement -- surprise reaction.

Hooray, I'm free. The wind was completely knocked out of me and I couldn't move, but let the record show I was free. All part of my plan.

Coal Golem had less of a sense of humor about it than Badger. He pulled back his fist.

And Peregrine jetted in to whisk me to safety.

Not really.

He tried. He gave it an A for effort. He did the swooping thing, but Badger intercepted him and they both crashed to the ground.

Peregrine was ready for it this time, so he was able to throw off Badger without doing a header.

Nothing stopped the swing of the boulder-sized fist.

I got a bit of a roll going, but too little too late.

Coal Golem's fist descended fast.

A red wall of light appeared between me and death.

The Golem made contact and the red wall held.

Well, good, and huh?

Peregrine got out of Badger's grip and threw him into the Golem, who didn't even register the impact.

I was the least of Golem's worries now. He started looking around for the source of the new parahuman ability.

Two tree trunks, glowing red and slightly transparent just like the floating wall, collided into Golem from two directions.

He staggered back and some of his coal cracked off, exposing a pale cheek.

That gave me enough time to get up. I rolled from under the wall, kicked up, jumped on the floating wall to give me a little more height, and landed the punch of my life to that exposed patch of flesh.

All of Golem's rocks cracked and turned to dust as the guy went unconscious.

Badger had a choice. He could keep the fight going with now three to one odds, or he could get the hell out of Dodge.

He attacked me.

His wild flurry of strikes were actually predictable now. I laid a chop to his neck, jumped to the side, and delivered a blow to his kidney. "Will you just go away already?"

He gave a wild kick with his hind feet, but was suddenly wrapped head to toe in red glowing chains.

Time to pay attention to my surroundings.

I looked for a possible source of this life-saving, red-glowing goodness. It wasn't hard. Thin filaments of light were attached to the outstretched hand of a man in a wheelchair across the street.

He had not been there earlier.

His hair was more grey than brown and his grey beard was completely wild and unkempt. He wore a stained flannel shirt open over a stained t-shirt, blue jeans, and old work boots. His upper body looked powerful.

"Get ready. I can't hold him much longer." His face was red and covered with beads of sweat.

I got ready.

The chains disappeared. I hit Badger hard and forced him into restraints. With any luck the cops or SSA would show up and take credit for the arrest of three parahumans operating without permission who'd caused massive destruction of property and endangerment of human life.

"It's you. I knew it." Peregrine was happier to see the guy in the wheelchair than I was, and I was pretty darn happy. He'd just saved me from a short career as street pizza.

"I'm no one," the wheelchair guy said. "You all okay?" He seemed to get his own answer, and turned his chair away.

"Wait!" Peregrine crossed the distance and landed in front of him. "It's you, the Red Knight."

The Red Knight! Founding member of the original Guard, Red Knight? Hero of the battle with Purge, Red Knight? That Red Knight?

I need a commercial break.

EIGHT

L ong story short.
He told us to get lost, Peregrine would not get lost, so he told us where to meet him and we all got gone before the cops showed up.

And met back up at his apartment, an efficiency thing in one of the few buildings in the area with a working elevator.

He lived a spartan existence. There was a bed, a table at wheelchair height, and a kitchenette that had plenty of dishes and an old tube mobile T.V. with a digital receiver.

He let us in his window once we were sure the coast was clear.

"Well, don't sit on my bed."

"You are... you are the Red Knight?" It wasn't a question, but Peregrine still asked.

"What gave it away?" he mumbled. "Look, I'm not that guy anymore. Warzone took that away from me." He punched his leg. "I'm just an old man, and I don't want anything to do with..." He waved at us, but I think he was looking at our suits.

"I've been looking for you," Peregrine said.

"Really?" This was news to me. Was that what Peregrine and Butterfly were doing working together?

Peregrine looked at me and scowled. I couldn't actually see his face, but we can assume there was some scowling. Then back at Red Knight. "I saw a report of a drive-by shooting foiled by a glowing red wall. The incident was a couple blocks from here."

He said report, but it was probably a couple posts on a Super stalker site.

"That? I knew no good could come from that." He looked away. "It was instinct... I threw the wall before I knew what I was doing."

"And the fight just now?" I asked.

"I heard the explosions and... well, I wanted to make sure no one was wrecking the deli. That's where I get my sandwiches on Thursdays. Look, why are you here? I'm sure Raptor made it clear I was not to be bothered."

I filled the silence. "Well, no. Raptor never really talked about you." I can play bad cop to Peregrine's fawning fan boy.

He gave a little laugh at that. "Of course."

"He never told us anything about those days," Peregrine said. "I only know about you because my brother was... really into the Guard. He had all the old stories and news clippings."

"Don't believe all those stories, kid." He turned away from us and wheeled himself into the kitchen.

Peregrine followed. "You started the Guard with Raptor and Landslide."

"And Imp and Wraith. I thought I could teach them something. Use their gifts to make this city better." He opened the door and pulled out a can of beer.

"You did, you set up the Guard," Peregrine said.

I wanted to step outside and ask Butterfly what the hell was going on. If they were looking for Red Knight, what were they hoping to get besides compromising his secret ID and an autograph?

"Your battle with Purge is legend and routed out the terrorist organization from the city, possibly the entire United States."

"Yeah, and at the end of that battle Wraith was dead, Imp a vegetable, and I..." He opened the beer and slammed some. "Aw, this stuff is awful." He took another long pull. "But at least Raptor and Landslide are still fighting the fight."

He spun his chair back around. "Raptor checks in from time to time, but I haven't seen him in a while. Last time he seemed a bit tense, even for him. What's going on?"

I didn't say it, I just couldn't. This was Peregrine's let's-kick-a-guy-in-a-wheelchair party. He could give the good news.

He didn't. He just stood there.

"Well?" Red Knight stopped in mid sip. "Oh, God." The beer slipped through limp fingers. "Did he send you? This isn't one of his stupid homework assignments, is it?"

Okay, so the guy knew Raptor.

"No, I..."

Red Knight finally caught on. "Which one? It was Landslide wasn't it? That idiot thought he was invulnerable, didn't understand that even he had limits."

"All of them." I said it because I guess Peregrine wasn't going to do the dirty work. "The entire Guard is gone." Yes, I said gone. I tried to form the words died or killed. I couldn't.

His mouth traced the words before giving them sound.

"All of them? Even the new guys? That archer and Watch or Clock something?"

"Clockwork." The anger made itself clear through the vocal distortion. "He betrayed the entire team. He had them all killed."

"Oh, I... I thought the one good thing about Raptor's new paranoia was it would keep him alive." The old man looked older. "I always warned him to be sure of his team before anything else. How?" He shook his head, like maybe he didn't want to know then steeled himself. "How?"

That was an interesting question. A dangerous question. We'd never talked about the nullifier as a team, but that was explosive information. If the nullifier got out, it would change everything. Not for the better.

"A trap." Peregrine settled on a compromise. "Clockwork lured the team -- Cat, Orion, Raptor, and Landslide -- to a trap. Silhouette and Shale."

That was a little too close for comfort. Red Knight might know that Shale and Landslide shared a bond, that if one died, the other died. It was only when they were both under the nullifier that they didn't have to worry about that effect. The reason Shale joined Clockwork was to get free of his brother Landslide.

I searched his face for any confusion, but he didn't show any. Maybe it wasn't public knowledge in Red Knight's day.

"Plus some other guys he brought in from around the country." I padded the stats. I wanted it to seem plausible the Guard were wiped out in one fight.

"So that's why you found me? You want me to help you what, get revenge, bring them to justice? I'm not as strong as I once was. That display at the gas station has tapped me for the night." He steeled himself. "But I owe it to Raptor and Landslide, at least. I'll do what I can."

Awkward.

"Well, no. We kind of already brought those guys to justice." And foiled their evil plan of evilness while they were being evil. "Justice-ish." I waved my hand a little.

"Oh, good." Red Knight looked surprised.

"Both Sill and Shale are in a deep SSA hole," I added.

Peregrine said, "It's been in the news."

"Not that we did it. The news kind of skipped that part," I said.

"Well, I'm impressed. Raptor didn't tell me you were that powerful to defeat two of the strongest parahumans working the other side. Wow."

"We had help." Hopefully he would think that help was the SSA and not a world-changing power-killing device powered by a parahuman. For an example taken at random.

"So, why are you here?" He looked from me to Peregrine.

I held up a hand. "I was just out for a run. I didn't know the band had gotten back together."

He looked at Peregrine, and so did I.

"We need you. We can't continue doing the Work. We're just a bunch of kids. We need someone who knows how to do all the things Raptor did. Setting up a secret base, funding ---"

"Those little snacks, the nuts and raisins. I love those." I was in shock and lost control of my lips. It happens.

"Training." Peregrine spoke over me. "The Guard are too important to this city, and now with Ceasar dead this city needs the Guard more than ever."

"Caesar died, too?" His eyes went wide at that. "I didn't think that could happen."

"Clockwork was thorough." Let's just leave it at that.

"A base was on your wishlist. Did Clockwork expose Gamma base?" Red Knight asked.

"He blew it up." I missed the Clubhouse so much. "Like I said, he was thorough."

"Blew it up," Red Knight repeated.

"Things got busy a week and a half ago," I explained. Did I want to be that busy again? "Peregrine, could we sidebar?"

It was against his better judgment, but he followed me over to the window. "Just throwing out a question, and I want an honest and thoughtful response. Peregrine, what the fu--"

"Peregrine, Raven, what is your location?" Butterfly asked.

"One second Fly." I turned back to Peregrine. "What are you doing?"

"I'm trying to do the Work." For some reason he seemed mad at me.

"The Work! What are you talking about? We were going to stop. We did what we set out to do."

"No! We stopped some bad guys. That's not the end of the mission, it was just one mission." He slashed the air with his hand. "You gave up. If you want to get back to Xbox and math class, go. I'm trying to do what I was always trying to do -- protect this city."

"If you knew anything about me, you'd know I'm a Sony guy, and..." Running out of righteous indignation. I needed a recharge. "And the last order we were given was to dissolve and fade back into our real life."

"This IS MY REAL LIFE!" he shouted. "I'm not like you, I got nothing else." He was in my face.

Not like me?

"Moron and Idiot! What is your location?" I think that was the most forceful I'd ever heard Butterfly.

"Which one is the Idiot?" Dibs on Moron.

"We're at--" Peregrine started.

"42246 Sanderson," she finished.

"You're good." Then to Peregrine, "She's good."

"Get out of there now!" Butterfly, again with the forceful. "An SSA division is converging on that location. It seems the Feds can figure out what a couple of glowing walls means, too."

"The SSA are coming," I told Red Knight.

"Oh, crap. I used my powers for vigilante activity. There's no statute of limitations on that." He'd replaced the beer he'd dropped and slammed some from the new can. "Get out of here kids. There's no point in all of us getting thrown in a hole."

The big black SUVs rolled up in front of the building right up onto the sidewalk. The sirens hadn't sounded, but the cherries were flashing. I could hear the screech of tires as the other exits of the building were covered.

"Go!" Red Knight ordered.

NINE

So we ran and got away.

The next morning the newspaper reported the arrest of the legendary Red Knight at an apartment building.

I went for a run and had a light low carb breakfast of scrambled eggs and some fruit.

Like Hell!

TEN

"We've got to go up," I said.

Several agents were streaming out of the back of the SSA vehicles. I called them SUV's, but they were more like troop transports crossed with a tank and given the heart of a monster truck.

"Can you fly with him?" I asked Peregrine.

"Fly with me?" The Red Knight did not like that idea.

"Not for very long," Peregrine admitted. Not like his ability to stiff arm gravity made any sense, but he could fly about one hundred pounds like it was a feather. At a hundred-twenty he started to sweat. Over two hundred and he was down to seconds of flight. Red Knight was a substantial, substantial man. His frame had both muscle and beer on it.

"You don't have time," Red Knight said.

"If they know who they're picking up, they might not have brought a flyer." I was grasping at straws. "You can't fly can you?"

He shook his head. "I couldn't even muster a stop sign right now."

Good. No reason the ability to make energy constructs could come in handy at the moment. "Not a problem. We've got this. Butterfly, we're making a run for it. Can you give us any help?"

"I will see what I can do," Butterfly responded. I think she already knew the situation had deteriorated.

I hoisted Red Knight out of his chair.

"Hey!" He realized what I was about to do, but didn't protest further. "This is how it ends, flopping like a bag of dirt."

"Bag of dirt would be lighter." Just an observation, not a judgment.

"My chair."

Peregrine tried to fold it up then ignored it. We would figure something out later. It wouldn't help us right now.

I nodded my head to the door. I wasn't going to be nimble with two hundred and seventy pounds of institutional memory on my back.

He cracked it. "They're coming."

We heard combat boots running up the stairs.

"Elevator!" I felt the Red Knight point, but he was swinging behind me so I couldn't tell where. We'd come in through the window so this was the first time I'd been in the hall.

"Where?"

"Left," he yelled.

"My left or your left?"

Peregrine motioned to a faded sign that said elevator.

I took point, in theory getting Red Knight as far from the SSA as we could.

We didn't close the door before we heard a crash of glass from Red Knight's window. And a growl and a howl.

I knew the SSA had a feral wolf man in town. I saw him

from a distance going over what was left of the Carlton. I'm not sure if he was a morphic or twisted feral. A morphic ferals turned into an animal, twisted were always stuck in bestial form. A little professional lingo for you to impress the ladies.

"Mint Am," I whispered. "Now!"

Hopefully Peregrine had come with a full complement of gear.

He had. He dropped the small vial of clear chemical, the mint Am. To a person with normal olfactory senses, it would smell like toothpaste. To a parahuman with a super sense of smell, it was a minty nuke. It could shut down a para's ability to use his nose for a day or two.

I put Red Knight down at the base of the elevator and started to force open the door.

A glowing red crow bar appeared at eye level. "Quickly." Red Knight's voice was strained.

I grabbed hold of it and jimmied the door open. The crow bar gave out, but the gap was wide enough for me to force it the rest of the way.

As luck would have it, the United States protectors, protectors who were alive because of me, were coming up the elevator shaft to arrest me.

Well, that was one way of getting out of summer school.

"Peregrine, now!"

While I was getting the door open, Peregrine had taken up the baton -- the grumpy and big, heavy baton -- and pushed past me into the elevator shaft.

They went straight down, then up slowly.

"Push it Peregrine. Push it!"

He started to gain a little speed.

I let the door close and leapt for the maintenance ladder.

It felt like cheating, using a ladder. I jumped up four or five rungs at a time. The elevator got to the floor we'd left and stopped.

I caught up to Peregrine on his ascent. "Come on P, get the lead out."

"Don't drop me," Red Knight protested.

There was no easy and fast way to transfer loads, so I just kept pace with them.

We heard some yelling and howling. Wolf-guy found our scent bomb. With any luck, they were dependent on Wolf-guy's tracking ability. Maybe reconfiguring their serch pattern would give me the seconds I need.

"They're in the elevator shaft," I heard someone yell.

Yep, poor guys are defenseless without their furry buddy. It's sad. "This is our floor." It was easier to get the door open from the inside out and Peregrine floated them both through.

Below me, the first SSA agent poked his head out the elevator maintenance hatch. I had enough warning to dodge the first couple of shots.

"Multiple targets, I repeat multiple targets," the guy yelled.

They already knew there was more than one. They'd said "they're in the the elevator." But now they had eyes on my uniform. Wouldn't take too much to figure out who was aiding and abetting.

Oh no, they might not be happy with me now. My spirit's crushed.

We were on the tenth floor of a twelve story building.

"Raven, window." Peregrine was down the hall and had chosen the north side.

I wound up and pitched one of my ball bearings through the window. I had a few of these bearings as my normal gear, but I was running low. One resource that I just took for granted when Raptor was around. Generally, I use them to knock adversaries in the noodle, but only as a last resort. They're the size of a golf ball and can kill a guy. It was nice to let loose and hit the window with a fastball.

Glass shattered and Peregrine was through it with Red Knight as quickly as he could. He dropped a little before he readjusted and started flying up again.

The north side was a mystery to me, so I took a quick look. A gutter drain, ten feet to the left. I hopped out the window and caught myself on a little ledge that ran under the window. I hand over handed it to the pipe and started going up the gutter. I lapped Peregrine quickly. He was really struggling under Red Knight's weight.

That made me nervous. He was not going to be able to jet away. He was barely going to be able to limp away with Red Knight. He had already spent a lot of juice flying civilians to safety in our Coal Golem slash Smokey fight. He might not even be able to get himself away.

I rolled onto the roof. The east wall, the side we'd come in, had a way out for me.

There might have been avenues of escape the other ways, but I hadn't cased the joint. Butterfly was right. I am a moron.

And the hits kept coming.

An SSA flyer crested the south side of the building. I'd seen him before. He was one of the flyers securing the crime scene in front of the Carlton. I wouldn't have mistaken him in his customized uniform of purple with a yellow bomber jacket and matching boots. He was surrounded in a yellow distortion.

Not only did this guy land gracefully, the four people with him landed gracefully.

For a second I thought there were five flyers, but the four were attached to the fifth guy with a translucent yellow distortion.

Three of the others were kitted out in standard SSA black combat armor. The fourth was dressed in blue and had an old style triangular shield strapped to one hand. I had never seen that guy.

"One Tango on the roof, Zuu Hotel," Purple and Yellow said into his radio.

Oh, yeah, two can play that game. "Whiskey, Tango, Foxtrot," I yelled back.

Purple raised his hand in the universal sign of "I'm about to do something so much cooler than you are."

I ran and rolled. Not only did I miss getting hit by a distortion field, one of the guard guys launched this net gun at me and I just missed that, too.

Come on, net guns?

Before the net gun guy could switch weapons, I closed the gap and delivered a couple of cracks to his head until he raised his arm and gun to defend himself. Then I worked the side and punched him right under the armpit.

One of the agents shot his fancy net gun at us. He must have decided that he could net us both and sort us out later.

The agent I was fighting was bent over. I jumped on his back, sprung into the air, and somersaulted. By the time I landed the net had passed under me and wrapped up the agent I had been fighting but good.

"Okay, I'm confused. Are you on my team?" I said to the agent as he tossed his net gun.

Another distortion field tried to grab me, but too slow.

There was only one more net gun, and I used the third agent as interference between the two of us.

Before he could get a new weapon I was on him. I grabbed a smoke grenade, popped it, and tossed it at Purple.

It never touched him. His yellow shield intercepted the grenade, but smoke started to billow out.

I hit the agent a couple more times and knocked him on his butt. He was armored enough I didn't have to pull my punches, but I wasn't knocking him out of the fight for sure, either.

And I got grabbed.

Yellow lit up my suit and I couldn't move. And believe me, I was trying. Last week I got wrapped up like this by Silhouette, powerless and terrified. I hated it. At least Silhouette would have killed me. He would have played with me for a while, but he would have killed me in the end. These guys would drop me in a hole for at least a decade. They might even bring my mom into it somehow.

"This is Oracle. We have one Tango down."

"Butterfly," I whispered into the radio. "If you're going to do anything, it's now or never."

"I need more time," was her robotic response.

"Hey, you," I yelled at Purple. "Oracle is it?"

He floated me over to him. The shield guy was keeping an eye on me, while the agents were helping each other up.

"Where are your friends?" Oracle asked.

"They're more like associates." I had to clear the confusion, it was ruining my street cred.

"Where did they go?"

Some days the universe just hands you a straight line like that. "Behind you."

Peregrine had floated up and had used me and the smoke to keep people looking the wrong direction. He set Red Knight down and collided with Oracle, classic head butt to the back of the head.

The yellow glowing field cut out. I landed and mule kicked under the shield guy's shield.

Peregrine unloaded all his pent up kung fu on the agents. Let the record show, I softened them up for him. Not that Peregrine needed it, if I'm going to be honest. The man was fast, and could attack you from every angle. I knew that from experience. The agents were in for a flying bucket of suck.

Speaking of buckets of suck, Peregrine left the shield guy for me.

Shield guy hadn't recovered fully from my sucker punch, so I pressed my advantage. Shield didn't have a full face mask. Silly, if you ask me. I love my full face protection. So that's why I aimed for his chin.

I landed two solid punches that knocked him back on his heels. For the third, he picked up his shield and stopped my fist.

Ouch.

And then he started fighting back. So not fair.

He was good, better than me. And he used the shield like it was part of him. I can't say I've fought that many shield carriers. It's a mentality issue. Bad guys want offenses, and that's who I fight. Good guys who want to protect would have a shield. I don't fight that many good guys as a rule, and Raptor never trained me against shields.

It was unsettling.

Wamp! I ate the shield in an uppercut and staggered back.

Peregrine flew in and took over the fisticuffs.

In the spirit of keeping track of my surroundings -- I'm learning -- I looked around. We were doing way better than I'd thought. But they didn't have to win, they just had to slow us down.

Dozens of agents and at least one more super were now trying to get to the roof.

Oracle was dazed, but he sat up and peered around for a target.

"Peregrine, behind you," I shouted, but not in time.

His body lit up with yellow and he stopped in mid-air. This was a different kettle of fish though. Peregrine wasn't me, he could fly. His body jerked back and forth in Oracle's mental grip. This looked like a new experience for our boy in purple and yellow. Oracle seemed to jerk around under Peregrine's attempts at freeing himself, his face going from surprise to concentration.

With Oracle's focus elsewhere, I ran at him and spun in the air to deliver my trademark double boot to the head. And failed. A shield got between me and my target. It was like hitting a brick wall.

I fell, and he landed on me hard. He twisted me and I was pinned, face down in the roof.

"Give it up, kid. You fought a good fight, but I don't want to hurt you." Was it Clint Eastwood under that mask? It sounded like Clint Eastwood. All the damage I'd done to his jaw and he was still able to sound badass and gravely.

"So what's your thing? Were you bitten by a radioactive spaghetti western?" I made a good effort to break free, and he manhandled me like I'd said something about his sister.

"Something like that, Raven."

"You know about me. Cool." I looked over at Red Knight.

The original Guard's hand was stretched out, glowing red, but then it flickered out. First his hand dropped, then he seemed to pass out.

"Bloodhunt confirmed you were at the Lennbrook

building, right where we found Silhouette and Shale."
Bloodhunt equals Wolf-guy, noted.

"You're welcome." If he'd wanted to chat I would have
let him and use that opportunity to make my escape. I have
a move that allows me to escape every hold. I call it my
Always Free move. It hurts, and I have to bend in crazy
awkward ways. I pushed hard and did my move.

It did not work.

I may have to rename that move.

Shield guy slapped me around and forced me back into
a pin. "You've got skills, kid, but you did not take down
Silhouette and Shale."

"You think I've got skills? Thanks." That was
encouraging. I needed a pick-me-up right then.

"We know you're working with a parahuman capable of
dampening powers." He'd put one plus one together and
gotten five, but an understandable mistake. Butterfly had
turned on the nullifier long enough for me to beat six shades
of crap out of Silhouette and Shale.

Good times, good times.

Some SSA supers must have been caught in the field,
too. It would be great if everyone thought it was a unique
super and not a mass-producible device. "He died, shot
himself in the face." Let's pin that on Clockwork. "He was
no friend of mine."

"Three," Butterfly said.

"His profile fits Clockwork," Shield guy said.

"Two."

"He set us up, set up all the Guard." I did not want
anyone to think I was working with Clockwork.

"Where are the rest of the Guard? Where's Raptor?"
Shield asked. "He always said this city was his, but where is
he now?"

"One."

"Blue Fish!" Flare yelled over the radio.

Shield was ready for an escape attempt, but escape was not my plan. I peeled off his visor and closed my eyes.

Even through my eye shield, it was painfully bright. Flare must have dropped everything.

Shield pulled his hand to cover his exposed eyes. Peregrine got free as Oracle did the same, and the agents that were regaining their footing screamed in pain.

I broke Shield's grip and connected but good with my elbow. He dropped off me, his nose gushing blood.

"Incapacitate Oracle and they will not be able to follow you." Butterfly was still all robot.

"How can you be sure?" Flare asked.

"You are not swamped by other flying supers," Butterfly said.

"Fair enough."

That made sense. Shield was blind and in pain. It was like getting up to bat for t-ball. I spun kicked him into next Tuesday.

Oracle had balled up. A distortion shield bubbled around him and he rubbed at his eyes.

Peregrine kicked it hard, but got no where.

"Flare, if you would do the honors?" I asked.

Flare was panting. For some reason the blinding attack was harder on her than death beams. Go figure.

She reached out her hand and gave two blasts.

Oracle's shield dropped.

I closed the distance. "Oh, I love the boots." And I kicked him in the head. "One Oracle incapacitated."

"Go! They're bringing in helicopters," Butterfly said.

"Damn." Flare wasn't the best stealthy flyer. She had to glow in the dark like... well, a flare, one would say.

"Where do we go?" Peregrine had picked up Red Knight again.

"Hastings and 5th." Red Knight moaned. "Alpha base."

We looked at each other. It was close. We could make it.

"Go. I'll meet you there," I told both of them. Flare was worse at flying weight than Peregrine. I was hoofing it out of here. "I have to go the long way anyway. They have a scent tracker with them."

I took the time to jam something in the door and pop a smoke grenade I found on my way out.

ELEVEN

I doubled back, ran through a sewer tunnel, did some crazy roof to roof stuff, and rode a panel truck for a couple of miles. If Bloodhunt still tracked me down, then it was just meant to be. Raptor had always told me that the armor had some scent-killing properties, but they didn't seem to work on Bloodhunt.

Butterfly talked me into the abandoned factory that was Alpha base. Raptor had called the Clubhouse Gamma base. I'd just assumed it was one of his mind jobs, but if there was an Alpha site, was there a Beta, too?

Flare came out to direct me the rest of the way.

The second I saw her I gave her a big hug. She was not ready for it and I could tell she thought it was awkward, but screw that. "You saved me, thank you, thank you, thank you. My children, should I ever have any, thank you." Another big hug.

"Need to breathe," she mentioned, and I set her down.

"I can't believe you got there that fast," I said.

"I didn't. Butterfly called me the second Peregrine got involved with the conflict at the gas station."

"Why didn't she call me?"

"I did. You didn't answer," Butterfly said. I was still on the channel with her.

I had turned off my call function to dodge Mom. I turned it on. My mom and the untraceable group call number were in my caller ID. How long would that number remain untraceable now that Raptor wasn't around supporting it?

"If she didn't call you, then why were you in the field?" Just a little accusation in her voice.

"Family stuff, I needed to clear my head." I shrugged.

You get good at reading body language when you can't count on expression. She was looking at me, appraising my motives.

"Honest, I wasn't patrolling or anything. I'm clean. I don't have a problem. I can quit any time." I held up my hand, palm out. "How's Ballista?" I knew his real name, but I thought of him as Ballista.

She relaxed a little. "Really well. Still exhausted and sleeping a lot, but he is ... good."

And by "good" she meant not brain damaged or any physical deformations. Both can happen with a surge, and Ballista's surge was triggered by the nullifier so who knows what could have happened.

"That's awesome." I relaxed a little too.

"Let's join the others." She nodded the way she'd come.

I made careful note of the twists and turns it took to get to some big chunks of machinery. She moved a valve to reveal a code pad. It looked old fashioned compared to the stuff we used in the Clubhouse. She punched in a code she let me see.

The whole metal gear box thing slid away with a squeak.

"Welcome to the Fox Hole." Red Knight still looked ashen, but was sitting in a beat-up wheelchair.

Peregrine was there as well. I knew he would be, but I can dream.

You could have fit the entire Alpha base into a corner of the Clubhouse and not noticed it if you weren't looking for it.

The center was dominated by a big boardroom table surrounded by well used chairs. There was a counter of computers, all the cutting edge technology of 1997. And a pile of boxes sat in the corner.

Red Knight saw what I was looking at and squirmed. "Well, I've been using this place as storage." He patted his chair. "That's why I had an old chair stashed here."

"Fair enough." Made sense to me.

He pointed at each door in turn . "Kitchen through there. Gym through there, bunks through there, and shower through there." He looked at Flare. "Not a lot of privacy in the locker room."

"What?" Flare was surprised, but it wasn't her modesty that was the problem. "How did you protect your identities?"

Red Knight seemed confused as he looked at each of us. "What do you mean? Wait, you don't know who each other are?"

Flare shook her head, but I waved my hand a little.

I knew who Peregrine was, and I had seen Flare unconscious when I'd rescued her last week. Don't let the long blond hair fool you -- it's a wig. She's actually East Asian, and hot!

Peregrine knew who I was, and we all knew Ballista's face and first name. I'd also seen Butterfly out of her costume. She wasn't naked or anything, just out of her costume. It was totally innocent. She's really cute, too. She's got these freckles and dimples.

"Raptor has a lot of procedures in place to keep our identities a secret," Peregrine said.

"Like total paranoia." I ignored Peregrine's present tense use of Raptor and his protocols.

"Wow. Well, I can't blame him after what happened with Osprey and his family," Red Knight said.

"What happened to Osprey and his family?" This was the second time today it had come up. Oh, wait. It was the next day. Forty-eight minutes into the next day.

"You don't know?" Red Knight couldn't believe our education was so lapsed.

"I know." Peregrine didn't seem proud, or interested in sharing with the rest of the class.

"Well, I guess you all have the right to know," Red Knight said. "It might make it a little easier to understand Raptor and his precautions." He still didn't look ready to tell us, but finally began. "I'm sure you know grief can trigger a surge. Well, when Hawk died, or rather was killed by Jackal--"

And everyone gave me an accusing look.

Red Knight picked up on that, but didn't press. "Well, the first group of apprentices that Raptor trained -- Hawk, Osprey, and Shadow Hawk -- they got close, like brothers. And Osprey shared enough of his personal life with Shadow Hawk that Shadow figured out who he really was. Maybe Osprey just told him, I don't know. When Hawk died, Shadow Hawk surged and surged hard. He was off by himself so there was no one to help talk him through it.

"It was bad. Total personality disintegration. Raptor tried to take him down and get him help, but he didn't realize just how fried he was. If you ask me, he didn't want to know. And Osprey's father and brother paid the price. After that Raptor broke the number one rule and called in the SSA.

"It didn't work. SSA didn't put enough resources to the hunt, and the next thing we knew Shadow was working for Caesar. Then he left the city and popped up now and again on the West Coast."

That explained what Mrs. Raptor had said. Dominoes played in Hell. Hawk's death triggered Silhouette, and that caused Osprey's tragedy. If Jackal was to be believed, Silhouette was chased out of town by Caesar after an action even too bloody and chaotic for Caesar. "At some point he changed his handle to Silhouette," I said.

"When he started working for Caesar." Red Knight nodded. "I was out of the team by then. Of course, Raptor kept me up to speed." He laughed. "Even asked for advice from time to time from his former mentor."

We were silent for a while. It all made more sense now. Why Raptor didn't want any of the apprentices fraternizing. Peregrine and I knew each other before I became a member, and I'm a para 1 and he's a para 2. You don't have to worry about surges being dangerous until you get to para 3.

"So what are you all planning on doing?" Red Knight asked.

"What?" The question was so obvious but such a blow. I started to get tired. I don't have to worry about surging, blowing up, or going psycho, but I burn adrenaline by the bucket and then crash and crash hard.

"Whoa." Flare was holding me up.

"Sorry." I did not remember her crossing the room to support me.

"Sit." She kept one hand on me and angled a chair.

I shook my head and stood. "No, if I sit down I'll be out for a week." I was on sturdy footing and started bouncing on the balls of my feet. "I'm good. Just have to get the blood pumping a little." Great way to get the blood pumping? Pick a fight with my old chum. "So what was your plan?" I directed the question at Peregrine.

"What?"

"You and Butterfly forming your own dynamic duo?" I asked. "You were working a mission by yourself."

"It wasn't a mission." Butterfly had powered down and now sounded human and defensive. "We were just going to track down Red Knight."

"Well, I'm glad you did," Red Knight said. "That gas station fight would have resulted in a lot of deaths."

"We can't keep doing this. I can't keep doing this." Flare waved her hands over her uniform. "We aren't the Guard. Next time you're pretending to be the Guard I won't be able to save you. The SSA are all over this city. Maybe they can keep a lid on the supers until things settle down."

"You're right, Flare. You're right," Red Knight said. "This isn't your fight. You all did enough."

"I didn't sign on to 'do enough,'" Peregrine directed at Red Knight. "I signed on to be a Guard. Nothing has changed."

"Are you kidding me?" Flare's aura ignited for just a second. "Everything CHANGED! Orion is dead, Raptor is dead. Cat, Landslide, they're all dead. We would have been dead too if Raven hadn't rescued us."

"Just want to give a shout out to Butterfly. Team effort." I tapped my helmet.

Flare looked at me, but that didn't seem to be the point. "We might have powers, but that doesn't mean we're invulnerable. I'm the most powerful of the team and the last thing I remember was the chaos of the Carlton fight and then I woke up in the back of a stolen van."

"That's what being a Guard is." I used a quiet voice. "That's what we signed on for."

"Not me! I signed on to learn how to use my powers before I blew up and hurt my family. I think they'll be plenty hurt if I end up dead!"

How did I end up on team Peregrine again, when I wanted to be on team Flare? But here I went. "This city needs the Guard more than ever." What was I even saying? Was I ready to sign on with JV squad? Even with Red Knight's help we weren't keeping the streets clean.

"This town needs more than a couple teenagers playing superhero. The Carlton, that thing at the office building, the explosion at Bio-Globe that killed that CEO. This town has gone nuts!" Green flashed in patches around her.

Did she have issues like this outside of her uniform? Maybe she just never got this pissed at anyone else. "The CEO thing was Raptor. It was a cover for his death. So that isn't anything we have to worry about."

That got a lot of looks.

"What?"

"You knew Raptor's true identity?" Peregrine was shocked.

"I'm pretty sure his true identity was Raptor, but his civilian ID was this Archibald guy."

"He's right, but I'm interested in how you know." All eyes went to Red Knight, then back to me.

I checked the time. "I rescued his widow from a group of Headsmen like six hours ago."

More looks.

"It's been a busy day." What?

"And you're not patrolling?" Butterfly had the decency just to send that to me.

"What did the Headsmen want with Julia?" Red Knight was suddenly a lot more interested and he seemed to take on a different persona. His fingers were steepled, and he leaned back in his chair. "Or rather, if it's the Headsmen, then I should ask what does Jack Midas want with Julia?"

I shrugged. "She didn't really talk that much. She's some kind of kickass secret agent. Told me to go home. I heard them question her, some egoist named the Confessor. He was really interested in the Phoenix."

That got Red Knight's attention. It might have gotten everyone else's attention too, but they were in masks, so I couldn't really tell.

"And what did she tell them?" Red Knight asked.

"She didn't know where it was. Only three people even knew about it." I tried to think back. "Boslin?"

"Bosin?" Red Knight asked.

"That was one."

"Not too helpful. That's me, Edward Bosin. Pleased to meet you," Red Knight said. "Who were the other two?"

"Mr. Y." That was the last name she'd said. I was trying to remember the other.

"Doesn't ring a bell," Red Knight said. "Was the third Franklin Kause?"

"That was it." Frank, but probably the same guy.

"I'm glad you saved her, but this doesn't change anything." Flare jumped in while Red Knight was mulling over the information.

"I disagree, Flare," Red Knight said. "I disagree most hardily. Everything has changed."

"What do you mean?" Peregrine asked, suddenly more alert, like a terrier told to go fetch.

"Ask him what the Phoenix is," Butterfly said on the common channel.

Sure, I'll play. "What's the Phoenix?"

His bushy eyebrows raised and lowered. "I'm surprised you don't know."

"Really? Did you meet Raptor?" I asked.

Red Knight gave a small smile at my joke. "The Phoenix is -- was -- Archie's backup. All his important data from his company and his vigilante activity was stored in the Phoenix."

"Do you know where it is?" Flare asked.

He shook his head. "It was right there." He pointed at an empty corner in the Alpha base. "I don't know where he moved it."

We knew there was a massive database on every parahuman in, well, the world. But he'd never called it anything.

"So some of Raptor's files end up in Midas' hands." Flare shrugged. "Not ideal, but--"

"We're in those files," Butterfly said.

That shut Flare up.

I repeated what Butterfly said for the radio impaired in the room.

"She's right," Red Knight agreed. "The Confessor isn't looking for information about you. I doubt they know Archie is Raptor."

"What are they looking for?" Peregrine asked.

"My guess?" Red Knight put out his hands. "Industrial secrets. Midas must have found out about Archibald Valtire's computer backup, but there's no way he's connected that Archie to Raptor. I'm sure Midas will be pleasantly surprised if he finds the Phoenix."

I took that seat that Flare had offered. "Well, crap."

"We would be completely exposed, and it's not even what they're looking for," Peregrine said.

It would mean turning ourselves into the Feds and begging them to protect our families. We would never have a free day for the rest of our lives and our families would be relocated to some farm town or something. If the SSA protected them at all.

"I'm sorry, but you'll have to postpone retirement for at least until we get the Phoenix," Red Knight said.

I asked for Butterfly, "What would be the parameters for a search?"

"Well, we have to find Frank," Red Knight said.

"What was his last known location?" Butterfly asked through me. I could hear her starting to tap a key.

"Last time I saw him?" He pointed to a different corner of the conference room. "Day after the battle with Purge. Maybe it was only hours after the battle with Purge. The base was turned into a medical bay. A doctor saved my life, just couldn't save my legs. Frank, or Imp as you know him, could jump into people and control them for short periods."

"He could possess people?" Flare thought that was disgusting.

Red Knight nodded. "The guy he was riding died with him inside. His mind was gone. A complete vegetable. I asked Archie where he put him, but he just told me that he would be well cared for. I was too stuck in my own misery to push the issue. And later, well, I trusted Archie's word."

"That narrows things down," Butterfly said. "It isn't that common of a condition. Assuming Archibald Valtire didn't skimp on care, even if he hid the money trail, there aren't that many facilities to give that level of care."

"If they stayed in the city," I pointed out.

"Archie would keep him close," Red Knight said. "I'm

sure he visited every once in a while. Kind of thing Archie would do."

"Well, if we're looking for a high end facility that's capable of giving that level of care there are three places." The tapping of Butterfly's computer could be heard over the channel.

I passed on the info to Red Knight.

"Any with connections to Bio-Globe?" Red Knight asked.

"Yes, Apex care." I repeated Butterfly's reply.

"Then let's get going," Red Knight said.

"Are you sure you should? You're wanted by the SSA now," Flare said.

"I've been wanted by the SSA for twenty years." Red Knight waved his hand.

"But now they know your name," I pointed out.

"I could stay, but do any of you know what Frank looks like?"

He had a point.

"How about we send you a photo of any candidates? Look, it isn't going to be easy sneaking around a hospital in uniform, never mind a guy in a wheelchair." Yes, I am that big of a tool. I regretted it the second I said it.

He didn't look slapped. He looked crushed. "Yeah, when you're right you're right. The guy in a wheelchair will wait by the phone. Or I can drive us there."

I loved this man. "Drive, you say? Tell me more."

"I have a van." He nodded his head toward the door already designated "bunks." "I store it in the garage, because parking is way too expensive in the city."

"We shouldn't," Flare began.

"I love this idea." I jumped in. There was no easy way to get across town for a guy like me. Getting to the docks was a piece of cake compared to this journey. "Let's do a pro-con list." I counted them off on my fingers. "Traffic won't be bad at this time of night, I wouldn't have to walk, we could move safer with all the SSA looking for us, I wouldn't have to walk, it would keep us together instead of spread out, and this is a big one, I wouldn't have to walk."

TWELVE

Butterfly directed us to Apex Care. If it didn't have the name on a sign right out front, it would have looked like a very nice office park. The area was light years away from the Kages. All the street lights worked, the pavement was smooth, hardly any graffiti.

"I'll check it out." Peregrine moved to open the back of the van. Of all of us, he was the least interested in driving around town in a van. He liked flying and didn't glow like Flare. This was a major inconvenience to him and was driving him nuts, pun intended.

I wouldn't say that made the drive sweeter, but it did. It did a lot.

"Red, we clear?" Nice thing about Red driving is we didn't have someone in costume stuck in traffic.

He took a good look around. "Place looks how a private clinic should look at 2:38 am. Wait, that isn't right. The main doors are open."

That was good enough for us. We piled out of the van. It was just the three of us. I'd lobbied hard for Butterfly to join us but she wasn't having it. She didn't trust herself in the field. I couldn't blame her. I'd seen firsthand what had happened. But I'd also seen her sneak around a building. She was amazing. I couldn't think of a better guide.

We did not need a guide today.

The front entrance had large glass doors that allowed you to see a tasteful front room with an admissions desk and comfortable waiting area. At the moment, the glass had a massive hole, with only tiny bits of glass still connected to the brass hinges.

"This was caused by a parahuman electrical blast," I said with authority.

"How do you know?" Peregrine doubted my analysis.

"Because I fought a super working with the Confessor who did this kind of thing." I pointed at the electric scorch marks on the floor.

"Whatever." Peregrine was not impressed.

We were already moving but Peregrine pulled ahead and Flare glowed and took to the air.

"The Care facility has a private suite on the seventh floor," Butterfly told us.

"Sounds like the place." Flare flew directly up.

"Can I get a lift?" I asked Peregrine.

"No. I don't have anything extra after carrying Red Knight around his apartment building."

I heard most of his excuse over the group channel. He was following close to Flare.

"I wish I could fly," I groaned through my teeth.

The building was one of these modern lots of glass and windows things. I wasn't making it up the outside of the building and going in alone was stupid.

"Let's go." Red Knight was out of the van and spinning his wheels toward the broken glass. "We don't have a lot of time."

"Good thing you have some backup, RK." I caught up with him. "You know, while we're here, we might be able to upgrade your chair."

"Ha," he responded. I think he was pumped to be back in the field, because he was in way too good of a mood. "We have to be quick. Police will be here soon. A place like this has to have some kind of alarm system."

I beat him to the elevator and hit the button.

The door opened.

I jumped in the elevator before the doors opened completely and collided with Arc and the Confessor.

Awkward.

If I could fly, I wouldn't be dealing with this crap.

I started swinging elbows and knees so hard and so fast I didn't have time to call for backup.

The Confessor reached out for me, but I angled his hand to Arc, and Arc screamed.

I followed up with a kick to Arc's head and he stumbled.

The doors were open enough now, and the Confessor stumbled out. I must have scored a hit because he was clutching his side.

"Why do you want the Phoenix?" I yelled.

That got the Confessor's attention, and he ate a small red glowing wrecking ball to the head.

He must have had a helmet under that scary hood because it didn't knock him cold. Instead he staggered and collided into an exhausted Red Knight.

"Red, watch his hands!" I tried to warn him.

I wasn't fast enough. Red had wrapped the Confessor in a half-nelson as they flopped around on the floor. Both of the Confessor's hands landed on Red Knight's head.

Red Knight screamed and went rigid as a post. His legs

didn't move, but everything above the waist seemed attached to cables trying to tear his body apart.

I grabbed the Confessor and pulled him off of the oldest living Guard.

In the reflection of the lobby glass I saw a blue light building behind me and dived into Red Knight. He was still stiff as a board and I rode him a few feet, enough to miss the arc of electricity.

Ding. Another elevator opened. This one was empty.

I rolled Red Knight into the elevator and missed another electric bolt.

"Raven! Get up here, there are Headsmen!" Peregrine screamed over the radio. I could hear the report of suppressed gunfire and Flare's returning blasts.

"They're down here, too!" I yelled back. I reached up and pounded a floor button and the door close button.

Arc rounded the corner and held out his hand, a blue nimbus forming.

The doors closed.

I felt sure he would still shoot, but maybe he was faking. Or he figured it wasn't worth it. No, not faking. A zip pop echoed.

I pressed the button for the floor Peregrine and Flare were on and rode the elevator until it reached the floor I'd panic-selected first. I got ready for anything.

The doors opened.

A guy in his eighties wearing a bathrobe started to move his walker, then stopped when he saw us.

"We can make room," I offered.

He made no move to enter.

"No?" The doors shut.

"Red, are you okay?"

He didn't look good. His teeth were clenched together

and his fingernails were digging into his palms. Every muscle seemed locked.

"Red?" I tried to shake him. That's a thing, right? You try to shack unresponsive people?

It worked.

His body went limp, and he gasped like he hadn't been able to breathe until now. "Holy crap, what was that?"

"The Confessor. He got my leg and it locked up. I think he did the same thing to your head."

"Egoists. I hate egoists," Red Knight said through gasping breaths.

"Are you okay?" I asked. Because that's the next thing you do, right?

"No. My back is broken and I don't have a chair again." He pulled himself up to a sitting position. "What's it with you and your rescues?"

I had nothing to say to that.

The report of gunfire could be heard before the doors opened.

"You have anything left in the tank?" I asked.

"A little." He had one hand on the elevator handrail. "Enough."

He better have.

The doors opened.

I did a quick "peek and back" that I'd seen on TV that looked cool, so I tried it. The Headsmen were falling back to the elevators, either trying to escape that way or down the stairs across the hall. These guys were some vanillas like I'd fought when I was rescuing Raptor's widow.

Yes, the official story is that I was doing the rescuing.

Mostly.

It was a team effort.

In those situations everything is fluid.

Flare was corralling them this way, but unable to get a clear shot. She could have her force wall up and be bulletproof or shoot rays of kick butt light. It was tough to do both. I've seen her do it, though.

"Peregrine, location?" I asked over the radio.

"Flare is moving them to a hall with a window. I'm coming in from behind."

In my peek I'd spotted the window that he was referring to. He would have to go soon if he was going to get them from behind.

"Now!" Flare shouted.

I'll take that as my cue.

There was nothing fancy I could do. No room for cool acrobatics. I just ran flat out. I had one of my two remaining ball bearings in my hand, just in case the gunmen turned around.

One realized I was coming, but before he could adjust, the window exploded in a shower of glass and Peregrine clotheslined both of them.

Before Peregrine could return I was on them, peeling weapons from their hands.

One punched my face. I let him.

He pulled his hand back in agony.

"Dude, I'm wearing a helmet. What's wrong with you?" An uppercut and he was no longer going to be a problem.

The second guy drew a knife, but a flash of green light knocked him on his back. He was still moving but making moaning noises.

Gunfire erupted behind me. There was a guy behind us who'd come out of a closed residence's door.

The spray of bullets hit a red glowing wall of brick and then a red anvil dropped on his head.

Then Peregrine did something I'm sure was remarkable, but I missed it and the third gunman was down.

"They were doing something to that room when we got here." Flare pointed back a couple of rooms.

"A little help." Red Knight had half his body out of the elevator and the doors were closing on him then opening with a ding.

"Right." I picked him up again. He was not light. As luck would have it, this was a hospital and the room that ambush guy had snuck out of still had the door open. I saw a wheelchair.

I fetched the chair. The bed was occupied by an old woman. She didn't even twitch. "Sorry ma'am."

She probably wouldn't be using the chair anytime soon.

Mobile once again, Red Knight wheeled his way to the room in question.

Unlike the rest of the rooms, this door had a sophisticated electronic lock, but it was completely fried.

"That's him," Red Knight said. He wheeled himself right next to the bed.

This room was nicer than the one I'd just been in. It had a little balcony with a view of the river and over to the skyline of the Island.

The beeps of the monitoring machines and the squeak of the wheelchair were the only sounds. That and the labored breathing of the shell of a man in the bed.

He was well taken care of, his hair cut, and he was clean.

I noticed two thumbprint-sized burns on his forehead, worse than the ones given to Julia.

"Hi, Frank." I don't think Red Knight thought he would get a response, but he did.

Frank twitched and jumped at his name, his eyes wide and panicked. "Edward?"

We all stepped closer. Red Knight grabbed his hand and Frank squeezed it. "Purge. Did we win?"

"Yes, Frank. You did it. Saved the city," Red Knight said. "You got the bomb out in time."

Frank relaxed a little. "Good, good. Archie was right, we shouldn't..." He trailed off.

Red Knight shook him a little. "Frank, stay with us."

His eyes focused on Red Knight. "Bosin, sir. What's the mission?"

"There was a man here. What did he want? What did you tell him?"

"A man?" Frank was trying to think. "I can't remember, so foggy, so much. Oh God, I killed him. That guy, Stratosphere. I killed him!"

"You saved all of us," Red Knight said. "Stratosphere, Warzone, Devastator, all of Purge. They were trying to hurt so many people. You saved us."

"Stratosphere didn't want to do it. He was so afraid. I made him. I made him fly higher and higher."

"You didn't have a choice. If you hadn't controlled Stratosphere, made him fly the bomb up, Archie would have done it. You did the right thing."

"Did I?"

"What about the Confessor?" Red Knight tried to get Frank back to the now.

"Confessor? So much to confess." He almost faded out again.

"Police and SSA are converging on your location," Butterfly said.

"We have to go," I told Red Knight.

"Where's the Phoenix?" Red Knight tried. "Frank, where's the Phoenix?"

"Yaltin!" He screamed. "Yaltin would know. Mr Y would know. He would know."

"We're leaving now!" Flare said.

Frank had one more second of coherence. "Am I being punished for my sins?" His eyes went blank and his body eased.

"Police are coming. You have got to go."

Red Knight seemed as drained as Frank. "We're all being punished for our sins. Sleep well, Frank."

He didn't seem like he was willing to move, so I wheeled him out of the room at a run.

THIRTEEN

W e got into the van with Red Knight at the wheel. We got a minute out of the parking lot when he pulled over to let the SSA and Metro race by, sirens blaring.

My heart was pounding, and I could see the rest of the team was ready to bust out of the van.

The last siren passed and Red Knight started the van moving.

I had a second to think. "I know that name, Yaltin."

"Really?" Flare said.

"Yes, I know things. What do you mean 'really'?" What did she mean *really*?

"I know you know things. It's just pretty specific."

"Could Yaltin be the Mr. Y?" Butterfly asked.

I ran Butterfly's question by Red Knight.

"It would make sense." Red Knight nodded. "It was a classic training technique to thwart egoist assaults, think of the people with cryptic code names that even if they had the name, it wouldn't help. I could see Julia trying that."

Though it didn't stop her from giving up poor Frank or

Bosin. But maybe she knew they didn't know anything. Yaltin was the important person.

"You said you know Yaltin. Who is he?" Butterfly asked.

We have *got* to get Red a radio. I repeated Butterfly's question before answering. "Julia told the Confessor that if he wanted ransom, he should contact Yaltin."

"Why were you there?" An edge of accusation crept into Peregrine's voice.

"What's that supposed to mean?" I asked.

"You just happened to find Julia in her moment of need?"

"We're not accusing you of anything." Flare cut in before Peregrine could accuse me of something. "But we were all going to quit, and it isn't even twelve hours later and we're fighting paras across the city again."

"Raptor would give us these scavenger hunt missions," I said.

Peregrine nodded, but Flare shrugged.

"We would get a text from an 808 number-"

"Mine were 907," Peregrine said.

"Whatever. It would be a different number but the same area code. We would go there, find a letter, go back to our nest, decode the number, and do the instructions. I got one of those calls just after we all went home from the funeral."

"Why didn't you call us?" Butterfly said.

"I didn't know that the Peregrine and Butterfly dynamic duo were still fighting crime." Why didn't I call them? Because if it was from Raptor, he would have called them if he'd wanted them there. "I don't know. I just figured it was a computer glitch."

"A glitch? You traveled an hour or more out of your way

to chase down a glitch?" Butterfly was accusing me of something.

"Julia had this James Bond watch thing, and she sent a call for help. I helped." This was a lot less sneaky than running around looking for Red Knight. I was the victim here.

"Did you get the letter?" I didn't even think Red Knight was listening.

"No. I mean, I got it." I fished it out of my pouch. "But it wasn't for me. I can't decode it. I figured she must have screwed up and given me Peregrine's last instructions."

Peregrine snatched it from me. Don't know what he was going to do with it. Did he have his library with him?

"This isn't based on a book in my code library." He reluctantly handed it back to me.

"You have the ISBN numbers of your code library memorized?" Bull.

"Yes," Peregrine said.

"Code library?" Flare asked.

"Classic cold war cipher technique," Red Knight said. "We used it in the early days of the Guard. A list of numbers relates to page numbers and a number of the word on the page."

"Yes, but add three or four more layers of BS and you have Raptor's system," I agreed.

Red Knight gave a laugh at that. "Archie always made things more complicated than they needed to be."

"Orion didn't make you use a code?" I asked Flare.

She shook her head. "If he wanted to call me, he would call me. He wouldn't even text."

"Well, sure, if you want to just trash the rich apprentice tradition." I put the letter back in my pouch since I didn't know what else to do with it.

"Clockwork and I communicated with a code that derived from Pi," Butterfly said. "So the letter is not for me either, though I doubt there was much chance of that."

"Okay, we'll deal with Raptor's note in a second." Red Knight pulled the van into a gas station. "We need to find this Yaltin. I'm sure if you hadn't gotten there when you did, Frank would have been killed. They're not going to leave loose ends, especially since they know we're right behind them."

"There is an Isaac Yaltin that works for Bio-Globe. In fact, he is Archibald's partner," Butterfly said. "He owned Bio-Globe when it was a startup and tried to sell a patent for a GMO carrot. Then Archibald bought seventy percent of the company and switched their focus to parahuman studies. They made the only test with a one-hundred percent accuracy rating in detecting manifested parahumans, and the cuff, the main way law enforcement apprehends supers." Butterfly read us the Wikipedia page, or whatever.

I noticed Flare put her hand on her wrist. Clockwork had used a cuff to keep her sedated. I can't imagine how that experience must have felt.

Peregrine relayed the information to Red Knight this time.

Flare noticed me looking, and dropped her hands. "Fine. Where does this Isaac Yaltin live? Let's try to get in front of these assholes for once."

"He lives on the Island." Butterfly gave an address.

I groaned. It was almost an hour drive out to the Island, depending on traffic on the Bridge. It would be rush hour by the time we got headed back home. It was past 3:00 am now.

"But because of the explosion at the main Bio-Globe

facility he is staying on this side of the river." Butterfly was quickly hitting keys. "Bio-Globe has a house that they use for executives and special guests. At the level of damage control that is happening, I assume he will be at that house."

"Damage control?" I knew the place had blown up.

"The facility that was destroyed was their testing facility. There were hundreds of tests still to be processed. The company is claiming they don't know when or if they will be able to resume processing samples. Everyone is up in arms and wants the company to share their method with other companies to get the processing back in service. They are calling it a matter of national security."

"That sucks." For them, I guess.

"That's it," Red Knight said. "That's why they want the Phoenix." He pounded the steering wheel.

"National security?" That didn't sound right.

"In a way. Somehow they found out about the Phoenix, but not that it was Raptor's master backup. They think it's the chief executive officer and owner of Bio-Globe's master backup."

"They want the parahuman testing technique," Flare said.

"That's awful, kinda, I mean... So?" I still didn't want my ID exposed to Jack Midas, but it didn't really raise the stakes for me if some other company was testing for supers.

"If Midas gets that test he's not going to sell it to a rival company. He would sell it to a rival nation. He would sell it to all the rival nations." Red Knight was getting revved up.

"Not sure why we're out of 'so' territory," I put in.

"It's the worst kept secret that China and Russia, as well as North Korea and a handful of other nations, have parahuman military programing. It's the next arms race. Who can weaponize more parahumans? If they got their hands on a test that could process their entire population, it would give them an edge over countries that respect people's privacy."

"Not sure I know of a country like that." There were all kinds of ways to "give permission" for a parahuman test. Any scholarship, military service, or most medical fields required screening. More fields were being added every day. Soon I wasn't going to be able to ask if a person wanted fries with that without being screened.

"It could change the international politics overnight," Red Knight said. "We have to get the information."

"And destroy it," Flare said.

"Destroy it?" Peregrine wasn't opposed. It was more of an "I'm interested, tell me more. Is there a number I could call for more information?" kind of destroy it.

"If no one has this test, great. That ends the second-class citizen debate once and for all," Flare said. "We all know the direction this is heading. If we can stop people from being shut out, well, it will be the most good we've done as Guard."

"Do we have the right to make a choice that affects millions..." I started. "Just kidding. Yeah, destroy it, I'm cool with that."

"Destroy it," Red Knight agreed.

Peregrine nodded.

"BF?" I asked.

"I would like to review all the data before we burn the entire data backup. The Raptor stuff might be important. Even if we are not going to use it, perhaps his files on criminals will be useful to the SSA," Butterfly said.

"Modified yes from Butterfly," I informed Red Knight. "We should review it first."

Good, the team was pointed in the same direction. We

all agreed what to do. We didn't have to change the world in ways we couldn't comprehend. Check that action item.

"Next thing on the agenda, let's try to save Yaltin."

FOURTEEN

Red Knight made sure to drive the speed limit. He wasn't going to risk getting pulled over. I knew it was the smart thing to do, and still faster than if I'd just hoofed it, but the waiting was excruciating.

Hopefully, this Yaltin guy had security.

"It's just down the road. We should park here. I'll come if you need me." Red Knight seemed less enthused about being in the field than last time. Nothing like getting knocked on your back to remind you you can't walk.

Still, he'd saved my bacon a couple times already, and I'd known him for like four hours.

"Okay." Flare popped the door and we piled out the back and dispersed.

Peregrine took to the air right away.

Flare and I ran for alleyways on foot.

"You okay?" I asked.

"Why?" She gave a non-answer.

"Just seem tense."

"I am tense." I thought that was all I would get. "I'm not like you and Peregrine. I wanted out."

I thought about our conversation a week ago, a lifetime ago. "I thought you loved this. You said this was the best thing that had ever happened to you." I was paraphrasing. Tough to quote and run.

"That was before Orion died, my brother was kidnapped, and I was at the mercy of a pack full of psychos," she snapped. "This is stupid, and we almost paid for it with our lives. I never want to be in that position again."

We got to the alleyway behind the set of buildings, and she started to glow. "Keep up." She took to the air.

Not sure if she was telling me to keep up the pace she'd set, or keep up with events. I went on a private channel with Butterfly. "Did she just say brother?"

"Yes, she did." Butterfly was as confused as I was.

"Do you think she meant Ballista?"

"It sounded like it, but maybe not. She's upset. She could be talking about something else that happened before."

"Doesn't really fit the context of the conversation." I dive-rolled over a trash dumpster and kept going. "They don't look that much alike," I pointed out.

"They don't," Butterfly agreed. We'd all seen Ballista's face when we were trying to save his life/not die horribly. I'd seen Flare out of her uniform when I'd rescued her and Peregrine from Clockwork. Afterward, Butterfly had to do the medical stuff on her and Ballista to make sure everyone was okay.

"Huh," I said.

"She probably just means someone who feels like a brother," Butterfly said.

"Yeah, probably. Like brother in arms. We're all

brothers and sisters of the Guard." Sure, that's it. Nothing to parse over and analyse here.

That's when I got clotheslined by a metal bar that looked like an arm.

I bounced off some trash bags. Good thing it was trash day.

"We're too late," Peregrine reported over the radio. "They've been here and gone."

"They're still here!" I shouted.

My opponent didn't look like much -- in a dark, evil, self-confident ninja "not much" kind of way. He stepped out of the shadows, dressed in black. I could see extra padding from some kind of body armor. And a visor that covered his entire face. The suit was way too tight to confuse him with a female. He had guns, but they were holstered.

"I repeat, I have a super here."

He walked like a cat. There was no sign of the monster strength he'd used to stop me in my tracks.

He held up a small device, and put his fingers to his lips. "Shh," he whispered.

"Butterfly, Flare!" I kipped up and assumed a defensive posture. A defensive posture of getting the hell out of here. "Even Peregrine! Peregrine, can you hear me?"

No one responded.

"Look at the blood. They killed him." Flare was angry, but also shaken. "They just crushed his head. Who would do that?"

"I know! I know!" I was running the way I'd come. Total coincidence it was also the opposite way of the mysterious Ninja guy.

I lost track of the scary Ninja dude, then I heard some whistling of air. He landed right in front of me.

I hit him.

I have weighted gloves -- I'm not stupid. But that hurt. It was like punching a rock.

And the rock hit back.

Usually, I have a little speed edge on strong guys. Not him.

I got a block up. That didn't cause insane amounts of agony. But the next block delivered insane amounts of agony. He pushed me back, and I fell face down.

I dodged and rolled up, but he wasn't pressing his attack. "Little Birdy," he said.

"It's Raven." Might as well get it right. When he tells his buddies over beers, I'd hate for him to have a confusing narrative.

"I know."

"Who are you?" Why not ask?

"Just a Phantom."

"That is way cooler than Raven." I had to give him that. "Can we find a peaceful solution?"

"That's why I stopped you." He tossed me another device.

I caught it, and almost threw it back at him before I realized it was an egg timer. With less than two minutes left. I turned it over, just to make sure it wasn't a bomb. Nope. Looked like a regular twisting dial egg timer. "Thanks. I have one at home, but it isn't this nice."

He laughed softly. "That's how long your friends have to leave the building."

"Guys!" I shouted.

"You just have to get through--"

If his next words were going to be "the alley then make a turn at the donut shop", I was going to feel silly. I just jumped to the assumption I was in a fight to the death to save my team.

He ducked both of my feet in a flying kick to his head. I landed and swept his legs.

No one was more surprised than me when he fell on his ass. I dropped a kick right on his throat, but he rolled and made his only strike.

He didn't have an angle, so I don't think he could have gotten much power behind it. I still dodged.

We were both standing. He blocked a kick with his shin and it felt like I'd banged against another bronze statue shaped like someone trying to kill me. He pressed the advantage, I gave ground, then delivered another jumping kick.

He didn't bother dodging this one, but I wasn't really trying to hit him. I landed on his shoulder and jumped up to the fire escape of a nearby building. There were two ways to get past this guy.

That gizmo he had was blocking my transmissions. If I got out of its range, I would be able to transmit. If I could get a building in between me and him, maybe that would do it. "Guys! Get out of there!" I started yelling again and again.

I broke my own personal record scaling four floors. He just stood down there looking at me. I felt like a monkey at the circus, but what else was I going to do? Maybe I was close to getting away of his jamming or maybe he was bored. But once I reached the fourth floor, he jumped. It looked effortless, and he landed on the same fire escape I was on.

He made it look easy.

And to give the devil his due, he made it look cool.

I hit him. I hit him a lot. There was no sudden transformation into iron, but it didn't matter. I was fighting a very skilled martial artist in the confined space of a fire escape balcony with a five story drop.

So, almost easy.

I got a good shot in his side and he went against the wall. I did it again and the metal of the fire escape whined right before I hit. And that hurt. I'm sure I hit him but it felt like I'd kicked a brick wall.

I guess his break was over. He came at me swinging. He didn't move as quickly as he had a second before, but I couldn't block his strikes, either.

He forced me back, and I flipped off the landing, snatched a railing, and dropped to the third floor fire escape.

"Why are you doing this?" We could still see each other through the metal grate.

"Just curious," he said.

I thought about busting through the window next to me and making a run for it through the building. But I didn't know the building, and if he followed, I would put the lives of any residents in jeopardy.

New plan -- I go through him.

I dropped, using every other fire escape to slow my descent.

As I assumed, he dropped.

Falling right into my plan.

I got a kick in the second he touched down. But my heart wasn't really in it. It was to test a theory. Sure enough, he was a rock.

While he was all dense, I was betting he couldn't move as fast. I delivered a fake punch to his face. He didn't block it quickly. Was that because he couldn't move fast in iron mode, or because getting hit wouldn't matter if he was in iron mode? I guess I would find out. I turned the strike into a grab, pulled the jammer from his belt, and smashed it against the wall.

"Guys! The place is going to blow. Get out of there!"

The egg timer went ding.

Boom, boom, boom.

FIFTEEN

I don't know what happened to Heavy Metal Ninja, or HMN, if you've known him as long as I have. The explosion went off and I was hit by a little of the debris. I hadn't been paying attention, but my fight had brought me closer to Yaltin's place than I'd thought.

The entire top floor of the building was on fire.

I looked around for signs of anyone -- good guy, bad guy, whatever. "Peregrine! Flare! Report!"

"We're okay," Flare said. "We're okay."

"Report!" Butterfly yelled. "What's going on?"

I didn't know, but... "We're all still alive. I think."

"You think?" Butterfly was a little panicked.

Did I say that out loud?

Peregrine touched down about ten feet to my left. Flare's green glow did a circuit around the flaming tower and landed on the other side of me.

"What the hell?" Peregrine seemed like he was accusing me. "Where did you go? Why did you break coms?"

"I think the words you are looking for are, 'thanks man, you saved my life again.'"

"How did you know there was a bomb?" Making vague accusations is Peregrine's love language.

"My new best friend, Heavy Metal Ninja, told me." I looked around for him but didn't see anyone.

"Raven, start making sense," Flare said.

"Some guy, a super, probably a P2, jumped me when I was following you guys. He told me the place was about to blow."

"And you told us to get out?" Flare asked.

"There was this whole hardcore Kung Fu fighting deathmatch and radio jamming thing first. But skip to the middle part, and yeah. I broke the jammer and got the call in right before the building blew. I thought I was too late."

"You almost were. If we hadn't both been standing by a window..." Flare gave a shiver. "Thank you." She folded her arms.

"If it wasn't for the 'ninja', we all would have blown up," Peregrine pointed out.

True, but I was still handy in the entire process. "He was probably the guy who set the bomb in the first place."

Flare nodded. "Why did he fight you? Did you see him?"

"No, total ambush. Said he just wanted to see what I was made of or something."

"He also knew how to jam your radio and that he would need a way to jam your radio," Butterfly said. "They know we're following them and that we're close."

"No we're not. Not now," Flare said. "Yaltin was dead when we got here. He must have talked."

"Why do you think so?" I asked.

"They killed him after mutilating one hand." Peregrine sounded like he was going to be sick. "They only had to get through the ring finger."

"Oh, God," Flare said. "They crushed his head. It was so awful."

"And they just covered up the crime scene." I looked again at the burning building. "We've got to get out of here." First responders would be here soon.

I started running back to the van, but Red Knight met us halfway. We all clambered in.

"Thank God. I was terrified that you were in there." He threaded the van through the back alley and out onto the main street.

Peregrine filled him in. Flare just sat with her arms around herself, not paying attention to the bouncing of the van through the back way.

I tuned out what Peregrine was saying. He was always better at after-action reports.

"Hey." I moved to sit right by Flare.

She pulled away a little.

"Are you okay?" Because saying "you are not okay" wouldn't help.

"I'm fine," she snapped. Then, "I'm fine," with a little more believable sound.

"No, you're not." Okay, so I guess I pointed it out anyway.

"You don't understand. What they did to that man, Yaltin." She shuddered. "They ripped him apart. It was awful."

It must have been something. Last week we'd walked into a charnel house of horrors and seen what was left of Caesar's chief lieutenant. That hadn't rattled her like this, although she'd already been rattled before she'd gone in.

"I'm done," she whispered.

"Okay."

"I'm done," she whispered even more faintly.

I didn't know what that meant. "Like done now, or like done after we take care of the Phoenix?"

A half-laugh sounds weird through vocal distortion. "Not like you. I'm actually done. But I'll help until we get the Phoenix or whatever. I don't have a choice."

"What are you guys talking about?" Peregrine was at the front end of the van and had noticed we were having a private moment.

"Just planning a book club. It was supposed to be a surprise, but I guess the cat's out of the bag now," I explained.

"We've got to plan our next move." Peregrine was taking his frustration out on me.

"What next move, Floater?" At least I could be professional. "We don't have a next move. We've been a step behind the Confessor all night and he just closed the door on any other opportunity. We're done with moves."

"Of course. Let's give up. Your happy place." He waved at me like I was a waste of his time and turned back to Red Knight.

"I'm not giving up. We've been going hard for like twelve hours and we have nothing. It's three in the morning and we're out of leads. We need to get some sleep and hit it again fresh."

So, looking back on it, I was trying to defend Flare, who needed a minute. Silly of me, but I also got to rage at someone. That ninja guy pretty much owned me in that fight. It was a weird fight, too. Like déjà vu. Almost like I'd fought him before, but I would have known if I had. I mean, I just haven't fought that many skilled martial artists.

"I'm fine," Flare said. I guess she figured out that I was trying to be all chivalrous and stuff.

"No, Raven's right," Red Knight said. "We've hit a dead

end. We can't just keep banging our heads against a wall. You guys fall back to your nests, or home. Get some shut eye. I have a few contacts from back in the day. I'll reach out, see if I can get something." He didn't sound too confident that he could find "something."

"Okay." Peregrine needed to hear it from anyone else but me. What a tool.

"Fine," I agreed.

Flare didn't disagree.

"I'll try to backtrack information about Yaltin and Frank. Maybe I can find an intersection," Butterfly added. At least someone could do something.

"Thanks, Fly," I said.

We drove around until we got back in our regular stomping grounds. Peregrine was the first to duck out of the truck.

Now it was just the two of us and RK, but Flare didn't seem to want to talk.

I didn't press her, but stayed until she asked to be let out.

A few blocks later, I felt like taking a run and called for a stop.

"Raven," Red Knight said before I dipped out the back.

"Yeah?"

"She'll be fine. She's tough stuff."

"Sure, yeah, I know."

"Get some sleep. We'll figure it all out." He seemed sure.

"Yeah, assuming it isn't already too late, that they got all the information they needed from Yaltin." Just a little perspective to keep everyone at the proper level of terror. "You should get yourself a burner phone," I told Red Knight. "Butterfly, what number should I give him?"

She rattled a number off and I gave it to Red Knight. He scribbled it down on a paper pad he had in a dusty tray on the dash.

"I'll be seeing you." I slipped out the van's back door and headed for an alley.

I liked the van, but it felt good to be on the street, up a fire escape, and on a rooftop again. "BF, you still there?"

"Yes." She must have been working hard on the computer data mining angle because she sounded pretty robotic.

"Do you think we already failed? You think the Confessor has the Phoenix?" I started moving in an easy rhythm. I'd run on these buildings three times in the last seven months, so I knew them like the back of my hand. Yes, three times is a lot to a kinist, my super power makes twice overkill.

"I am unable to postulate. We do not know what Yaltin knew."

"He must have known enough. They stopped torturing him and just killed him." I jumped over an alley, rolled, climbed up the brick wall to the next roof, rolled to a stand, and hopped hands then feet across some industrial air conditioners. This was a fun run. I should do it more often.

"We do not have an alternative. We have to hope." A little bit of the human crept back into her voice. "Like Red Knight said, we are at a dead end. We don't have any other leads to follow. Hopefully his contacts will get something."

I stopped on the edge of the building, gazing at a thirty foot drop. A jump and mid-air somersault could get me across to the next building. "Of course, I've been running all over for the last..." *How long had it been?* "Ever. I have a contact I can check with."

"Who? No! I thought you said you were going to destroy the idol." Butterfly's focus was all on me.

"He helped us out a lot last time. He didn't have to."

"I... Maybe you should ask Red Knight. I'm sure he's worked with criminal informants before." Butterfly was a little hesitant.

"Sure. I'll call back if I find anything."

"I don't think you should trust Jackal," Butterfly said.

"I don't trust him, but he might know something. We have to at least try." I ran along the edge of the building to get a head of steam and leapt.

This felt right. Like I was finally doing something.

SIXTEEN

The idol was right where I'd put it. I'd been talking to Jackal when Raptor's widow had texted me. I'd been about to break the thing, but I didn't. When I wasn't communicating with the criminal mastermind and sociopath, I wrapped the idol in a plastic bag and taped it to the inside of an abandoned building's roof intake vent.

Jackal was in prison, serving a billion-and-a-half life sentences for all the crap he'd pulled. His power was the rare ability to copy other parahuman abilities. He'd told me that the more powerful the ability he copied, the faster he lost it. The lower octane para abilities he could copy permanently.

Most of his permanent powers were enhanced senses, but another power was the ability to communicate through wooden carvings.

A little over a weeks ago, Peregrine and I had found one of his idols in his old abandoned base. He'd helped us defeat Clockwork. I literally could not have done it without him.

If it hadn't been for him, I and the rest of the world would be scratching our heads about how Caesar, the

Guard, and the entire Federal government Superhuman Suppression Agency had all died within twenty-four hours.

I took hold of the statue. There were other clairsentients in Raptor's files. Cat, the deceased member of the Guard, could communicate through his cat, Feral, now my cat, Feral. I'd done it once or twice while Cat was training me. Tons of other supers could do it too, but I didn't know how it worked.

Jackal had told me he could project into my inner ear, but I suspected that was crap. I suspected it was more mind-to-mind psych stuff. Not scary. Not scary at all. I didn't really know the limits of his power, so I didn't bring the idol anywhere near a place that had anything to do with my real ID.

Raptor had taught us that egoist attacks weren't confusing. If someone was reading your mind, you knew. Egoists forced you to think about what they wanted to know. Sounded unpleasant. Raptor had also said it could go both ways. You could get glimpses into the mind of the egoist.

Well, this didn't feel like that. It felt much more like the handful of times I'd talked to Cat through Feral. Certainly nothing like what I saw the Confessor do to Julia.

The statue of Anubis looked like a knockoff from a souvenir shop in a fake Egyptian exhibit. It wasn't quite six inches, wood carved, and painted. I looked at it. The yellow eyes were not glowing. I am not a master of this thing. Most of the time Jackal got in touch with me.

My point is, if he could read my mind, he could already have all the details about me by now. I'd been plugged into this thing but good for a day solid.

"Jackal?" I didn't know how to turn it on. He'd told me just to hold it once, but he'd been expecting me to contact him. The last time we'd talked, I'd told him not to expect any more communication. "Jackal, I need to talk to you."

The statue did nothing.

Come on. I shook it and tapped it. I know, I know, but that's what I do when something doesn't work. "Jackal!"

Nothing.

I put it down on the tar paper roof and sat across from it. What did I really think he could do for me, anyway? He was a convicted criminal not a genie. He just knew the underworld better than... well, anyone else I knew. Raptor hadn't gotten to the actual investigative part of our training.

Minutes ticked by. Nothing. I could always try again in the morning on my way back to Alpha Base.

I picked it up and it flared to life. I almost dropped it.

"Good God, Raven, what time is it?" He yawned.

"I don't know, close to four." I yawned, too. Not sure how I knew he was yawning, but they're still contagious.

"Okay, give me a second." I got the impression he was slapping his face.

Was this his two-way mind-reader thing Raptor had told me about? It was creepy.

"What you got?" Jackal asked, a little more alert.

"I need your help." That was hard to say.

"I was already there," he said as one word. "Let's make this quick. I'd like to get back to sleep. Busy day today."

I didn't know why one day at prison would be busier than another. "What do you know about a parahuman called the Confessor?"

"What did you step in?" He seemed a little more interested. "I leave you for eight hours and you're hip-deep in Jack Midas' people."

"I already knew he worked for Midas."

"Sure. He's an egoist, not a very strong one since he

needs to operate by touch. But he's good at forcing people to answer the questions put to them. They always have to answer the truth, but it depends on the will of the person on how useful the information could be. I worked with him a few times."

"Really?" *Of course, really. What did you think he was doing while setting up a criminal empire, selling band candy?*

"A few times. When I worked for Caesar. Mindraker handled all that kind of stuff in-house. He made the Confessor look like a hack. But when I went independent, I had to hire out. What's this all about?"

"I need to find him." That's all he needed to know.

"Oh, you coy little minx." I thought he was going to push me but he didn't. "Okay fine, be that way. But this information isn't coming free."

"What's your price?"

"I need you to help me make something right, or at least as right as I can," Jackal modified.

"How?" Said the fly to the spider.

"I'm setting things up. In a couple of days I need you to deliver a package."

I was not going to start moving drugs or weapons for him. "What's in the package?"

"Money. I'd have someone else do it, but you're the only person I trust not to take any off the top." Jackal sounded different. He certainly hadn't been arranging packages last time we'd talked. Something had changed. Made me think about his "busy day" comment.

"Why wouldn't I take any off the top?"

"It's for a widow. Her husband worked for me and got killed. Saved my life, Caesar got close. Set a trap. Shortly after that Raptor changed my address. I owe him. I want his family taken care of."

What am I supposed to say to that? "Fine, I'll deliver your money."

"Done and done." I'd just shaken hands with the devil. "Why do you need the Confessor? That is to say, are you looking to hire him, or be all heroic on him?"

"The last one."

"Okay. Well, I have a number I could give you. But he doesn't live in the City."

"How can you be sure?" Jackal might have more freedom to communicate with his former associates since Caesar had died, but he'd still spent the last five years in prison.

"It's a rule. A rule I know the Confessor didn't break."

"He's a criminal. Why wouldn't he break rules?"

"Because this wasn't a law, it was a rule! A rule put down by Caesar. No egoist could spend more than three days in the city without permission," Jackal said. "The penalty for breaking that rule was rather permanent."

"But the Confessor works for Midas. Why would he care what Caesar says?" This made no sense.

"Because Caesar was very scary. Midas might make a good show of being independent, and in a lot of ways he is. But the Confessor knows better than to go to war over Caesar's rules."

"Well, he's in town now. Where would he stay?" I asked.

"The Confessor had a room at the Carlton whenever he had a job in town. I don't know which one. He was good at keeping his ID a secret."

"But the Carlton was Caesar's place." Even I knew that.

"Exactly. The Confessor wanted to make it very clear to

the real boss of the city he was following the rule. Also, I don't think Midas knows his identity. Caesar did, because Mindraker could detect other egoists." He said it like that was supposed to make sense.

Whatever.

"Well, the Carlton is closed for remodeling." I'd been there when some of the toughest supers in the city had ripped the place apart. "I think it's still an SSA crime scene."

"Then what's the next nicest hotel in the area?"

"The Golden View." That was a Midas-owned hotel.

"The Golden View, I know it. Owned by Midas. Makes sense."

"Alright I'll check it out." I got the plastic bag out.

"Wait just a second."

I stopped.

"What's this all about? Why do you need a mindreader for hire?" Jackal seemed a little worried. "What have you gotten yourself into?"

I wrestled with what to tell him. If he wanted to, he could be really useful, but everything I told him was ammunition he could turn on me and then maybe my team. He was the man responsible for Hawk's death, which had started a chain of events that created Silhouette and killed Osprey's family.

If I didn't owe my life and the life of my friends to him, that would be easier to keep in mind.

"He's looking for something, something that might expose my identity and the identity of all the apprentices. I think he found it. We need it back."

"Oh, yeah, that could be bad. Are you sure he's working for Midas? The Confessor had an arrangement with Midas, but still worked his own contracts."

"He's working with the Headsmen." That was really the only clue I had that Midas was involved.

"What's this thing that might have your identity?"

Did I really want Jackal to know what could expose me? Would that be trading one villain on my tail for another? "It's a data backup. I guess Raptor started it way back in the day and it might have my address."

"Back in the day, huh? Alright. Well, I'll ask around on the inside. If you needed current info that would be tough, but there are some people in here that were working the city before Raptor. I'll see if I can find anything."

Ah. Now would the entire prison of criminals know about the Phoenix? I think I'd done enough damage. "No, you don't have to do anything like that. This lead is good enough."

"It's no problem at all. You watch yourself. I know you're not telling me everything, but this sounds dangerous. If the Confessor's coming to Darhaven now, this is bigger than just some vigilante names. The SSA have never been this thick. Whatever he's looking for can't wait. How did you find out about this? Are you sure you can trust the source? You might be pawns in a larger game."

"I'm sure of the source of the information." It wasn't like Julia had faked being tortured. She hadn't even sent us on this mission.

"Okay. Well, the sun will be up soon. If we're going to check the place out, I suggest we get there now or come back in plain clothes closer to seven."

"*We* aren't going anywhere." I straightened out the bag. "Thank you for the information. I'll be in touch."

"You should really take me with you."

I put the idol in the bag and started rolling it up. "I got this, thanks."

"Check back soon. Something about this isn't sitting well. I'm worried about you." Jackal was a little muffled through the plastic.

You and me both. If Red Knight was right, this could threaten the global power balance as well as put my mother in jeopardy. "Yeah, I'll check back soon."

The idol stopped glowing and I retaped it in its hiding place.

SEVENTEEN

So I went to the Golden View under the cover of dark. Not actually to the Golden View, but the tallest neighboring building.

I'd never really gotten this close before, but I'd always used the tall building with the golden circle around the crest as a landmark. It was visible for miles and sometimes had spotlights from the roof if they had a big name show playing.

The words Golden View were spelled out down the wall. Above the V was the trademarked Midas touch, a cartoon hand that would tap the V and the sign would change from blue to gold.

Raptor never put this area on my patrol. Probably just like the Carlton, he didn't want me bumping into a big time player.

The first sixteen floors looked easy enough to climb. There were plenty of handholds with the kind of brick they used. The top fifteen were a lot trickier. It was slick windows. Maybe if I got closer, I'd figure something out.

I made it around the building, staying in the shadows.

Through careful observation and razor-like investigative skills, I noticed the Confessor wasn't hanging out a window.

I thought about calling Butterfly and sicing her on the hotel, but it was four in the morning. If she had an opportunity for sleep, she would be doing it. Besides, did I really have a reason to think this was the place?

Screw it.

I went back to my nest and caught a couple hours of sleep until the sun came up.

I put on the nicest clothes I had in my nest. Jeans with no rips, a white button-up shirt, and my ratty chuckies. The white button-up was a surprise find. It was in the back of my locker. I'd forgotten all about it.

It was wrinkled, and I didn't have an iron, but it would do. I guess.

I took the bus to the hotel. It felt weird seeing the city from this low. The bus probably made better time than I could just running. But it felt like it took forever.

The hotel seemed more imposing from the ground, too. I felt small and shabby. I looked at everyone coming and going from the building. No teenagers and no one in a wrinkled button-up.

The door guard or bellhop or whatever saw me and kept an eye on me as I walked by.

I hunched my shoulders and kept walking. My "plan" of entering in the front door went up in smoke. I did not line up with the dress code and stuck out like a sore working-poor thumb.

Fine. The front door was out, but they had to get stuff inside for all the rich, rich people. I would just use the tradesmen's entrance.

I tried to walk around casually while still casing the area. In the daylight I could see getting to the sixteenth floor would be easy, and after the twentieth floor there were balconies that might as well be a ladder for a guy like me. It was just those pesky four floors in between that would pose an issue.

I kept looking for something -- not that I wanted to scale thirty floors -- but I would if I had to.

The alley was blocked off by a fence. I did a quick look around. No cameras and the coast was clear. I got a running start, ran up the wall, flipped myself over the fence, and landed on my feet.

Felt weird doing that in civies. I compensated, but it was still weird not feeling my uniform boots underneath me when I landed.

I kept walking like I owned the place.

My first test was a couple Hispanic guys in hard hats and reflective vests. I think they were from the city. I gave them a nod and kept walking.

I don't think I even got a look from them.

Around the corner I saw a group of people, most in the same hard hats and reflective vests, and two others in blue blazers with a gold patch over the chest. Two work trucks from the county were parked taking up most of the alley.

I made a path like I was going to just walk straight, but darted around the end of the van.

I gave a heart beat. No "kid, get away from there!" so I must not have been noticed. I peeked in the van. A few spare vests and hard hats were hanging from the back. I slipped on a vest and pulled down the hard hat over my face as best I could.

And kept walking.

I got in line behind some workmen handing out crates

to bring into the building. I was coming up with a cover story, but when it was my turn, they just handed me a crate.

I followed the guy in front of me, keeping my head down until I got past the guy in the blazer with the walkie-talkie.

A quick check to make sure there were no other blazers, and I started looking around for my next move. Nothing in the loading dock screamed "evil," or even "pretty bad." No one was in red robes stroking a white Persian cat, either. I was stumped.

I set the box down where the crew ahead of me did, but started walking the other way.

"Hey." A guy in a helmet, probably the foreman. "Where you going?"

I didn't look back, just pointed at the blue sign that said "Restroom" and walked faster. He didn't follow me, so I guess it worked.

There were a few people in this area. They were a mix of men in blue jeans and tool belts and men and women in the white shirt and bow ties of hotel housekeeping.

I held the door open for a few guys in overalls. I got a look from one but he didn't say anything.

Inside the locker room there were a few people talking in Spanish. I walked by them and hit a row of lockers.

Some had locks, some did not. I started going through the open ones. Empty, empty, empty, balled up blue jeans, empty, a blue jacket and bow tie.

I stuffed my hard hat and vest in the same locker and pulled on the vest and clipped on the bow tie. Thank God it was a clip on.

I tried the shoes I found in the same locker, but they were too tiny. I put my chuckies back on and went out again. Back in the hall there were a few more hotel staff, and

I fell into step behind them as they stepped into the elevator.

I got a look from one of them, but they didn't seem to care enough to say anything, either. He just pulled his card on an elastic cord and slid it through the reader, then selected a floor.

I was going to need one of those cards.

We rode the elevator in an awkward silence to the tenth floor. The door opened for a housekeeper with her cart. I quickly got around her and did a brush pass with her cards. I'm not a pickpocket. I'm sure with a little training I could be very good, but Raptor didn't focus on that. Still, there wasn't much to snatching a card off an apron. I just hoped she wouldn't get into trouble for losing her card.

The tenth floor was a different world from below at the tradesmen's entrance. Exposed concrete block and scuff marks were replaced with tasteful art and thick blue and gold carpeting.

I passed a family of guests. The daughter was chasing a much younger brother. They had the family resemblance that screamed siblings. Their mother followed a little behind, texting into her cell phone. She didn't spare me a glance.

Tenth floor did not scream "evil lair" to me. That seemed better suited to the penthouse. I found another elevator and tried the card. It didn't light up the penthouse button. I pressed another button, and it got me to the twentieth floor.

That's where I'd have to start.

The doors opened onto a dining room with a breathtaking view of the entire city. The restaurant, The Golden Ledge, was doing a brisk breakfast business. A few people were waiting to be seated.

I kept walking right past them.

"Hey, you!"

Damn it, busted.

I walked faster and turned the first corner I came to.

I heard some footfalls behind me and a voice speaking into a walkie talkie. I couldn't hear what he said, but I doubt it was "All clear, nothing to see here."

I tried my key card in the first door I came to. It was a suite. I heard the shower running.

"Hello?" A woman had heard me enter.

I tried a falsetto. "Housekeeping."

"Ah, not now, please," the woman said.

"I'll come back later." I whipped off the jacket and tie, tossed them in the closet right by the door, then exited the room.

The security guard -- it was indeed a security guard -- had already run by the room I'd been in. He was looking right and left down a T intersection at the end of the hall. He must have heard the door open, because he spun around.

I tried to be cool. I looked right at him and gave him a wave.

He started walking in my direction, talking into his mic again. Crap, crap, crap, crap on toast and lightly salted. Crap.

I tried to walk purposefully, like I belonged there, but nothing about me indicated that I did.

I turned toward the elevator. The door opened and two big burly types in security guard uniforms stepped out and spotted me.

The way I'd come was blocked and I couldn't go down in the elevator, so I started walking toward the second hallway.

I wasn't sure I could fight my way out of this, but even if I could, that was the last thing I wanted to do. I'd rather not hurt anyone, or tip my hand that I wasn't just a punk trying to get as far into the hotel as possible on a dare.

"Sir," one of the guards said.

He called me sir. That was nice.

"Ryan!" a high pitched voice called out.

EIGHTEEN

My heart crawled right up my throat. They'd made me! How the hell had they done that? I didn't even have any ID on me.

I looked in the direction of the voice. A little brown-haired girl, maybe six years old, was running at me. I'm embarrassed to say my first thought was she was some kind of parahuman that could shrink.

Then reality set in. "Helen?" I hadn't actually seen her in a year, maybe longer. But I'd seen pictures on social media.

I bent down, and she jumped into my arms. "Ryan!" She gave me a big hug. "Dad said you'd visit."

"Ryan." Dad may have said it, but he didn't believe it. He was more surprised than I was.

Well, not more surprised, but a near second place with honorable mention. "Dad." I forced a smile and stood holding Helen.

I tried to look at the guards without looking at the guards. They seemed a little confused, but weren't willing to make a scene.

"It's so good to see you." My dad stepped in and gave me a hug.

I thought he would take Helen back, but he didn't. He just stepped away.

"Are you coming to breakfast with us?" Helen asked.

"Um." I looked at my dad for a cue. Was I invited? Because I could eat, and it would be great to lie low until the heat cleared.

"Of course he is." Dad moved his head toward the restaurant. "They're ready for us."

I carried my half-sister like a protective talisman, keeping her between myself and the security as we passed in the hall.

A woman was waiting for us when we reached the restaurant. For a second I thought my stepmother would be joining us, but it was a woman I didn't recognize. She looked maybe early twenties and Hispanic.

"This is Nanny," Helen said, as if introducing people was something she was practising. "Nanny, my brother, Ryan."

Nanny smiled and held out her hand. "Maria." She had a little accent.

"Ryan." I smiled and shook.

She seemed a little embarrassed. Maybe I shouldn't be carrying Helen around. It wasn't like I did it much. We barely had any contact at all.

"Nanny and I are going swimming after breakfast. You can come, too." Helen's huge brown eyes were so hopeful.

"I can't, not today." My disappointment matched her own. "But I'll make it up to you."

Her spirits lifted. "We're moving into the city. I'll have a new school, and you can come over and we can play and have fun."

"That would be great." I wasn't even lying.

We were directed to a table by a window where you could see the bay and docks. From up here, it didn't look like a pit of soul-crushing poverty and corruption.

Helen was amazed. She pointed out things and asked what different buildings were, dominating the conversation until I finished my waffle. Say what you want about the one percent -- they know how to make a waffle.

"It is time to go," Maria finally said. Other than a few shushing noises, she hadn't said anything since she'd given her name.

"Swimming!" Helen jumped up and down in her chair.

Maria nodded and took her hand.

A few feet away from the table Helen ran back to me and gave me a hug. "Thank you for dining with us." She stumbled over the word dining like she'd heard it, but didn't know what it meant.

"Thank you."

I watched my sister bounce back to Maria's outstretched hand, and they snaked their way around other customers and servers.

"So." Dad drew my attention back to him. He still seemed casual and relaxed, but willing to get down to business.

"So." I was not willing to get down to business. "Is that a new nanny?"

He allowed himself to be distracted. "Been with us eight months...no, ten."

I kind of flailed around for something else to talk about. "She seems quiet."

He flashed his perfect white teeth. "I think our Maria has a little bit of a crush. Not immune to the old Blackwater charm."

Yuck. "Dad, she's like twenty million years younger than you."

Dad threw back his head and laughed. I hadn't seen him laugh that easy since before Mindy... well, for a long time. "I wasn't talking about this Blackwater." He pointed at himself. "I think her taste goes to the newer model."

What? Whatever. "So thanks for breakfast. You were right about the waffles."

"I know, right?"

"But I have to..."

"Why are you here?" Now he was really ready to get down to business.

Pure coincidence. You were the last thing on my mind. "I just didn't feel good about how I left things last night." True. Well, trueish. "I just wanted to apologize."

He held up his hand. "No apologies. I wish I'd handled it differently. I just... being back in that house... puts me in a bad place."

The place where Mom and I live? That bad place?

He must have read some of my emotions on my face. "Sorry." Then, "I'm sorry for all of it."

"It?" What was that supposed to mean?

"I got lost. I made a ton of mistakes, and every one of them I can't make up for. I hurt you and your mother." His gaze held mine for a second before he looked away. "For the longest time I couldn't even ask for your forgiveness. I didn't think I was worth it."

Oh, the angsty teenager bile I wanted to spew at that straight line.

"But I'm asking for it now. There's nothing I can do to make up for the last decade. Once I got out of the bottle, I tried to make things right. Every time I tried, I just made things worse."

Probably not worse. When things are that bad, you can't make them worse.

"I just felt you were happier if I stayed away."

Damn straight.

"But that hasn't helped, either. Mark told me you're flunking out."

Mark Spiker, Dad's inside man, was a teacher that I did back flips to never take a class from. He was a friend of my dad's from the neighborhood. He felt it was his duty to keep Dad up to date on all my business.

"I hear you don't have many friends, and what friends you had you grew away from," he continued. "Your mom says the only person she knows you hang out with is the Smith kid."

Smith kid?

"What's his name, their youngest?" He tapped his forehead. "Cameron, that's it."

"I wouldn't call him much of a friend," I said under my breath. "More of an associate."

"Makes sense, I guess."

It did? "It does?" I asked when I realized I hadn't actually asked anything the first time.

"Well, you're both from the same neighborhood, and you both lost an older sibling to gang violence."

"What?" *What? What? What?*

"Yeah, his older brother. Got shot in the head, point blank range. They had to have a closed casket." His gaze got far away and lines on his face made him look old. "It was just after Mindy, before I completely destroyed things with your mother. But I was well on the way. I went to the funeral. Don't know how drunk I was."

"I didn't know."

"I wasn't even the whitest person there." He gave a

laugh. "Two kids were in the back of the room, about Thomas' age."

"Thomas?"

"Cameron's brother. I don't think anyone else knew who they were. They were left alone, just like me, but they were an even bigger mess than I was."

"What did they look like?" This couldn't be, could it?

"Tall freckled redhead kid, and thin pale goth kid." He shrugged. "I only noticed them because they sat in the back with me, and weren't family."

Thin pale goth kid -- that would describe Silhouette. Gears kept shifting. It made sense. Two weeks ago Cameron and I had found Hawk's helmet, the one with the bullet hole. Cameron had completely lost his stuffing. I'd thought it was just the last straw in a crap sandwich day. But it would explain everything. *Everything.* Why he hated Jackal so much. Why he wanted to be a Guard so much. Oh hell, half the axe he had to grind with me was explained. For some reason Raptor had given me Hawk's old uniform. I'd known it was Hawk's. But I hadn't known why it pissed Cameron off so much. Why Raptor hadn't let him have the Hawk uniform when he'd joined up.

"Oh, hell."

"What? You didn't know."

I shook my head. "Cameron doesn't talk about his past." For that matter, I'd never talked to him about Mindy.

"Well, I hope I didn't complicate things. I just assumed you would know."

Did it change anything? Peregrine was still a first rate tool. Did a sob story give him an out? Yeah, it did, at least a little. "No, it's good I know."

We sat in silence. I didn't have anything to say. I just kept flipping over what Dad had said. In the last year and a half, Peregrine had been one of three people I'd spent the most time with. Raptor had had us training with and against each other. My existence had seemed to offend him, like he didn't think I was worth his or Raptor's time. He'd always kicked my ass.

Did this change anything? Yes, but how and what?

"Have you thought about my offer?" Dad finally brought things back to crap.

"What? No, I mean, yes I've been thinking about it." *No, I have not been thinking about it. I have tons of other things on my mind.* I hadn't even known what he was talking about at first.

"I know it would be weird." He'd said it, but I didn't think he really understood the sheer magnitude of the hurricane of weird it would be.

"I just think I need time to patch things up with Mom. It would be good for us to work things out."

He looked very uncomfortable.

"What?"

"I don't.... Your mom is hurt. I know she feels guilty that she can't help you." He was looking at his plate now.

"That's not true."

"Of course it isn't. I told her that. But she takes on responsibility for the men in her life."

Wow! That was an ugly mirror. I'd just gotten dumped into the same asshole bucket with my dad.

"I will make it up to her." My conviction was clear.

"That's what I always thought, too," he said. "But that's not to say you can't. I just think it might need more time. You have a family -- your sister and brother, me. You can prove yourself to your mother and get to know us."

"It would kill Mom." I didn't mean to say it out loud.

"She's the strongest person I know. If you proved you

were serious about turning things around, she would take you back in months."

Take me back? She hadn't thrown me out yet.

"Just think about it. Shar and I would love to have you as long as you need a place."

I didn't know what to say. This was not how I thought I was going to spend my morning. I couldn't even formulate a reply.

My dad's eyes tracked to the left and his face changed into one of his charming smiles and a nod. "Listen, I have an 8:00. I can push it back if you want me to."

I glanced at who he was looking at. A group of men in suits had come into the restaurant and were being seated at a longer table. "What? No, no. I have to go..." And try to find an evil mind reader. "Do some things."

"Okay. It was really good to see you." He got out of his chair and made his way to the other group.

I stood and looked at my dad. A kid from the Kages seamlessly approaching the powerful and becoming one of them. He made them laugh and smile. Mom always said he could be a charmer, but how could he be taken seriously by that crowd? It blew my mind.

Maybe I wasn't the only parahuman in the family.

"You here for the talk, too?" A woman had approached me, and I hadn't even realized it.

I jumped, and she giggled.

She wasn't a woman. Well, I mean she wasn't an adult. She was probably about my age. "You can't handle your caffeine."

"What? No." I leaned in conspiratorially. "It's the neighborhood. I don't usually slum it like this." I waved my hand limp-wristed at all the suits.

She laughed, which was good. Real good. She was

blond, with blue eyes that almost knocked me down, but her laugh was better. Wow.

"So, are you here for 'The Talk'." She mimicked a deep adult male voice for The Talk.

She'd said that before, but I hadn't known what she was asking about.

"You know, the talk," she said without the emphasis.

I did not.

"Well, it's about time you took your future seriously" She used the same false male voice.

"Oh, the *talk*."

"This is kind of the standard Talk breakfast location." She pointed out another man and his son. The son looked about twelve and was shrinking under the power tie and glower of his father.

"I wouldn't call it a talk so much as an ongoing epic poem." Epic poem's a thing, right? I had a vague memory of talking about an epic poem in fourth period English.

She laughed again. "I know what you mean. I'm about to be seated for part one-hundred-and-twenty of my Talk." She looked around. "My dad's still in the restroom. He got in a car accident yesterday."

"Crap!"

"Yea, he got banged up really good and broke his arm. Makes everything take longer." She had a flash of worry cross her face, then she hit me with her smile again. "I'm just glad he wasn't driving. He's a clutz behind the wheel."

"So give me some pointers. What do you tell your dad when he wants to know what you want to be when you grow up?" I just wanted to keep her talking. Just for a minute or two. I could spend a minute or two.

"Well, right now, it's a toss up between pole dancer or

owning my own food truck." She held out her hands, weighing her options.

"Can you cook?"

"Mac 'n Cheese."

"There you go, you've got the food truck thing down. Combine the two and make a killing." I would buy mac 'n cheese for that act.

"Sofia." A man stepped up next to the girl I'd been talking to.

Man, I had to get out of there. I was not in the zone and aware of my surroundings. Shale could have snuck up on me in this place. I was out of my element.

"Daddy." She seemed genuinely happy to see him and gave him a peck on his unbruised cheek.

I haven't seen a lot of car accident victims, but I have seen a lot of fight aftermath. This man had been in a brawl. Probably mugged by some thug and didn't want to worry his daughter. I could respect that.

"Who's your friend?"

Sofia giggled. "Sorry, we hadn't gotten to names."

"Ryan," I said.

"Ryan, are you Mark Blackwater's son?" Sofia's father asked.

"Yep. You know my dad?" Visions of family picnics danced in my head.

"Not really. I met him at the mixer a day ago, but the resemblance is uncanny." He reached out his hand from force of habit, forgetting he had a cast on it. "Sorry." He held out his left, and I took it. "Guy Cranston."

His thumb was smooth, like all the prints were burnt off it.

I pulled my hand a little faster than was polite. "I'm sorry to hear about your accident." The height was right.

The impact on the chin and eye. "Wrist breaks can be nasty."

"Thankfully it's just a bone." He touched about where the bone had broken. "The doctors feel confident I'll heal completely. Just a blow to my pride in the long run."

"Good." Oh, did I miss my helmet. When no one can see your face, you forget how to keep a poker face when things go sideways. I was the thug who'd beaten this guy up. He was the Confessor. Subtract a little for boots and costume and he was the right height and build. "Did you get the guy?"

He looked confused.

"The other driver. Did the other driver stop?"

"No, a hit and run I'm afraid," the Confessor demurred. "I got a description of the vehicle to the police. I'm sure they'll find them. It's all up to the insurance companies now."

"Are you two visiting the city?" If Jackal was right, the Confessor could not live here.

"Right now, but my business situation has recently changed. We're looking at moving here full time."

"I've been telling him to do that for years. He always comes into town for two or three days, then back again," Sofia said.

"Well, sorry it was such a poor welcome to the city." I took in his injuries.

He smiled.

"Well, I'll let you guys get back to breakfast." I took a half step away.

"Actually, about that." The Confessor turned to his daughter. "My ten o'clock just got bumped up. I'll have to meet the client earlier."

"Daddy." She was disappointed. "You don't have to take this. This client is way too difficult."

He smiled. "Contracts are contracts." He looked at me. "Nice to meet you, Ryan." He gave his daughter a half hug.

She did not look approving, but pecked his cheek.

We both watched him leave.

"Does he look nervous to you?" I asked.

"Ever since we came to the city this time. I think the deal is falling apart, and he's freaking out." There were more thoughts on her face, but they were wiped away with a smile. "But I'm free for breakfast. Any plans?"

I don't want to be a superhero anymore. Forget all of it. The danger, the late nights, the not being available to talk to girls.

"I can't." The regret was real. *I have to follow your father to his evil lair.* "I have to get to work."

"Fine." She got a pen from her bag and grabbed my hand. "When you're off work and visiting your father, give me a call. We'll be here the rest of the week." She wrote her number on my palm, Sofia, and a little heart.

That was the hottest thing ever done to me.

She gave me a wink.

I almost collapsed.

"I will." I looked at the number. "I will." I took a step backward and bumped into a server.

Fortunately, the server had game and deftly recovered. Didn't even give me a look. This was fancy.

"Sorry," I apologized.

Sofia giggled behind her hand.

I got out of there with no other damage to my dignity. Dad was knee deep in some sales pitch, so didn't even see me leave.

All to the good.

I walked past the security guards. They didn't look at me this time, and I got to the hallway for the elevator without incident.

I saw the Confessor enter the elevator. I hit the stairs and started running down the steps. I didn't see any cameras, so I turned on full speed. Jumping from floor to floor. The floor numbers were painted in large gold letters. I counted them in my head.

Main floor.

This was a fire exit, so it was locked from inside the stair well. I tried the key card I'd lifted from the maid. The door swung open. People were already entering the elevator, so he'd beaten me to the floor.

The crowd was thicker now than it had been just an hour ago. Mostly going, but some people coming.

There. He'd exited the building.

I've followed a lot of people -- not in a creepy way, but in a crime fighting for justice way. But it had always been under the cover of shadow. I felt exposed and might as well have been waving my hands in the air with sparklers.

There was another exit, so I went out that door.

Down the steps to the sidewalk and around, keeping a throng of briefcase clones between me and my target. Raptor had talked about this once or twice, but I'd never actually done it. I wracked my mind, trying to remember what he'd told me.

No, it was Cat. He'd said something about lead. Was I supposed to give a good lead, or not give him a good lead?

I was sure I shouldn't stand out from the rest of the group or be someone he'd just talked to. Damn it. Overall I was glad I hadn't bring Jackal's statue. I would have had to smash it the second Helen saw me. But he would have known what to do here.

I settled in on a half a block. I still felt exposed and tried to walk purposefully and casually, just noticing stuff out of the side of my eye. Not looking right at him.

A cab pulled up and the Confessor got into the rear passenger side.

And he was gone.

I looked around for inspiration. I could hail a cab but I had no money. I didn't know the area and doing a parkour run not in uniform would be stupid.

He got away. I couldn't even get the plates without making it obvious.

"I got your name, Guy," I whispered. "You can run but you can't hide." Unless you get in a car, I guess. Then you're all with the hiding. But the takeaway is... I have a lead. Probably.

NINETEEN

It wasn't an easy run to Alpha Base in broad daylight. I had to keep circling back trying to avoid areas where people congregate. I couldn't trust to shadows to conceal me.

That being said, it felt so good to be behind my mask again. I felt exposed doing the Work in plain clothes. My real identity for anyone to see. Made me shiver.

I was exhausted -- from the run, but more just the nature of sleep deprivation. I hadn't gotten a solid six hours in more than a day and I was feeling it.

It was already ten-thirty. We hadn't set a time to meet, but I felt it wasn't this late. I got in through the door Flare had shown me the night before.

"Fly!" I was surprised to see Butterfly there.

She looked up from the computer she was working on.

She was the only one in the base's front conference area. I could hear someone talking through the door.

"Raven." She sounded happy to see me, though it's tough to tell through a voice modulator.

"Did you get my message?"

She nodded. "Guy Cranstan. I haven't been able to run much down yet. I've been following up other leads."

She must be tired, too.

"That's the Confessor. I'm sure of it." Pretty sure. I mean, what are the odds he has the exact same injures as the guy I was looking for?

"Tell Red Knight. He has me doing a pretty deep dive on Bio-Globe employees." The computer beeped and she turned back to her work.

Fair enough. We had to circle up and come up with a new plan. "Where?"

She pointed at the door Red Knight had called "Gym" last night.

I entered it carefully.

This was a much, much smaller workout space than the Clubhouse. I missed the Clubhouse.

A rock climbing wall, a set of free weights, and an industrial strength treadmill were around the edges. The center was an area about twice the size of a boxing ring, all padded.

In the center, Ballista was forming a ball of light about a foot off his palm.

That was new. Last week he couldn't make any manifestations without slamming his palms together, and he had to release the ball right away. The result could either level a building or pop like a soap bubble. And his aim was crap. Still, he'd pulled my bacon out of the fire more than once and he was the most powerful parahuman on my Christmas card list. He was just too young and inexperienced to use all his power.

"Good." Red Knight stood a little to the side with a red translucent wall between him and Ballista. "Now focus on turing the energy outward."

I couldn't see Ballista's face. He had his backup mask on.

The bubble started to shimmer.

"Stop," Red warned.

He didn't stop.

I dived behind the guy in the wheelchair.

The bubble started to twist. "I can't."

A red globe materialized around the twisting, out-of-control bubble right before it exploded.

The explosion broke Red Knight's control bubble, but it didn't hurt Ballista at all. I just saw a flash.

"I lost focus." Ballista sounded like an ashamed robot.

"Sorry, B. I didn't know you guys were in the middle of...that." I got up from the mat.

"Sorry? That was fantastic!" Red Knight beamed. "That was the most control I've seen you use yet. In two hours you went from making explosions to suspending your orbs. That's way better than I thought I would see during our first session." He wheeled over and clapped Ballista on his shoulders. "You did good. Now hit the showers, and get some lunch. We'll put in a few more attempts before the day is out."

Ballista seemed encouraged and went to a door that joined to the locker room.

After the door shut, Red slumped in his chair. "Wow, that kid is powerful. It was all I could do to contain that pop."

"I've seen him drop Shale on his ass."

"He told me all about your little adventure last week." He wheeled around so he was looking right at me. "That kid's got some hero worship."

"Yeah, but his heroes are dead." I looked the way he'd gone.

"Not the old Guard. I mean you."

"What?"

"Oh, come on. You saved his life from the likes of Silhouette and Shale and you stayed around him and helped him through a surge when the smart money was on running."

How much he did tell him? Did he talk about the nullifier? I guess I didn't really care, but I made a mental note to talk to Ballista about need to know information. I wasn't worried about Red Knight knowing about it -- the guy was a legend. But the more people who heard about the nullifier, the more opportunities for an egoist to find the information.

"So Butterfly told me you gave her a name to look up?" It was a little tough, but he started wheeling himself off the cushie mats.

"I identified the Confessor." I said it with definite triumph, but he didn't look convinced.

"How can you be sure?"

"I talked to him, saw his injuries, and felt his thumbs. It's him." Probably. I mean definitely, probably.

"Walk me through how you found him."

I did, explaining how I'd gotten through the hotel security to the restaurant. I modified the story at that point, so that instead of my sister saving me, it was Sofia who struck up a conversation with me and then introduced me to her father. I didn't need anyone learning my dad and siblings were in town.

"Any why did you pick that hotel?"

"Well... I figured... since the Carlton was closed, the Golden--"

"Ballista told me about Jackal." Red Knight did not approve.

"Yeah, he pointed out that an egoist was only allowed to spend three nights in the city, and that the Golden View was a logical place for him to stay while he was working."

"You have to be careful with Jackal." Red Knight wheeled off the mat and over to a small and well used satchel by the weight bench. "He was after my time, but he's crafty. The more you tell him, the more he'll use you."

"He saved all our lives last week." Though Red Knight's warning mirrored what I'd been telling myself.

From the satchel, he pulled a folded copy of the Darhaven Press. "He kept you alive, and for that I owe him." He handed me the paper. "But he didn't do it for free. Corbin Lassiter, a.k.a. Jackal, gets a new trial. Eleven days ago, proof was released that Judge Mortimer Kurt, the presiding judge in Jackal's case, was accepting bribes and being blackmailed."

The information that Jackal had directed us to find. That had been his plan the entire time. "He played us. He played me." I wanted to crumple the paper, but I folded it and handed it back to Red Knight. "Did Butterfly tell you?"

He nodded. "She put it together."

"He told us NOT to put the information on the web."

"Which helped push you into doing it." Red Knight was right.

"Still, a new trial. That doesn't mean he gets off."

"In this town?" Red Knight gave me a pointed look. "He doesn't have Caesar tightening the screws. It's been five years. Who cares enough about Jackal to keep him behind bars? If he has any resources left, he'll apply that to his defense."

I'd just let the man who killed Hawk, Peregrine's brother, loose. "How did Peregrine take the news?"

"Poorly," Red Knight said. "Flare not much better."

"They blame me for working with Jackal." I was blaming me now, too.

"No. Well, Butterfly doesn't. Ballista doesn't. The other two weren't there when he saved your lives multiple times," Red Knight allowed. "I'm not saying you didn't do the right thing. You made a deal with a devil to fight a bigger devil. That happens in the Work." He said it, but he clearly wasn't comfortable having said it. "Raptor was always better at that than me."

"What?"

"Nothing. Look, just talk with the team before you involve Jackal again. He isn't to be trusted and he has his own agenda."

"He led me to the biggest break we've had in the case." I was more defending me than him.

"I hope so. Sometimes a car accident is just a car accident." He raised his hands to forstall more debate. "It's more than worth checking out though. We'll have Butterfly up his name in her queue and I'll go stake the place out."

"You? But I --"

"You've already been identified to the target. We don't need him to put the same pieces together on you that you did to him," he countered. "You know I'm right."

"But you're wanted by the SSA," I pointed out.

"That was hours ago. The SSA have moved on from little old me. Besides, this won't be in an area where the Feds are thick," Red Knight said. "But I'm not in charge here. We'll talk about duty assignments as a team." He spun his chair toward the conference room.

That was a lot different from working with Raptor.

I followed. "What did you mean about Raptor and deals?"

He turned on me. "Shouldn't have said that." He ran his

hands through his hair, trying to brush some life back into his mind. "I didn't sleep that well last night. I'm making stupid slips of the tongue."

"Julia said it was funny Raptor told me not to kill people. Like that was Raptor's last priority, even though he made that the first part of our training."

"Julia was a little bitter."

"I got that." I nodded.

"She wanted him out of the life. He put together Bio-Globe from a crashing startup and made it one of the biggest biotech firms on the east coast. Maybe one of the biggest companies on the coast. She wanted to retire, have babies, see the world."

"And Raptor wouldn't leave the city." I finished the sentence.

Red Knight shook his head. "No, he loved this city. He felt he could make a difference. But in the end he was consumed by it. He made deals with the big players, because he had to. That fight with Purge? It was Caesar that gave us the intel. It saved thousands of lives."

I was silent.

"I know why Raptor made the deal he did, but I couldn't stomach it. Legs or no, I don't think I would have stayed in the Guard. I couldn't see how we could clean this city up if our hands were dirty."

I stayed silent.

"Sorry, kid. I should have kept my mouth shut." He directed his chair to the door again.

"What about Section 5?" I asked

He spun around at that. "Where did you hear about Section 5?" He sounded almost afraid.

"It was something Julia said." That didn't calm him. "She said that's where she was trained."

His eyes kept on me, searching for something. I don't know what.

"That's it." I held up my hands defensively. "That's the only time I ever heard about it."

He watched me then exhaled. "Fine. Sorry. It's just, that was one of the things I agreed never to talk about."

"To who?"

"I don't suppose it matters now. Archie. Archie swore me and the entire Guard to secrecy." He obviously took the oath seriously. I thought that was the last I was going to get out of him. "Section 5 isn't a secret. It's the covert investigative arm of the SSA."

Not a secret? That was news to me. "I've never heard of them."

"They might not exist anymore." He shrugged. "It was a scandal at the time. When the Superhuman Suppression Agency was chartered they had 5 sections. The first section is the division of heavy hitting supers you saw last week. Section 2 is the crime unit, 3 is analysis, 4 logistics, and 5 was the undercover unit to investigate threats. A few senators thought it smelled of secret police." Red thought for a second. "Or maybe 3 is logistics. Whatever, it doesn't matter. It almost crashed the entire program, but after Purge let go downtown Darhaven and leveled three blocks, the politicians got in line with a groundswell of support." He laughed. "Not that the people who actually fought Purge got any of that support. The fact the Guard saved thousands of lives wasn't brought up." He rubbed his legs.

"Why does Raptor have anything to do with Section 5?"

"It was one of the deals I was talking about. He made some deal with them. He would pass them information and they would stay out of the city. Julia was his contact, and that relationship went... well. At least for a while."

"I don't get it. Was Julia still working for Section 5?" Then would Section 5 already know about me? Know about all of the team?

"I don't know. I haven't heard anything about Section 5 in years. The division was probably pulled and quietly mothballed. Just when you started talking about them again, I thought maybe I was wrong."

I followed him out of the training room.

"Okay, Butterfly. Do you have that list?" Red Knight asked.

"Still working on it." She seemed disappointed in herself. "Bio-Globe has excellent security. I think Clockwork may have designed some of it."

"Makes sense," Red Knight said. "Do you know any of his backdoors or whatever you call them?"

"I do, dozens. If he made this, he did not seem to leave any."

"There's gotta be something," I said. "He was playing Raptor. Just in case he got caught, he would have a way in."

She nodded. "I'll keep at it. I have other attacks lined up, but this could take weeks."

"Then we have to focus on the Confessor," I said.

"I agree with Raven," Red Knight said. "Peregrine is keeping an eye on Bio-Globe for the time being. I'll go to the hotel and scope the place out." He held up his hand to forstall any debate. "A cardboard sign, and I will blend into the background like a kid who was just there can't."

It wasn't like I could go back there in plain clothes and just walk around. I could hang out with my family maybe, but that would just put them in harm's way. "Fine, what should I do?"

"Get some sleep. Go home and get some sleep," Red Knight said.

"I can't go home."

That got a raised eyebrow from Red Knight.

"Mom stuff."

He nodded in understanding. "She know?" He waved a hand at my uniform.

"No, God no." I shook my head. "I think she thinks I'm getting into drugs or something. I just need to get this Phoenix and fry it. Then I put this behind me and make it up to her."

"That sounds like a justification you've been rattling around in your head for a while."

I shrugged. "I can't tell her the truth. Just this job and then I'll retire--"

Butterfly laughed.

"What?"

"You think you are going to quit? This is what you want most of all, more than all of us except maybe Peregrine."

"Yeah, well. That was before. Now it's just too dangerous."

"It's always been dangerous, but now it's become more real," Red Knight said. "Now that you don't have Raptor, you're walking without a net."

Maybe.

"Trust your team, trust your training," Red Knight said. "It will get you far. In a way, Raptor still has your back."

Except I really know nothing about him.

TWENTY

I only meant to get a couple of hours crash time in the bunkhouse. I mean, I was in my full uniform and helmet. Not the most comfortable pajamas. Unlike the Clubhouse, I didn't have my own little locker room I could have crashed in. This was just a set of six dusty bunks.

I was out the second I was horizontal and the next thing I knew it was 4pm. I'd been asleep for six hours.

I checked my message feed.

Nothing.

At least I hadn't missed anything. If the team had been counting on me and I hadn't woken up, boy I don't know if I could have rebounded from that.

There was also nothing from Mom. Maybe she'd heard from Dad and knew I was okay.

I'd picked the top bunk, so I didn't notice Flare was laid out in the bunk below until I climbed down. She didn't seem to mind being in full gear, either.

I quietly got out of the bunk room and shut the door behind me.

Butterfly was still working at the base computers.

"Any luck?" I asked.

"Luck is not a quantifiable trait," Robo-Butterfly said. "I have not had any progress." Her fingers were moving over the keyboard so fast I couldn't see them.

"Anything on our boy, the Confessor?"

"Yes."

"What did you find out about him?"

"He is a consultant. He makes high six figures officially, but more is probable. His most important client is Midas Enterprises, but he 'consults' all over the country. He is married and has a daughter who is eighteen. He lives in Connecticut. His last consultation was with Green Solutions, the distant second supplier of parahuman testing. Green Solutions' best accuracy rating achieved is sixty-seven percent. I do not know his current location. Further conversation about the topic is possible but has reached a point of diminishing returns."

Okay. "Well, I see you're hard at it. I'll let you do your thing."

She creeps me out when she gets this way, like *she might shoot me to reduce distractions* kind of creepy. I backpedaled out and started the long daytime route back to my nest.

By the time I got to my nest, I had worked the kinks out from sleeping in my uniform and was feeling normal and awake.

To my surprise, Feral was sitting on my cot, curled up.

"How? How do you get in here?"

He didn't answer so much as look at me with annoyance for waking him up.

"Boy have you missed some interesting stuff," I told my cat. Or I told my owner, depending on perspective.

"Did you know that Raptor was a spy for SSA and killed people?"

He was unimpressed.

"Sure, I'm always the last to know."

I stripped out of my uniform and showered. The water was always cold, but felt good.

I let the tepid water run over me. "I don't even know how much I should care. It wasn't like he even trusted me with his face. Did you know he was married?"

Feral actually hissed at that.

"I don't know, I kind of liked her. But she was scary as hell." So, I had to agree with Feral.

I shut off the water and toweled off.

"The Confessor could already be out of the country with our names and addresses. We have no way of knowing."

He purred.

I pulled on my pants. "You think so? Well, I suppose he wouldn't leave his daughter if he was ready to skip town. In fact, I'm kind of surprised he brought her on this business trip." Then the shirt. "I mean, why put her in harm's way if he didn't have to? They live in Connecticut for crying out loud. Super villains are crazy."

I headed to the door. "You coming?" I asked him as I was about to leave.

He got up, stretched, and padded his way to me.

I caught him when he jumped and gave him a good rubbing.

The second time carrying him down the pitch-black tunnel was easier, my para-ability giving my muscle memory perfect recall of the last descent.

My head was still working the angles of the case. I felt like there was a piece I was missing. I'm ashamed to say it, but I wanted to go dig up the idol and ask Jackal. Red Knight was right though, I couldn't trust him. He played me to get his new trial. Also, growing dependent on him was a good way to end up dead. I would just have to trust the team. That felt right.

Feral kept pace with me on the walk home, but when we arrived he stopped right in front of me. I almost tripped over him.

"Feral? What the hell?"

"Watch your mouth," my mom said.

So I was so up in my own business I hadn't noticed my mom on the concrete stump in front of our home. She was smoking.

"I thought you quit." I hadn't seen her smoke in years.

She laughed without mirth and tapped some ash. "Your father has that effect on me. All the Blackwater men." She took a drag and blew it out in a geyser of smoke.

I took another step closer and realized her eyes were red and puffy.

"Mom." I don't even know what I was going to say, but I didn't get that far.

"No." She cut me off with a wave of her cigarette hand. "No, I can't take it." She sobbed into her other hand, then looked at me. "Your father told me you stopped to see him for breakfast."

"Yeah."

"And you couldn't call me?" I think she was trying to not say that. It came out as a panicked blurt.

I opened my mouth. What was I going to say? *I didn't mean to run into him, I just didn't want to blow my cover.*

"How did you even know what hotel he was staying at?"

She didn't really care about the answer. She was just talking to keep from falling apart.

"The Golden View is the nicest hotel in the area. I figured it was a safe bet." Which was why I was there looking up the Confessor.

She made an inaudible "Oh."

I took another step, and she started crying. A shake of her head. First the word was just formed on her breath, then I heard it. "No."

"No?" No, what? I stopped where I was.

"I can't. I can't do this anymore."

"Do what?"

"Pretend that I'm doing anything for you at all!" More tears now as she stood.

"Mom, let's go in and talk about this." The street wasn't busy, but I didn't want to perform my little street theater for everyone.

"No. This isn't home for you anymore." With her cigarette hand she pointed at two trash bags I hadn't focused on yet. "It's not like you even live here."

"Mom."

"No. You don't respect me, you don't listen to me. You barely even live here."

"That's not true."

"Yes, it is."

"No, I respect you." Is what I was trying to say.

"Then where have you been?" She put it right on the table.

Awkward pause. "Around?"

"Doing what?"

Come on, Mom, not now. "Stuff." Yes, I know how lame that sounded. "I'm sorry. I just have a few things to set right, then everything will be better. I promise."

"You promised all last week, but the second your friends called I didn't see you until 1am. That's not making things right." Another drag on her cigarette.

"It's important," I said. "But it's almost over."

"What? What is so important that it's more important than me, than graduating? What?"

Maybe she had a little hope that she could get through to me, that she could get answers to the questions crushing her.

I couldn't. Not out here in public. I might have told her, told her everything. Raptor, Jackal, Red Knight, the Phoenix, everything. If we'd been inside, alone, I think I would have.

I couldn't.

I took another step forward.

"I mean it." She got in front of me.

"I know." I stepped around her and picked up the two bags. One was clothes and one had my game system and a few games that I never had the time to play, and some other things that went clink.

I walked down the steps.

Feral hissed.

I turned back to face my mom. I don't know where I found the strength. "Mom?"

She was looking at me, caught in mid-tear wipe. "What?"

"Feral's dish?" I held up the non-clothes bag.

She nodded. "And the cans of food you had left."

"Thanks." I had no idea what to do next, what to say. "Mom?"

"What?"

"I'm sorry. For putting you through this." I held up the bags. "Putting you through all of it."

She started to cry, sob.

I'm smooth like that. So smooth.

I left my mother crying on the steps, smoking a cigarette.

TWENTY-ONE

So for those paying attention at home, Raven zero, cruel insensitive world five million and five.

Where the hell was I going to live? Sure, I could crash in my nest for the near future. But eventually I would need stuff like money and food. And to somehow graduate. I wasn't going to put my mom through all this and then fail to eventually cross *that* finishing line.

Also, in my free time I needed to find the Phoenix before everything went public. I had nothing, totally stumped.

What do I do?

Feral was no help, not even a little. He just wandered behind me making hunger meow noises until I got back to the nest and fed him.

On the upside, Mom gave me all the snacks I'd originally pilfered from my nest stores. I nibbled on an energy bar while Feral munched down the cat food.

"*You're* the one screwed here? Do you think my stepmom will take in a mangy old fleabag like you?"

I think that worried him, not at all.

"I have to go talk to my dad. See if his offer is still open."
I banged my head against the wall. "Well, nuts." I'd never
thought it would come to that.

I looked over at my mask. "Screw it," I told... me... it...
my alter ego... whatever. "And screw you!" The nearest
thing I had to hand was the empty tin of cat food and I
threw it at my helmet on the shelf. "I've got nothing else you
can take from me!" That wasn't fair. "I've got nothing else to
give you, to sacrifice to you."

I peeled myself up from the bean bag and took the four
steps to my mask. "I don't know what I was thinking. You
were stupid. Everything I did, everything I gave up, and for
what? For some do-no-harm make-a-difference crap that he
didn't even believe in." I pointed up to make sure my helmet
knew I was talking about Raptor.

"Damn it." I swiped my hand across the stand and
knocked it down. Then flopped back on the bean bag.

Feral hopped on me and licked my face.

Let the record show, it was not my tears. He was licking
my face. Under my eye.

I blew my nose.

"What am I doing, Feral? I can't do this without Raptor
and the last thing he said to me is I'm not good enough." I
banged the back of my head against the wall in time with
the desperation throbbing in my head. I started running my
hand over Feral.

He purred.

"Fair point. It wasn't the last thing he said to me. The
last thing he gave me was a note that I can't decode."

I petted the cat while I chewed one more energy bar.
"Fine, let's get this over with."

I'm still more of a dog person, but I appreciated Feral
sticking with me. I didn't have a plan. Just showing up at my

dad's room with a cat wasn't a great move. But what else did I have?

I stood at the bus stop for somewhere between three minutes and a century, and just couldn't take it. I just couldn't take sitting and waiting for the world to move. I started to run.

At first I thought I would leave Feral behind. I almost picked him up, but he was gone. He appeared twenty feet ahead of me, licking his paw. As if to say, is that all you got?

I smiled. "That's how it's going to be?"

I put on the speed.

I was in plain clothes. I may have looked suspicious running the street at well above a jogging speed, but I didn't care. I just had to run.

I came to the first wall. I could go around or over.

I went over. It was actually easier than in full gear. I got to the top of the wall. Feral got up and stretched, then jumped to a ledge and started padding away.

"How do you do that?" I pulled up my hood just in case I ended up on someone's social media post and ran along the brick wall.

I started to push it.

I was up on the roofs moving faster than I should be. I knew the route, but it was still ten o'clock at night.

I got to the building across from the Golden View. Funny to say, but it kind of snuck up on me.

Feral padded in front of me and under my waiting hand.

"What took you?" I gave him a good rubdown. "That could be my life." I nodded at the tower. "Boom, I win the lottery and just pretend the last year and a half didn't happen. Show I can keep my crap together and prove to my mom that I'm not a screw up."

He butted my head and rubbed his back into my face. "Yeah, I have to be honest. I'm a dog person. I'm just saying. If I find a labrador or corgi, I'm kicking you to the curb."

His tail twitched under my nose.

I looked at the tower, trying to figure out where my dad was staying. Or, and purely a secondary consideration, if Sofia was taking a late night bath on her balcony.

Neither were discernible.

"Well, let's go beg." This would be a great time to not disappoint me, Dad. A great time.

I got down to street level. I don't even remember the climb other than it was way easier without my uniform. Without my gloves I could get my fingers into the smaller cracks.

And walked up to the front door. I looked around for Red Knight. He was supposed to be staking out the place, but I didn't see him.

The door guard or bellhop or whatever let a couple through, but got in front of me. "Can I help you?"

I looked him in the face and inhaled, but his expression changed from intimidating to friendly service. "Ryan, I presume."

Nothing freaks me out more than when someone knows my name that shouldn't. A professional hazard. "I--" Should I punch the guy and run?

"Your father told us you might be stopping by." He held the door open for me. "Oh, and he gave me this."

He passed me an envelope with my name written on it.

If this was in code, I was still going to punch this guy in the face. Not because I wanted to, but because there was just no other option. "Thanks." I took the note and felt the climate shift as I entered the air-conditioned comfort of the other half.

The lobby was huge, all marble and small clusters of chairs. It was after ten, so it was also empty. Just the two people I'd come in behind, the woman's heels clicking on the marble floor, and a pretty woman behind the front desk.

I opened the letter.

Ryan, I just got off the phone with your mother. Sorry it went this way. You're welcome to stay with us. The front desk will have a key card, room 1808. Your room has a post-it note on it if you arrive after we're all in bed. We'll talk in the morning. --Dad.

The lady at the front desk did indeed have a card key for me, and I went to the elevator bank.

It opened and I entered.

Feral was already in the elevator waiting for me.

I looked around, but no one was watching. "Feral, you can't be in here." I was pretty sure they had a no pet policy, though thinking of Feral as my pet was getting harder and harder.

He crouched at my feet and gave me the, "I'm jumping, you can catch me or I can use my claws all down your chest, stomach, and groin. Your call," look.

Jump.

I caught him. Good human.

"Fine, but if we get busted, I don't know you." I pressed the eighteenth floor, but it didn't work. It took me a second to figure out I had to swipe my room key. I guess when I'd been sneaking around earlier today, it had made sense that I needed a key card, but now that I was here legally, I'd just figured I could use the damn elevator.

I swiped the card. A little red light went green and Feral leapt out of my arms, colliding with the number selection so about four other floors lit up.

"This is why I'm a dog person. Lassie would let me go directly to my room." I hit the 18.

Feral didn't look interested in being held anymore, but he did seem agitated. Normally he was pretty calm, but he was walking back and forth like a caged animal.

To be fair, that is what he was.

The first false floor opened, then the second. At the third, Feral darted out the doors.

"What? Come on." I followed. "Feral, you can't just walk around up here," I whispered.

I reached down to pick him up but he got just out of my reach and scampered down to the end of the hall.

"Fine, go walk around and get put in the pound. Don't expect me to bust you out." The elevator had closed behind me, so I punched the call button. "I am not running after you."

He raised his leg to the corner, like a dog would. Cat's don't pee that way, do they?

"Oh, come on!" I rushed over, but of course he just kept ahead of me. This would be great yearbook footage to play for the entire school. I was just inches from grabbing him as we went down the hall, around a corner, and then he was gone.

"What the hell? Feral," I hissed. "Show yourself or someone is getting a trip to the vet." I poked my head around the corner. Luckily no one was up to see my antics. Down the hall, in front of a door to a suite, Feral was sitting casually licking his paw.

"Are you done?"

He gave me a look. It was a cross between "whatever do you mean?" and "what took you so long?"

I walked up to him carefully. I didn't want him to jet off again.

Like he hadn't just been a total spazz, he let me pick him up.

"Did I mention I'm a dog person?" I am so a dog person.

And I heard a sound. A muffled sound, but I knew it. It was the sound of a body being smacked with more force than was non-para possible.

The smackie didn't even have time to yelp. Just hit the floor.

I looked at the cat in my arms. I think Feral winked at me.

More sounds of a fight, a little less one-sided.

I could get in there. Bust down the door or try the housekeeper's key. But what would I find? And more critical, I wasn't in uniform. I would be Ryan, concerned citizen -- no helmet or armor plating. No cool leather.

I popped up my burner phone, dialed the Team number, and rattled off the code to Butterfly.

"Raven?"

She didn't recognize my voice unmodulated. This did not feel good, like I was walking in front of my English class naked, kind of exposed. "Yes, patch me through to Red Knight."

"What's going on?"

"Is Red Knight at the Golden View still?" I hadn't seen him.

"Yes." She was frantically punching buttons. "He isn't picking up. What's going on?"

"I don't know. Get Peregrine and Flare here stat!"

"Here?"

"The Golden View."

"Why are you there? Are you out of uniform?"

All good questions, Butterfly. "Just trust me. See if you can find out who's in room 1712."

"I don't have to, That's the suite for Guy Cranston."

And Sofia was in there while a parahuman was ripping some vanilla apart. "Crap. I'm going active. Unmasked."

"No! Let me get the others. You can not go active unmasked in Jack Midas's hotel!"

Something else broke, and muffled gunfire sounded.

"Don't have a choice."

Feral make no comment as I dropped him.

You can Google this, how to make a t-shirt into a ninja mask. I'd had time to kill in study hall one day and had looked it up. Cool thing about being a kinist -- you do it once and you're a pro for life. I tied off my shirt in a minute. Now I didn't even have the protection of a shirt, and I looked like the dirty laundry avenger, but it was what I had.

I tried the door. Locked.

So either they'd known the person going all medieval on them, or he was a para and had entered through the balcony.

I swiped the maid's key and the light went green. Yes!

I opened the door quickly and jumped to the right. The room had the same basic layout as the one where I'd hidden my stolen disguise. I went straight into the closet.

I don't think anyone saw me. They were way too busy getting the crap beat out of them. Three guys in suits -- nope, there were five -- but one and two were already on the floor bent in ways that were not healthy ways to be bent. So three guys were fighting a ninja in the main living room of the suite.

Not just any ninja. It was my buddy, Heavy Metal Ninja.

TWENTY-TWO

So at this time I had to ask myself, *huh?* Why would Heavy Metal Ninja be here with the violence? Wasn't he working for the Confessor? Were these aggressive contract negotiations?

Another suit, weapon drawn and one hand on Sofia, kept his body in between her and HMN as he pushed her toward the door.

At this point I also noticed the Ninja-sized hole in the glass door to the balcony. Even though they knew him, he'd used his powers to get in.

The Ninja noticed Sofia and her guard. He lost interest in his dance partners, flipped over a couch, and landed a punch right into the guard's neck. It was so hard the man dropped.

Sofia yelled and stepped back.

Giving the first three some room. They drew their pistols and got a bead on the Ninja.

Sofia was totally in their backfield, and they were beyond caring at this point.

It was possible the Ninja might be hurt by bullets. But Sofia would certainly be hurt by bullets.

I moved. As fast as I could, I jumped out of the closet, vaulted over the kitchen counter, and tackled Sofia out of the way.

Guns started going off.

The Ninja just stood there and took it. Bullets bounded off his back.

Cracks spiderwebbed from the Ninja's feet in the fake wood tile and bullets ricocheted off him. He didn't bleed. His clothes ripped apart from the bullets, but he didn't bleed.

"Go, go, go!" I forced Sofia up and into the room she'd come out of.

"Who are you?" She pushed me away. "Who is that guy?"

"I'm Raven. I'm with the Guard. I'm here to help you. We've got to get out of this building."

"Like hell! I'm not going anywhere with you."

One of her bodyguards screamed and then stopped screaming.

She reconsidered. "How can we get out of here?"

I tipped the mattress over the door. "Get onto the balcony."

"Can you fly?" She was not really buying that I was with the Guard, but she was willing to entertain the idea. Desperation is a powerful thing.

"Something like that." I beat her over to the door and assisted her getting to the balcony.

I really could use some back up here.

The door to her unit splintered. The bed bought us another heart beat.

"Hold on tight," I told her.

She looked at me, over the edge, at the door, then back at me. "What?"

A bodyguard bought us a second, but he was dealt with quickly and finally.

She threw her arms around my neck and wrapped her legs around me in a figure four.

"That tight," I pointed out. She didn't loosen her grip.

"Here we go!" I rolled over the railing, rotated in the air and caught the balcony railing below.

She screamed.

Hold on, hold on. I didn't have an extra hand if she let go.

I swung out over the seventeen-story drop, kicked my legs, and flew back into the patio on floor sixteen.

I landed back first, trying to shield her from the impact.

"Oh, God. Oh, God." She had not lost any of her grip.

But now I needed to get up. And breathe and stuff. "Okay," I said. "That worked. You've got to get up. We're not safe."

"Oh, God. Oh, God." If anything she held on tighter.

I peeled her hand away and rolled her off me. "Shh." I heard someone on the balcony above us.

It wasn't going to be rocket science to figure out where we'd gone. I was sure he had the skills to make the jump down just to check out the possibility.

Then something broke, a vase maybe, and whoever was on the balcony went back inside to investigate.

I didn't realize I was covering her mouth, but I removed my hand and pointed at the door. We tried it and it was unlocked. I mean, who would bother locking a sixteenth floor balcony?

"A cat!" I heard the Ninja curse.

I had Feral to thank for the distraction. We got into the unit below.

The lights were off. The coffee table had manila files strewn on it and a closed laptop. The sink had some dishes, and a half-eaten pizza was on the table.

This was how crazy my day had been -- that pizza looked good. I was so hungry.

So this was not an empty unit. And I'd just led an assassin into the guy's room. Damn it.

I forced the maid's key card into Sofia's hand. "You have to run now. Find some place to hide."

"No." She shook her head. "Where are you going?"

"I can't let him follow us through the hotel killing people. I'll take him down upstairs."

"You can't. He's a parahuman." She matched my hiss whisper.

"So am I." No big deal. Except I can't beat this guy. He totally owned me our last fight, and I was in armor then. This was going to hurt, probably briefly.

She shook her head and grabbed my hand. "Trust me, if you go up against him, you'll die." She pulled my hand. "The only way you're going to live is if you come with me."

"Hey, that's my line." But she was right. I was a dead man in another one-on-one with the Ninja. So I let her pull me.

If the guy, and I'm guessing guy here -- the pizza was a meat lovers -- who was a guest of the hotel got hurt, well, how would I live with that?

We got out into the hall and went directly to the stairwell.

She pulled the door open and Heavy Metal Ninja was waiting for us on the other side.

I kicked the door shut before HMN could react. "Run."

A fist punched through the door right were the lock was.

Sofia was already running so I jumped the other way and avoided the door slamming open as HMN burst into the hallway.

He looked my way, saw Sofia, and started after her.

I couldn't blame him. A moron without a shirt didn't rate on his threat-o-meter.

But talking threat, I'll bet he hadn't thought a cat was a big deal, either. Part of the Ninja's mask, right by his eye, revealed a new scratch. I knew it was Feral. I recognized the brush work of a master. Feral had just shown me that HMN could be hurt, could be made to bleed.

I kiped up into a run. Before he realized I was following, I jumped, got more momentum pushing off the wall, and kicked him square in the head.

He spun and I kept up the pressure. If he got a second to get all invulnerable, this would be a lot harder.

I got under his defenses and felt a rib crack. Not sure how badly, but it had to take some spring out of his step.

He scissors kicked my legs out from underneath me. I turned the fall into a kick to his abdomen, aiming for the same spot in his ribs.

He exhaled with the kick, and I beat him to a standing position, firing in with a right hook that should have ended the discussion.

It did not, as it happened, end the discussion.

He caught my hand, and it was like punching a vice. Turns out I needed to up the pressure. Huh, life's like that. At least mine is.

I pulled my fist away and did a spin over his arm to get more leverage that freed my fist. He didn't care at all about the double kick I delivered to his temple in my escape.

"Well, that's surprising." HMN stood, not even bothering to block a few more shots I delivered. "Raven? Is that you?"

He'd recognized me from my fighting style. That was never anything I'd had to worry about before.

"No. Who's this Raven?" I said, but in a really cool deep voice. It's called a disguise.

"Raven, run!" Sofia screamed down the hall.

"Don't know who she's talking to." I shrugged and looked around.

His hand shot out with such force that my block didn't change its trajectory. He put his hand around my throat and lifted me up. "I didn't want it to end like this." He squeezed.

I couldn't breathe. All my twisting and hold breaks didn't matter to this guy at all.

I heard a loud buzzing, then a siren.

Doors started opening all along the floor and people were putting their heads out.

Sofia was standing by the fire alarm. "You ready for your World Wide Web debut, asshole!" she yelled.

He was not.

He must have lost focus because a strike that he'd ignored a second ago sprung me from his grip. I landed and struck with a side kick to his damaged side.

He howled in pain and took a couple steps back. I was up and running.

A lot of people were flooding into the hallway in varying levels of confusion.

I would not have done that. It was possible Heavy Metal Ninja would have started slaughtering people. But Sofia had called it right. He didn't want to be seen any more than I did. He went for the stairwell.

I caught up with Sofia. She was panting and still looked terrified.

"Okay, good. Thank you for saving my life," I told her.

She looked at me and started laughing. "Isn't that my line?" She was still panting.

"Who was that guy?" We both asked at the same time.

"I don't know," she said. "You're the superhero."

At least she was going to verbally give me that one, but the look on her face said she still wasn't sure. I couldn't blame her.

"Well, you may not have superpowers, but you work out," she allowed.

"Thanks." I guess. "Look, I thought he worked for your father."

"My father?" She looked at me like I was crazy. "Dad's an HR consultant. He doesn't hire death ninjas." She pointed at the way he went.

"Your father works for Jack Midas."

"Sure, but don't buy the hype, Uncle Jack just likes to play that image up for the press."

Uncle Jack? Question mark and exclamation mark! "Your life is different from mine," I pointed out. "Well, Uncle Jack is not playing up the image for the press, he's close to taking control of this city's underworld."

She gave me an eye roll.

"Whatever." I tried another tack. "Who were those five guys in your suite?"

"Personal security."

"HR must be a really tough biz to need five personal security."

She opened her mouth at that, but didn't have an easy explanation.

"I bet this is the first time he's let you come to the city."

She nodded.

"Why?"

"He said that things had changed in his business and we were moving into town full time. And I, well, I made him."

"Made him?" She didn't want to talk about something.

"Ever get a feeling, like a really bad feeling?" She nervously started twisting a ring. "I've been getting them a lot lately. And I just knew that if I didn't come, my dad would die." She teared up a little at that. "I know it's stupid. I even came down with a bad--"

"Fever, sweats, passed out? Just after you had this intense feeling?" I asked.

I could tell by her face that I had predicted exactly what had happened.

"I'll bet your father took you more seriously after your fever."

She had to think about it, but she nodded.

"You told me I would die if I didn't go with you. Was that the same kind of premonition?"

She shook her head. "No, that's crazy. I'm not a parahuman. I don't have powers."

The precognition stuff is tricky, She could be a P1 or a P4. There was no way of knowing by what she was presenting, at least not so new to her power. For her sake, I hoped she wasn't a P4. Precogs have a really tough time in surges. Don't know why, but very few survive intact. They all go a little nuts. Maybe it's a feature of living in multiple futures of fry during a surge.

"I think a rival gang was moving in on your father." That isn't all of it.

"Rival gang." She repeated the words as if learning them for the first time.

"There will be a lot of that going on in town," I

explained. "Part of what changed for your father's business."

People in the hallway had realized there wasn't a fire. Some decided to go down the fire escape and others shrugged and went back to bed.

"No, this is crazy. My dad does not have a rival gang." She shook her head and pulled back from me.

"Sofia, you have to listen to me."

"How do you know my name?"

Ah, hell. I'm smooth.

My flip phone beeped. "What?"

"Fire and rescue are dispatched to your location," Butterfly said. "There are also some sightings of a man in black jumping from the hotel to another roof, so SSA are at least investigating."

I looked around for a window. There was one at the other end of the hall. "Damn it."

"I can't raise Red Knight."

"What?"

"He made his last check in, and isn't due for another in five minutes, but what if..."

No. I was not losing another member of the team. I was not! I looked at Sofia, but she was already running at full speed away from me.

Crap!

I either had to look for Red Knight, or convince Sofia I was telling the truth. I couldn't do both. I had to pick one.

Crap.

I made my way to the fire escape and pulled my shirt back into regular shirt shape.

Crap.

I got to street level with a mess of other hotel guests. Just one more poorly dressed patron. I kept an eye open for my dad and his family and started walking the perimeter of the building.

"Fly," I said into my phone. "Do you know what side of the building he was on?"

"He moved a lot." She knew she wasn't being helpful. "Peregrine is still five minutes out."

"Five minutes? Where the hell was he?" In the dark, Peregrine didn't have to worry about being seen and he was fast. He could fly around the entire city in fifteen minutes.

"Tracking a lead down in the Flat Stones. I only now got through to him."

Can't imagine what lead he had in the Flat Stones. That was a few districts over.

"Flare?" I asked.

"She can't get close with SSA converging on the area."

She was right, of course. Flare would be spotted by all these pedestrians a mile off. And it wasn't like I wanted to flag her down and have a chat out of uniform.

Where was the magical cat to point me in the right direction when I needed him?

I started running around, scanning for anything, van or person. It wasn't easy pushing my way through the crowd of annoyed rich hotel patrons. I kept jumping and looking over the heads of people in robes and pajamas, then running and jumping for a quick look again.

I spotted the van.

I pushed through the crowd as quickly as I could without knocking people over. After I cleared the crowd, I got ten feet from the van and saw broken glass.

"No." No, no, just no.

There was blood on the steering wheel. Red Knight was on the floor of the van, a gash on his head and broken glass on his flannel.

I opened the driver's side door and felt for a pulse. I didn't even remember climbing into the van.

His pulse was steady.

I breathed. Not out of the woods yet, but maybe.

I shook him. He didn't respond.

I had to get him to Butterfly.

The keys were still in the ignition, so I turned on the engine and put the van into drive. Fun fact -- I don't have my license per se. Or really at all. My mom doesn't own a car and was never willing to use the company cleaning van to get me some time behind the wheel.

But how hard could it be?

Navigating at street level was a different beast as well. I knew where I was based on the landmarks I passed, and I knew where I had to go. But there were a lot of one-way streets in the city. And routes that were easy when I could jump a fence were far more complicated.

Something landed on the van.

Crap! I slammed on the brakes.

Peregrine fell off, but stopped his descent and glided right by the passenger door.

Thank God, a break.

"What are you doing?" he yelled.

"Driving. We need to get Red Knight to Butterfly. He might have a concussion."

"Do you know this is a one-way?" He pulled open the door.

I unbuckled and let him have the driver's seat. "Yes, I know it's a one-way."

"It's not the one way you are driving." He pointed at a sign that said "Wrong way."

Oops.

"Can you take over from here? I have to go suit up," I said.

He looked at me. "Why are you in your cives, anyway?" He didn't say "moron," but he had tone. He had lots of tone.

"It was all part of my plan." I didn't have to be as careful around Peregrine. We've known each other's identity since before I was in the Guard. "My dad's in town. He's staying at the Golden View."

"I thought you hated your dad." He pulled the van off into an alley and backed up so we were pointed in the right direction.

"Totally hate my dad. Just... Mom kicked me out." I said it so fast I hoped he didn't hear me.

He gave me an unsympathetic tisk. "Now, after all this time?"

"I've had it coming for a while." I had no defense.

"Well, whatever." He stopped the van at the corner. "Get suited up and meet us at Alpha for a debrief. We're just chasing our tails here. Something's got to give or we're all screwed."

He had a point.

TWENTY-THREE

S o I went back to my nest.

No Feral. I was nervous now. Maybe Heavy Metal Ninja had taken out his frustration about getting scratched a little hard. I'd just assumed Feral could take care of himself, but he could have gotten hurt in the fight. I didn't know what to do about that.

For all of you keeping up at home, we can all agree Feral is not just a cat. But what is he? Whatever the answer, invulnerable is not on the list.

Nothing I could do about that now.

It felt good to get into my uniform, like reattaching a leg. I called into the Guard's party line. "You online Butterfly?"

She was not.

Hopefully that wasn't a bad sign. She was probably just busy patching Red Knight up. No reason to panic, but I had to get the lead out.

I kept thinking about what the Heavy Metal Ninja attack meant. It could be that he'd felt ripped off by his employer, but I didn't think so. It seemed like he belonged to a different group all together, which meant there were three groups looking for the Phoenix -- us, the Confessor or whoever he was working for, and HMN's contingent. Whoever he was working with had a lot of faith in him, since the two times I'd seen him he hadn't brought any other resources to bear.

It would also explain why there was a change in MO. Imp's mind was read while Yaltin was tortured because the group that found him didn't have a mind reader, they had a killer. So what did that mean? What information did the Confessor have? What did HMN get from Yaltin? It wasn't enough to find the Phoenix, or he would have just gone and gotten the thing rather than raiding the Confessor's suite.

So even as lost as we were, so were the other two groups. At least we had that going for us. Maybe Raptor had hidden the data backup so well that no one would ever find it.

I was taking my least favorite route. There was this straight climb for four stories coming up, but it had been drilled into me to rotate my route just in case someone started noticing.

"Help! Oh God, help!" A woman screamed in absolute desperation. "He has a knife! Please, anyone."

Hey, I'm anyone.

I changed my trajectory and ran along the edge of the building.

A woman in her twenties, dressed for a party. A wiry white guy with a ton of tattoos slowly closing on her. He held the knife for intimidation, like he wanted her to scream. A scream wouldn't bring any help in this area. Not normally.

I dropped, stopped my descent on a window ledge, and back flipped in the air to land right in front of the knife wielder.

The knife guy dropped the weapon right away and threw up his hands.

A butter knife?

"Oh, thank god," the woman said. It wasn't the "thank god" of someone who was being saved from an ugly death. It was the "thank god" of someone who was thrilled she could finally get out of her heels. "You're Raven, right?" She rummaged in her purse.

"Yes," I said hesitantly.

"About time. We've been staging this little play all over the area. For two hours." She pulled an envelope out and handed it to me. "Thanks for trying to save me." She gave me a smile.

"Sure." I took the envelope. *Raven* was written on the outside.

Knife guy pointed at the butter knife. "Cool if I pick that up? Littering isn't my thing."

"No, go ahead." I stepped back from them. This was too weird. "Keep the city beautiful." The slogan on all the park signs just poured from my mouth.

The damsel-in-not-that-much-distress popped a piece of nicotine gum in her mouth and gave me a wink. "That was a cool flippy thing." She twirled her finger in a loop.

"Thanks. Well, nice meeting you." Didn't really know the protocol in this situation. Do you tip?

"You, too. Thanks for all the vigilante stuff. Big fan." The guy put the butter knife in his back pocket and gave me a thumbs up.

"Just doing my part." I slowly backed away from them.

The woman gave me a little wave and a suggestive eyebrow, but took the man's arm and they both walked out of the alley.

I felt a little foolish and exposed, so I didn't open the letter until I got up on a roof.

The paper was recycled, flimsy, and folded. On the back was a very good drawing of what I at first thought was a wolf. No, it was a jackal.

I read the note: Urgent! Get to the idol and give me a call. I have something you need to follow up on and soon.

Well, how about that?

The idol was close by, proving he could lock onto the physical location of his focus. He'd guessed that I had stashed the idol on my patrol. So somehow he'd gotten this note to some "actors."

Red Knight was right, I was letting Jackal way too far into my confidence. He could have led me into a trap with the same bait.

My pulse quickened a little.

I jammed the note in my pouch with the letter from Raptor. He might be playing me, but he might know something. And we needed something.

I thought about calling it in, but why fight about it? I'd just see what he had to say. It wouldn't put me too far behind and the others would want to know. The only information we had so far was because of Jackal and Red Knight.

I had to backtrack a little.

But when I reached the spot where I'd stashed the idol, I stood there for a ten count, waffling. Last chance. I could still walk away.

Fine.

I pulled out the packet of plastic and unwrapped it. The statue immediately jumped to life.

"Raven, thank God. You were making me nervous." Jackal actually seemed concerned.

"I'm fine."

"Have you been watching the news?"

"Been busy." How have *you* been watching the news?

"Supers matching the description of members of the Guard were seen at the explosion that assassinated the co-owner of Bio-Globe," he quoted.

Oh, that could look bad.

"They're spinning it that Bio-Globe is being targeted by terrorists. And they're not sure if you're with them or against them," he warned.

"Come on." This day just got better and better. Oh wait, it's midnight. This was a whole new day of suck.

"The SSA have given a statement that all vigilantes will be rounded up like all the other super-powered criminals." Jackal seemed like he was reading something from notes. "They have let the Guard flaunt the law for too long. With these acts of terrorism tied to them they at least need to be brought in for questioning. They're imploring Raptor and the rest of the team to turn themselves in."

"Well, it won't matter if we don't get the Phoenix first."

"Phoenix? What's that?"

Oops. Did I mention it was midnight? I was getting punchy. "What's your can't wait information?"

"I found out about a guy who might have information from the old days. He was a legend in my day working with Caesar, but I never met him. He goes by the handle Worm."

"Legend how?" Sounded like a sleeze.

"He was an information hound. Caesar always had him working on getting information from every corner of the city. He reported directly to Caesar. And I got an address for you."

"Do you really think this guy would know anything useful?"

"I do."

"Why would he tell me?"

"I'm not sure, but we can ask." Jackal did not sound like he just intended to ask.

"Alright, give me the address."

"No."

Going from punchy to pissed. "I don't know what you had to do to get me your letter, but then to jerk me around is a little much. What do you want?"

"Take my idol with you." The statue glowed yellow.

I weighed the ins and outs.

"You have a lot of good qualities, but negotiation is not one of them. If you're going to get anything useful out of this guy, you'll need me."

Let's just face facts. He was right. Besides, I couldn't think of a reason not to, except it was letting a known sociopath and force of evil ride in my back pocket. Again.

I slipped the idol in my pouch. "Let's go."

TWENTY-FOUR

J ackal guided me to an absolute crap hole. Cockroaches wouldn't be caught dead in this place.

I thought it was a condemned building, but the roof held my weight. The fire escape was a little more dodgy. I was ready for the wall to give out, which would force me to jump for something else.

I counted windows and made an educated guess which one was the Worm's. I jimmied the window easily enough. I have a tool in my gear for that purpose.

It did not open quietly.

"Who... who's there?" The voice was timid and terrified.

I didn't say anything.

"I said who's there?" He rounded the corner, a small revolver in his hand. It was shaking.

This was August, and it was hot. If this place ever had air conditioning, the landlords never fixed it and passed the savings directly on to themselves. He didn't even have the windows open, but he wore a knit hat, a blanket altered to be a poncho, and mismatched gloves with the fingers cut off.

His hair was short, and small circle-rim glasses rested on his nose.

I quickly took the gun. He might hurt himself.

"What do you want?" He backed away, tipping over a coffee table and not stopping until he hit the wall.

"I'm looking for the Worm." Yes, I said that sentence. I said it with pride and commitment.

"Why? What good could the Worm be to you?" he snapped.

"I think that's a very, very good question." This guy looked like crazy wrapped in nuts and smothered in fresh wackadoo. "Jackal, line," I whispered.

"Which one are you?" He peered at me over his glasses, then pulled his head back when he realized he was getting an inch closer to me.

"I'm--"

"Raven," he answered himself. And as if we didn't need to get any more screwball, it was in a completely different voice. "Yes, Raven. Apprentice to Raptor, a member of the Guard." He jumped on the couch and made marching motions up and down. "Good little soldier does what he's told." He saluted. "Yes, sir."

"Okay, I can see you're busy. I'll just let myself out. Good luck with that tea party thing." I took a step back to the window.

"Don't just leave!" Jackal spoke into my ear. "You have to ask him what he knows."

"The guy's a loon. What would I care what he says?" I whispered back.

The Worm flopped down on the couch in a cloud of dust. "The boy is talking to a voice in his head and he thinks I'm mad." Different voice and totally sane. "What do you want, Raven? I know your master didn't send you, not unless you can talk to the dead." His head tilted and he looked at me. "Unless you have a new master?" He moved his head back and forth as if trying it on for size. "Or you *can* talk to the dead."

"What do you know about Raptor's early days?"

"Raptor's early days? Oh, I know them so well. I know when he was born. The man, the man's pain that gave birth to Raptor. I know so, so much." His voice changed to the couch jumpy guy. "So! So! MUCH!" Then he was back to sane. "You're a kinist."

Not a huge leap, Most people would assume I'm a kinist or a feral. I didn't answer.

"And a powerful one at that." He inhaled through his nose. "Yes, a powerful one." He shook his head. "You could be an amazing musician or a surgeon. But what does the great bird of prey make of you? Someone who can break things. Break people. For the good of all." Sarcasm was heavy in the last sentence. "He always chooses the good for all." That was not a compliment. The Worm looked off into the distance of his cramped living room and his eyes glazed over. A second later he started mumbling to himself.

I could have brought seventy-five of my closest friends in and done a sing-along to the Village People's classic YMCA, and he would not have noticed. I shrugged and turned to leave.

"Ask your questions. It's the only thing I'm good for." I wasn't sure he was talking to me, but it was clear he was full of regret.

"I need to know where the Confessor is."

"No, you don't." He shook his head. "That information will not help you. You need to know where he's going. That I do know."

"You're well informed." If he was telling the truth.

"I am the Worm." He waved his hand. "Of course I'm well informed."

"Does the Confessor have what he came for?" Let's see how well informed he really is.

He shook his head and laughed lightly. "No, he came here in search of opportunity. But you've gotten in the way of that." He gave a little golf clap. "He's now close to failure and close to death."

I wouldn't feel too bad for the guy, except he was Sofia's dad. But I didn't know how to help him. "What did he come here to find?"

He looked at me, a little surprised that I was standing there. "A piece of history, a piece of the now, and a piece of the future." Another laugh, but this time it was manic. "He's made a deal. He thinks the deal will bring him money, money will bring him power, and with that power he will cut for himself a piece of Caesar's empire. And then have more power and money."

That tracked, but not why he was close to death. "Why is he close to death then?"

"He's not the only one who wants what he seeks."

"Do you know where..." I almost said the Phoenix, "what he seeks is?" Couldn't hurt.

The Worm shook his head.

"I'm aware of five people who knew about it," I said. "We're sure none of them know where it is now."

"Do you. Which five people?"

I didn't answer.

"The Confessor seeks Mr. Y," the Worm said. "He's been asking everyone, but no one knows him."

"Mr. Y was killed by some ninja." Gosh, when was that? Yesterday? "Yesterday."

That surprised him. "Just yesterday? Seems longer ago."

He knew where the Confessor was, but didn't check the local news? "It's all over the news. Yaltin was killed in an explosion."

He blinked, confused, then threw back his head and laughed. "Not the letter Y, the question Why."

"Mr. Why?" I think everyone can see how I'd made that mistake. It was a simple mistake to make.

He nodded. "Who is on first?" He laughed again.

"Okay." This was probably the best laugh he'd had in a decade, but enough already. "Who is Mr. Why?"

He didn't stop laughing. If anything, he started laughing harder.

"Who is Mr. Why?"

"Yes." He couldn't breathe now. "Yes you are right, Who is Mr. Why." He nodded and kept laughing.

"Okay, thanks for all the nothing. I got stuff to do."

"Sorry, Raven," Jackal apologized. "My source said this guy knew all about the city and what was happening in it. I guess the Worm is a little further gone than Micky the Shiv knew."

"A world where I can't trust Micky the Shiv is a world I don't want to live in," I murmured.

"Wait," the Worm said in between gasps of laughter. "I can explain." He rubbed a tear out of his eye. "I can explain."

"You know, if you have to explain a joke... it isn't worth it." I held up my hands, trying to shield myself from an explanation.

"It's Wraith. Wraith is Mr. Why." He was in a little more control of his breathing now.

Okay, that might make sense. I never did find out what had happened to Wraith. The blogs were sure he'd made it through the fight with Purge, but then he'd disappeared from the vigilante scene.

"Flesh that out for me," I said.

The Worm held up four fingers. "Wraith was never just one man. He was four. Quadruplets, one mind." He lowered all his fingers except his index. "In his Section 5 days, his code names were questions: Who, What, Where, Why."

"Wraith was part of Section 5?"

"They all were, all the original Guard." Then he corrected himself. "Except for one."

Did Red Knight know all the original Guard were Section 5? He'd seemed to know Raptor was, but that meant Imp, Wraith, and Landslide were Section 5, too.

"Most of the Guard were Section 5? Were they still section 5?" What about Cat and Orion? Were they Section 5, too?

He waved his hand and shook his head. "They weren't part of Section 5 for years. Shortly after their big fight with Purge, Raptor got some dirt on Section 5 and blackmailed them into leaving him and his band of merry men alone."

Blackmail? That wasn't what Red Knight had said. He said they'd cut a deal. Though he might not have known the ins and outs of the deal, since he'd left the team at the huge Purge battle. So if Raptor changed the deal after Red Knight left, then he might not know everything. God knows Raptor compartmentalized information.

Or -- and this was more probable -- Worm was wrong. Hell, Worm could be making this crap up on the spot.

"So where is Mr. Why now?" Jackal said in my head.

"So where is Mr. Why now?" I'd been about to get to that.

"Dead. Been dead for years. Caesar got ahold of him."

He looked thoughtful. "Or is it hims? It couldn't be them since there was only one."

Then why would Julia have listed Mr. Why as a person who knew where the Phoenix was?

"Caesar killed him?" I asked

"No, Caesar was not that merciful. He ripped them apart." The Worm shuddered. "Let one watch himself be disemboweled. That kind of thing? He thought it was great fun."

"That tracks. Caesar would totally experiment on unique parahumans," Jackal added. "Mindraker thought it was fun. Caesar was just there for the science." I felt Jackal shudder, too.

So another dead end, but the good news was the Confessor was at a dead end, too.

"Anything else you wish to know?" The Worm seemed eager now to talk since he'd gotten going.

"We got what we needed. Let's wrap this up." Jackal was half in thought, turning the information over in his head.

"Did Raptor make deals with Caesar?" I asked.

"Many," the Worm answered quickly, decisively, and without question. "Raptor operated in this city for over fifteen years. Do you really think he could do that without Caesar's blessing?"

"Enough, kid," Jackal said. "There isn't a reason--"

"What kinds of deals?" I cut off the crime lord in my head.

"There were a few people and places Raptor would never touch." The Worm seemed almost gleeful to smear Raptor's name.

Raptor had given us a list of supers that we could not mess with. We'd called it the R-LAB, Run Like A Bitch. But we'd thought it was for our safety. Could it have been part of the deal?

"And they would pool their resources for common enemies," the Worm continued. "If Raptor got too close to something, Caesar would call him off. Or if Caesar had a competitor that was getting out of hand, he would feed Raptor information and the competitor would be taken down a peg or two."

"Like Jackal," I said.

The Worm nodded. "There were others."

"Let's just let this go," Jackal said.

"For Raptor's occasional assistance and work to keep other groups out of the city, his Guard were not hunted down and eliminated."

"What about Wraith?"

"He was the price of resistance. Raptor didn't feel like paying a higher price, so he cut a deal. He had similar deals with Midas, Trident, The Miracle King. He was a player for sure, but he was part of the power structure of this town. The loss of Caesar overshadows him, but Raptor's loss has also put the city into confusion."

I shook my head.

"Raptor was very good at keeping the status quo going." The Worm wasn't paying attention to me. "He gave the sheep someone to look up to -- stop a purse snatcher, or an unapproved bank heist here and there. But he also made sure that the balance of power stayed unbalanced for Caesar."

"I don't believe you."

He shrugged. "I can't lie. Something Caesar did to me when he was... when he trained me." He pointed to his head and twisted his finger like a knife. "But he's gone. I can leave this city, this filth," he whispered.

"No, Raptor wasn't like that."

"Raptor was just like that!" The Worm was standing and pointing at me. "He came into this city as a front for Section 5. As soon as he could, he turned on them, and used Section 5 resources to set himself up in this city. I don't know how he got so well funded, but it must have been one of thirty-four companies or billionaires in the city. Then he let Wraith die so he could go on playing superhero." There was foam on his lip.

"You don't know what you're talking about!" I shouted.

"But the worst thing? He brought other little soldiers into his pretend war. Told them they were fighting the good fight. But really, they're the filth this city swims in. The Guard are the same as the corrupt cops, dirty councilmen, and the crime lords." He was spitting. "The city is better without him, and it will be better without you."

Oh, I wanted to hit this guy. "You're wrong." I turned to the window.

"I can prove it. I have proof in my room." He was pointing to the door off the living room. "Just come in here and I can show you exactly the type of god you serve."

"Get out of there," Jackal said. "This isn't right."

"What?"

"He hates you. Why did he answer your questions? I buy the can't lie thing -- I've seen Caesar do that. He had a small cadre of information gathers that reported directly to him. I never met any of them, but Worm must be one of them. But listen to him. He hates you. Why is he being helpful?"

"Is this a trap?" I asked.

The Worm slapped his hands over his mouth, but still yelled, "Yes! I called SSA as soon as you were twenty feet from my building."

He said more, but managed to jam his fingers into his mouth, so I couldn't understand him. That was okay. I think I got the gist.

"You've got to get out of there now!" Jackal roared.

"He said he had information in that room." I looked at the door. Maybe it was some files I could snatch or something.

"No, he said he had proof, not information. Who knows what he thinks is proof? SSA are not going to mess around this time. They think you blew up the CFO of Bio-Globe. They will come for you and come for you hard."

Damn it, he was right.

I was out the window, but while I was in midair to the next building, I noticed someone below me.

"Eyes on Target!" someone yelled below me. "South side. He's out of the building!"

TWENTY-FIVE

It was the guy with the shield. He was in the alley watching me execute my half-roll and grab of the neighboring building ledge.

I didn't have an option. I knew this area okay, but the only route I had memorized was the way I'd taken to get here. That would have to do until I could get to 5th and Hamline. From there I knew about a dozen paths that could get me under the cover of deserted buildings.

Shield Guy threw something at me, a disk of some kind.

I swung out of its way and it hit the wall with a splat. It was connected to a chain. I pulled myself up, flipped over the edge of the roof, and started running. I heard something like a winch spooling and Shield was right at the lip of the building.

He ran after me but I had some distance on him. We'd see what his 007 crap would get him in the long run.

I rolled over an air conditioner and heard the ping of something bouncing off the metal behind me.

Seemed they were not messing around this time -- they were playing with guns.

"Raven, stop!" It was the guy in the boots, Oracle.

I only knew this from Raptor, but most telekinetics needed to see their targets. If he got a good line of sight on me, he could just grab me with his mind and this would be over. I jumped off the building and did a dive roll right through a window, glass shattering.

The building wasn't abandoned. Something was actually still being made or shipped out of here, but no one was working at one in the morning. It wasn't tough for them to follow where I'd gone. Even in this town sometimes broken glass is a clue.

I ran, pulling open the door. I was in some kind of office cube area. I jumped to the first cubicle and ran from cube to cube on top of the half walls.

A window broke to my left. I didn't even look, I just dropped.

I made it about three-quarters of the way through the cubicle maze. They might not have line of sight on me, but if I didn't move fast, I would just be giving them more time to surround the building.

"Raven." It was Oracle again. Crap. "We have some questions for you. What happened at the Bio-Globe building?"

I heard other people moving out around the cube farm.

"What happened at Yaltin's apartment?"

"See? They think you guys are doing this stuff," Jackal pointed out.

"Not now," I whispered.

"You've got to get out of there," Jackal pointed out, again.

"Ya think?" I heard movement -- people starting to walk through the cube farm, at least four. That seemed to be how many people Oracle could bring with him on his flights.

"I don't think you had anything to do with it, but you've got to tell us who did." Oracle's voice was coming from too high. Either he was standing on the cube walls or he was hovering.

"Well, that sounds legit." Jackal did not think that sounded legit.

"Not helping," I whispered.

"Help, right. What's the tactical situation?"

I moved to another cube with a quick silent roll. One step closer to the door. "I'm surrounded. One parahuman telekinetic, four unknowns."

"How did they get in?"

I didn't dare answer. A uniformed SSA agent walked right in front of the cube I'd taken cover in. I was under the desk and he didn't spot me.

"They broke a window," I whispered.

"Cool. Go out that window."

"Oracle is right in front of the window."

"You're on a first name basis with these guys?"

"I met them earlier today, I mean yesterday," I answered.

"Okay, whatever. This is perfect. You need to neutralize Oracle if you're going to get away anyway. So pop him on your way out the window."

"Pop him?" Sounded easy.

"You know, a non-lethal popping," Jackal added, not really helpfully.

It was as good a plan as any. Downside, I didn't really know what was on the side of the building I was about to jump out of. I have a hell of a long jump, but I was not getting across a main street.

But at least I had an objective.

I moved back to the desk I'd abandoned. Quick peek around the corner and started going from desk to desk.

"There he is."

I didn't look at the guy who'd spotted me, I just started running for my objective.

A distortion of air came at me. I dodged, jumped, landed in a roll, stood, and used the momentum to pick up an office chair and hurl it at Oracle.

He batted the chair out of the way easily, but was distracted. He didn't see me coming at him like a missile just behind the chair.

I clotheslined him in the head. He was still floating, so I didn't get a good connection and he spun like he was the biggest goalie on a foosball table.

I landed in a handstand on the outside-most cubicle wall, and instead of bouncing off and out the window, I pulled in my feet and didn't let go.

One of their stupid net bombs fired right past me. If I hadn't seen the guy out of the corner of my eye, he would have gotten me mid-air.

I didn't think about it then, but that could have killed me. It would have wrapped my hands so I would have just fallen out the window. We were only on the third floor, but if I was all wrapped up I couldn't survive that fall.

I pulled my second ball bearing and threw it at his center of mass. "Grenade!" I yelled. Why not, right?

The SSA agent, now with an empty net guy, decided to take me seriously and leapt behind the corner of the cube farm.

My ball bearing was caught though, by a blue and gray glove. The Shield guy stepped out from cover and threw the ball back at me.

I dodged it, but he wasn't really trying to hit me. Just slow me down so he could close.

He closed.

I blocked his first shot, but couldn't get around his shield to land any of my own.

"You heal quick." The jaw that I thought I'd broken looked fine. Not even purple. I was disappointed. If I wasn't fighting the guy, I would have thought he was someone else. I mean, I could only see his mouth and chin below the visor. But he fought the same way, not using the same method, but the same way.

He did not chat.

Maybe it's just all the action movies that I grew up on, but I expect a little chit-chat. It seems rude if they don't give me a little banter or a straight line to work with.

He fought exactly like he had yesterday, so I got in under a kick I knew was coming. And punched right at his junk.

He had a cup, but still rolled with that punch. Now that he was off balance, I flipped him on his shield. And used the momentum to slide through the broken glass and roll over the edge of the window.

This was the front of the building so I didn't have any other buildings to go to directly. I slowed my fall by grabbing onto a few handholds and dropping to the ground in a roll.

The front of the building was all glass. The door lock was broken and roughly a million-zillion SSA stormtroopers were making their way up the stairs. This crew was on their way to support Oracle and the boys.

Fun fact -- there were another two shield guys in their mix, and man they looked just like the dude I'd just cherry picked. I mean, I could just see the jaw line, but they looked exactly like the other guy.

Funny old world.

"Target!" someone yelled.

I ran out into traffic.

A van came right at me. A soccer mom. Why was she out in the middle of the night? Go home! I dive rolled, up, jumped on top of a moving cab, and landed on the opposite sidewalk with a roll.

My heart was pumping at about a billion beats a second. I'd never done that before.

Right cross to the head.

I have a helmet so it didn't knock me out, but I did not see it coming. Another one of those Shield Guys was standing over me, shield in one hand and a net gun in the other.

Pop.

It was like getting shellacked in silly string, if the silly string weighed ninety pounds.

"Good run, kid." The Shield guy's voice was the same action movie gravel and badass. I mean, the *exact* same as the guy whose jaw I'd broken. This guy had a completely healthy-looking jaw.

"They got me," I whispered.

The Shield Guy pulled at my head, trying to find the release on my helmet.

I rolled, but he had his knee on me in a second, and I was pinned.

"There still may be a way out of this." Jackal was on the edge of his prison bunk.

"I can't move." There was no way out of this.

"That's the idea. Where's the release?" Shield Guy was manhandling my mask, looking for a catch.

"Do exactly what I tell you to do." Jackal told me what to do.

Sure, why not?

"I'm Section 5." I really tried to sell this. "I have nothing to fear, but you are in deep trouble." According to the Worm, Section 5 might not exist anymore, and this guy might not even have heard of it before.

"What did you say?"

"I'm section 5. Release me immediately or you'll blow my cover."

By this time we were joined by others.

"He says he's section 5," the Shield Guy on my back told someone.

That guy swore a lot. "I heard a rumor they were operating in Darhaven again."

"Orders?" my Shield Guy asked.

"Put him in the holding truck, keep his mask on. If he is Section 5, they will flip out if you break his cover." That was the voice of experience. "Somebody get Section 5 on the phone."

That's right boys, I'm section 5. For about five minutes. "Now what?" I asked Jackal.

"Hey, you still have your mask on. This is such a better place than I thought we would be."

TWENTY-SIX

There I was, in the back of their containment truck.

This was an armored truck, but it was even more armored on the inside. I wasn't in the net gun stuff anymore, but handcuffed to a metal table and sitting in a restraint chair that reminded me of a prison version of an amusement park ride.

"Can you call for help?" Jackal asked.

"They're still jamming me." I pulled at the restraints. They didn't even budge. The SSA hadn't bothered keeping an agent with me, but they had a camera pointed right at my head.

It felt like Jackal was pacing in his little cell. "We're out of options. Give me a number. I'll call your friends. We can get you out of this."

"No." I shook my head even though he couldn't see.

"Now is not the time," Jackal said. "You need help. You need the rest of your team."

"No." Well yes, I did need the rest of my team. I wasn't getting out of here by myself. "I'm not exposing them to the SSA." Or to Jackal.

"You can't just give up." Jackal was a little desperate.

"Yes. Yes I can. I've given up! I gave up my life for a lie Raptor told me. I bought it wholesale, just walked up to the trough and guzzled down all his crap. I already gave up everything. I'm the giving up king!"

"Raven, you have--"

"No, my name's not Raven. It's just a stupid codename that he picked out of a bird book. Probably didn't want to waste a cool bird of prey on the P1." It was all crap. "He lied to me."

"So he lied. Maybe he was this horrible guy the Worm said. Do you really think the entire Guard would follow him if they didn't think he knew what he was doing?"

Maybe not. "He could have lied to them, too. But it doesn't matter. I needed..." Him to be a hero. I needed him to be THE HERO. That would have justified everything -- the sacrifices I made, the risks I took. It all made sense for something good. Even if we couldn't get there, it still made sense if it was for something good. But it wasn't. "I'm just part of Raptor's machine to keep evil men in power."

Jackal cut me off. "No, you're a pissed off kid trying to do the right thing. But this isn't a moral puzzle, this is the rest of your life. Take it from a man who has spent five years in a box. You will look at this moment for the rest of your life with regret. You do not deserve what they're going to do to you."

"No, I don't, and I wouldn't be here if I hadn't sold my soul to that... liar." What did he want from me?

"Give me a way to contact your team." Jackal was urgent. "Right now there's still a chance. If they get your mask off things get harder. If they get you to a facility, you're done. How can I reach your friends?"

"I won't risk them." That was that. I was done. "Maybe this way my mom will at least understand."

"What are you talking about? This is a mommy issue?" Jackal jumped on my slip of the tongue.

"I didn't mean to say that out loud." Not even sure I did. More proof he was in my head.

"Look, if you think your mom was pissed because you were staying out all night, when she finds out that you were risking your life to commit a federal crime, I don't think understanding is the word she'll use." Jackal was definitely pacing back and forth in his cage. Maybe he wanted me to feel what the powerlessness of being caged really does to you.

"It doesn't matter..." I already twisted that all up. I couldn't really see a way to fix it.

"You know what your mom wants?" Jackal asked.

"A son who is less of a disappointment." Yes, that's what I said. I was in a dark place.

"No, what she wants is what every parent wants for their children. To walk to the grave as slowly as possible, financially secure. Grandkids are a plus. That's it."

I opened my mouth to protest, but he kept talking.

"Whatever you think you did to mess things up with her, none of that matters. You're not talking about going to jail where she can at least visit you. You're going to a hole where you will never see the light of day again. For yourself, for your mother, tell me a way of getting you help!"

I almost believed he cared.

A lock twisted and the armored door opened.

"He's coming to tell you that you're lying. They will unmask you and take away the idol. You have got to do this now!"

I said nothing.

An SSA agent in full combat gear slipped into the compartment and closed the door behind him.

"Raven! Damn it! Don't be a martyr!" Jackal hissed.

Jackal had once offered someone five million dollars to not kill me. Don't know if he was just talking out his butt, but he seemed to care what happened to me. Too bad the one guy I could talk to was a psycho killer. It would have been nice to have a direct line to Red Knight and actually get some advice I could trust.

The soldier seemed distracted. He made sure the door was closed, but not latched.

He looked at the small camera domes and seemed content with being recorded or something.

Folding metal chairs were strapped to the side of the containment truck. He pulled one off and unfolded it right in front of me.

His gear looked used, like he'd been wearing and using it hard in the last week. I didn't know the rank patches from Adam, but his name tag was visible.

"Hello," I guessed at his title, "Officer Robinson."

He looked down at his name tag, then at me. "You with the Guard." It wasn't a question.

"Yes, I'm an agent of Section 5 in the Guard."

"Who is this guy," Jackal asked. "Something isn't matching up. Is this guy actually an officer?"

"He's dressed like a grunt agent," I whispered.

"What?" Robinson asked.

"The longer you guys hold me, the harder it will be to explain my absence to the rest of the team," I said.

"You're not Section 5." He waved away my complaint. "I did a rotation working for Section 5. Just base security. Do you even know where Section 5 is located?"

"Don't tell him," Jackal said.

How was I going to tell him? I didn't know.

"I mean, say 'you are not cleared'," Jackal said.

"Okay, we both know I can't give that information out to someone who just says they're qualified." I tried to be cool, but I was not cool.

"Like I said, I did a rotation for Section 5. I know for a fact that they had no operations in Darhaven. Mission command had a guy thrown into the pit for a week for just going through the Darhaven airport."

That lined up with what Worm had told me about Raptor's deal with Section 5.

"Why do you think he wanted all assets out of Darhaven?" I just repeated Jackal word for word. "He didn't want anyone crossing my op."

Robinson looked like he would consider that, then shook his head. "No, you're too low a para level to end up in Section 5. I knew a P2 once, but he could turn invisible. You're what? P1 Kinist? You're a dime a dozen, and wouldn't get a second look from Section 5."

"Well, I guess we'll see." I tried to act like this would all be cleared up soon.

"Unit command is having a tough time connecting with Section 5 Control." He looked at me, like he was making a decision.

"You're not here to question me." At least Jackal didn't think he was, so I mimicked what he said, feeling more like a puppet. But at least I knew I was being a puppet this time. "Interrogation wouldn't be handled by a grunt."

"No, I'm not here to interrogate you," he agreed. "I was at the battle a week ago, that fight in the Lenbrook office building."

So was I.

"So were you," he said.

Glad to have my helmet still on. I could not keep a poker face.

"I heard you gift wrapped Shale and Silhouette for us." He didn't sound like he believed that.

"I had help."

"I'd like to hear that story." Still didn't really believe it.

"Classified."

He nodded. "I know, it's just I would like to know how you did it." He shook his head. "But that isn't what this is about." He removed a slender wand from his pocket. "I'm not here to ask you questions."

I tensed at the wand, but I recognized it. It was the high tech key thing they'd used to lock the manacles.

"Then what is this about?" Could it be my ticket out of here, or was this just a trick?

"Do you know what they'll do to you?" He didn't wait for an answer. "First, they'll give you to the brain surgeons. Section 5 has a pool of egoists, and they will rip your mind apart. They might just turn you into a vegetable, but they might try to reprogram you. They aren't good at it, but they're always up for practice. It will be hell."

This was a new scary face of freedom's protectors that I hadn't heard of.

"That is if Section 5 gets a hold of you. If SSA keep a hold on you, you will just waste away in a box about this size." He took in the container with a spin of his finger.

"SSA and Section 5 aren't the same thing?" Oops, just tipped my hand. Damn it! I suck at this covert ops crap.

He was already convinced I wasn't Section 5, so he didn't react. "It was once, but not anymore. Now Section 5 is its own little kingdom. I've never been happier to leave a division."

He didn't sound that happy.

"I don't like what they'll do to you. Don't get me wrong, most of the guys we take down deserve it, but not you and yours. I'm from Darhaven. I know what the Guard do, the hope they give." He dropped a neutral accent and sounded like he was from the Cages.

The hope was false and a show, but I wasn't going to correct him.

"I also saw all the explosives rigged at that office building. They were going to blow us all to hell. Most of the supers would have walked away, but me and my friends would have punched it." He looked uncomfortable at that admission. "I owe you my life. And a lot of good men and women owe you their lives."

"You're welcome." That was probably true, except the part about the supers walking away from it. The whole point of the trap was to kill the supers, and the nullifier would have done it, too.

"I can't say thanks, then send you to prison forever." He pointed the wand at the lock and my restraints pulled off. "Give me thirty seconds to start a diversion, then run south."

"South?" I was in a metal box. I had no idea which way was south.

"Left." He pointed. "I don't know how much help I'll be from here on out. I can only risk so much."

"You should come with me. I mean, you're busted." I stood up and got as far away from that chair as I could with one step.

"I'll be fine. I have a plan."

It better be a good plan. I was sure we were being recorded. "Good luck."

He sneaked out of the truck, again making sure that it didn't latch.

I started counting. "Do you believe the luck?" It was an actual question.

"Not really," Jackal answered, "but it looks like a good deed gets rewarded. Let's not overthink this. Keep your eye on the prize. You have a hell of a run ahead of you."

"Has if been thirty seconds?"

"Just about." Jackal didn't sound like he was keeping track, either.

Kaboom!

"That's thirty," Jackal guessed

I went through the door. Section 5 must really terrify these guys. I was just blocks from where they'd picked me up. They'd sectioned off the back corner with crime scene cones in a parking lot. I remember seeing an orange sign that gave early bird pricing. I don't remember the actual rates, but I recall thinking they were reasonable.

The parking lot only had the containment truck and three of the SSA standard attack vehicles.

All eyes were pointed at the explosion. A car was on fire, and I heard the crack crack of weapons fire.

Not sure if it was actual gunfire, rounds cooking off in the explosion, or firecrackers. As diversions go, it worked great. Everyone was either jumping for cover or returning fire. No one was looking at little old me.

I ran south, away from the explosion. I ducked through a tight alley and was able to get up to roof level by bouncing from wall to wall.

The entire time I kept an ear out for the sound of pursuit, but I didn't hear anything. Robinson had game, he knew how to run a distraction. I hoped he wouldn't get into any trouble over this. I didn't stop running for blocks and blocks. My lungs were screaming for air by the time I took cover at the top of a building under a billboard.

"Are you being followed?" Jackal asked.

I wanted to respond, but I was sucking air through the helmet vents. I knew how to spot a tail, but I doubted SSA would be subtle. "No, I made it." I could breathe fine now.

"Thank, God." Jackal sounded genuinely relieved. "One of these days you are going to run out of lucky breaks, kid."

My mind spun as the reality caught up with me, electricity shooting through my spine. I had been so close. By rights they'd had me cold. But I wasn't going to prison. I was free.

It was like waking up from a nightmare.

TWENTY-SEVEN

"You did it." Jackal didn't sound like he believed it. "I mean, I thought you were screwed." He laughed.

"I was. I got lucky." Very, very lucky. "What were the odds that an SSA agent would have morals and the balls to do something about it?"

"I've seen people like him before. You can't fake that level of disillusionment. He was weary of it all. If it wasn't you, he'd have found another way to screw over the SSA," Jackal said. "Just glad it was when we needed it."

"Yeah." I stopped to catch my breath at the top of a building that was one of my favorite places to rest when I was on patrol. I knew about seven ways off the building and I could see for miles. It was still black, but dawn was coming.

"So, we have to plan for our next move," Jackal said. "The Worm wasn't as helpful as I thought he would be, but he still gave us some interesting nuggets to chew on."

"Not as helpful!" I wasn't even mad at him, but Raptor wasn't there to take the heat. "Your 'tip' almost got me locked up forever!" I yelled. "And what do I know now?

That Raptor was one of the monsters that kept this city in the cesspool I thought I was fighting."

"You have got to focus on the problem in front of us," Jackal interjected. "There will be time to spit on Raptor's grave later."

"Did you do it?" I asked.

"Do what?"

I wasn't making sense, my head was spinning. "Did you make a deal with Raptor?"

Silence.

"When you were working with Caesar? Or when you were killing people for yourself? Did you make a deal with Raptor?"

"I never heard anything about any deal," Jackal said, but he wasn't saying everything. I was really going to go all teenage angst on him, but he continued. "I do know this. Raptor crossed Caesar regularly. If anyone, and I mean ANYONE, crossed Caesar once he was put in the ground. No one knew why Raptor was ignored. I never had the guts to ask Caesar or Mindraker."

"And now we know why."

Silence.

"What about you? Did you make a deal with Raptor?"

Silence.

"So help me, I will smash this idol to toothpicks if you don't tell me."

"Fine, you want to know, I'll tell you. I only tried to make one deal with Raptor. And he wouldn't play ball."

"What was the deal?" I was so close to smashing the damn statue, anyway.

He must have heard it in my voice, because he didn't hit me with silence again. "You don't want to know."

"Tell me." Jackal had played me, but he'd never directly

lied to me. I was sure he was right. I didn't want to hear this story. "Tell me!"

"Raptor, with a few of the Guard, hit one of my boltholes. I'd just paid for a load of weapons. Midas doesn't give them away, but he has the best connections to weapons. I knew a war with Caesar was coming soon. I needed every gun I could find." He fell silent, like mustering his forces.

"What do weapons have to do with it?" I asked.

"Just the crumbs Raptor followed." Jackal didn't think they really had anything to do with the punchline. "But it wasn't just a warehouse, it was the base of operations of my entire anti-Caesar campaign. They hit, and we fought. I lost one of my Para level 4s in that fight. But I also lost a hard drive. It had a lot of information -- bank numbers, everything. It was my war chest for a coming campaign, plus enough information to unravel my entire offensive."

"How did you get out?" If Raptor had decided to go after him, I couldn't imagine a situation where he'd let him go. Jackal didn't have any movement powers except those he could copy.

"I was able to get the jump on one of their new members." His voice wasn't guilty exactly, but not proud.

The penny fell in the slot. "Hawk," I finished.

"I copied his power of flight. He was fast. And I flew us out of there."

"Why didn't Raptor follow?" No one flew faster than Raptor.

"The P4 I mentioned needed a lot of attention." Jackal said. "It was a disaster. I lost one of the toughest parahumans on my payroll, and a lot of money in those accounts on the hard drive. And I ran and left a number of my people behind. The Guard rolled up most of them. My plans to take the fight to Caesar went up in smoke."

"So you shot Hawk? You shot him!" Why did I even talk to this guy? I didn't know if he was worse than Raptor, but he was just as bad.

"Not exactly. I tried to cut a deal. I made Hawk call Raptor to make a deal. I had to show my men I was tough, that I was still in the fight. Ruthless. A leader they would follow."

"So what was this deal?" The heat escaped me, but cold fear, anger, and revulsion churned my stomach.

"Simple. The P4 and hard drive for Hawk."

"And he didn't do that?" That seemed insane. "Why wouldn't Raptor do that?"

"I don't know. The Feds probably already had the P4. I can't imagine he gave up the hard drive. Doesn't matter. I didn't give the order, but the second Raptor said no, my right hand man pulled the trigger."

"He wouldn't make a deal to save Hawk?" To save an apprentice? Raptor had gone on and on about how he didn't want another Hawk, but this whole time it had been his fault. He didn't do a damn thing to save Hawk!

"He said no, and Simon pulled the trigger," Jackal restated. "I could either look like I couldn't control my people, or take credit." Now Jackal sounded full of regret.

"Credit." The word was disgusting in my mouth, one more slap.

"I kept control. Raptor, of course, came at me with a vengeance. In retrospect, it was probably Simon's plan. Get Raptor motivated to rip me apart." Jackal seemed to want to stop talking, but was unable to stop once the tragedy was queued up.

"That must have been awful for you." Hawk was dead because Raptor wouldn't deal and Jackal needed credit. "You both can go to Hell!"

I pulled the idol from my pouch. "I'm done. I'm done with you, I'm done with Raptor and this idiot crusade. I'm done being a hero, a patsy. I'm done!" I pulled back my arm and threw. The idol went spinning into the darkness. I heard it clank and knock into something. I couldn't tell if it broke.

But Jackal was gone.

TWENTY-EIGHT

I didn't dare call out to the Guard's party line just in case SSA were monitoring the phone or something. Maybe I just wanted to be alone with my thoughts.

I made it to the factory before 2am, but not much before.

I ran hard. I was doing that a lot. No phone calls from Mom or Dad. Not sure what I expected, but it would have been nice.

When I reached Alpha Base, I took my time finding a different route in, picking my way through the abandoned factory to the entrance.

"Where have you been?" I let Flare come up behind me. I'd heard her approach.

"I've been... getting into trouble."

She looked around, "Are you alone?"

'What?" Did she mean Jackal? "Yeah."

"You weren't followed?"

"No, I was not followed. I doubled back and did enough spin work that I'd spot anyone. I was trained by Cat on how to spot a tail." I didn't graduate with honors, but he once told me I wasn't a disappointment.

"We heard you were taken into custody," she said. "Butterfly was in a panic trying to find out where. We were all just waiting for the word, and we were going to roll out. But here you are."

"What did Red Knight say about that?"

"He talked us down. The original plan was to find the largest collection of SSA and rescue you."

"Peregrine in on your plan?"

"It was his plan, until Red Knight talked him round.'" She didn't seem to have a dog in the fight, but that wasn't how she'd shown up to planning sessions in the past.

"Red Knight was right," I said.

"I know." She pointed at my chest. "Obviously, you didn't need our help. You're *Raven* after all."

There was a little sting in that. "What's that supposed to mean?"

"Two weeks ago I thought you were just a well-intentioned, smartass slacker."

"Ouch," I said sarcastically, but ouch!

"But you're the one ready for the big leagues." Was she angry at me? Was she angry at herself? Both? She was angry at something.

"That's really not how I see things." On a scale of one to ten, ten being big league material, I'm a solid four. Well, maybe not that solid of a four. A three point five, easy.

"Oh, come on. The biggest super fight of the year at the Carlton and I was captured in round one." She rubbed her wrist. "I had to wait around for you to rescue me like some damsel in distress."

"Ah, there's a huge asterisk in that stat. I wasn't affected by the nullifier like you and Peregrine. And you may think I rescued you, but all I remember is running like hell while my friends were being abducted." I'd love to think of myself as the hero there, but I'd blown it. I had nothing.

"Then you rescued Red Knight," she said as if I hadn't spoken. "And now you escaped the SSA."

"I drove Red Knight home, and I had help with the SSA thing. I'll explain." Later. I just didn't have enough gas for this. "What's really bothering you?"

I thought she would take another verbal swipe at me. Like she resented not being needed or something. But her shoulders slumped. "It's Ballista, Red Knight, this base, all of it."

I didn't know where she was going with this.

"I thought I could put this all behind me." When she said "this," she spread her arms and flared green. "I'm in good enough control of my power. I can handle any surges from here on out. And David made it through his first." I already knew Ballista's real name, but it felt like breaking a rule to hear her say it out loud.

"You thought you were getting out."

She nodded. "Then Butterfly called. Peregrine had gotten himself into trouble, then we found Red Knight, and now a normal life is in jeopardy if we don't get this Phoenix thing. It all starts up again. I'm not like you."

"You've said that before. What do you think I'm like?"

"You love this crap. You aren't happy unless you're running around the city doing the right thing." She said "right thing", but not in a good way.

"That's not true. Not anymore."

She kept talking as if I hadn't said anything. "And Ballista worships the ground you somersault on."

How is that my fault? Because she sounded like that was my fault.

"He tries to make jokes like you and tries to put on a brave face, but he's terrified. All the things that they did to him..."

"That you couldn't stop them from doing."

She flared totally at that. Green fire danced all over her body. "What is that supposed to mean?"

"You're feeling powerless and small." I knew because that's how I felt all the time. "You can do all these amazing things, but when the people who counted on you to do something amazing needed you, you couldn't do anything. It's how I feel all the time. Every day. Except maybe for the amazing things part. If I can't acrobatic my way out of it, I'm out of tricks."

She glowed more. "Go tell the rest of them you don't need our help, before you need to rescue everyone again." She folded her arms and stalked away, green fire dancing around her in a corona.

How did I always end up just making her mad?

I entered Alpha Base.

"Raven!" Butterfly attacked me with a huge bear hug. "I thought they got you."

Red Knight clapped. "Good work. We were trying to track you through the SSA radios, but they had no clue what happened to you or how you got out."

"I had help." I returned the hug.

Butterfly seemed to realize what she was doing and let me go. "Sorry," she said in a small voice.

Sorry for what? At least someone on this planet was glad to see me.

"What's this all about? We ready to go?" Ballista scrambled out of the bunk room fastening his mask.

"It's all good, I'm here." I gave him a wave. "But I do appreciate the rally guys."

"See? I told you there was nothing to worry about," Ballista told Butterfly. "It was all part of some plan wasn't it, Raven?"

"Um, well, no. It was a lot of running and then more running," I said. "Red Knight, could I have a minute?"

He nodded, pointed with his thumb to the bunk room.

I exchanged a high five with Ballista as I passed him and followed Red Knight.

It took Red Knight a little wheeling back and forth, but he turned his chair around and looked me in the eye. "What's on your mind?"

"What kind of person was Raptor?" I had no one else to ask.

He exhaled. "I'm not sure I have an answer for you. I'm not sure I know. He was wicked smart and always working an angle. He always had the higher good in mind."

That was close to what Worm had said. "I found out that he had deals with Ceasar and Midas, maybe more. He helped them handle competitors so he could keep playing superhero."

"I see." Red Knight thought a lot about that. "Okay, I don't know anything about deals with Caesar or Midas. That was after my day. I was only with the Guard for those early years."

"The deals started just after Caesar tortured Wraith to death."

"Then I can't blame him," Red Knight said.

"What?" Because if he needed some extra blame for Raptor, I had plenty to spare.

"Caesar was a very powerful man. You don't take effective control of Darhaven without being a powerful man. Raptor did not have police powers. He was trying to give the people of this city hope. He couldn't always give them justice."

That wasn't what I wanted to hear. "According to my source, Wraith was Mr. Why. The question Why, not the letter. But Mr. Why is dead. He died years ago."

"Maybe not," Red Knight said thoughtfully. "Not if Julia believed he still knew about the Phoenix." He looked at me. "But I'm more concerned about you. If Raptor did make a deal, what does it mean to you?"

"What do you mean 'what does it mean'? It's obvious. Everything I thought was crap. Everything I was trying to do and risking was crap. My mom kicked me out of the house because of this and it is crap."

"Your mom kicked you out of the house because you were a superhero?" He was surprised.

"No, because I couldn't explain what I was doing. And that I'm not going to graduate." I threw up my hands and let them fall. I would have started pacing but there wasn't room.

"And you blame Raptor for your grades?"

"I'm blaming Raptor for lying to me. He sold me on a bill of goods he didn't even believe," I shot back.

"I think the issue here isn't what Raptor believed. It's what you believe." He held up his hand before I could reply. "You can't be a hero for Raptor. If he thought that's what you were doing, I'm surprised that he didn't fire you on the spot."

He did fire me.

"You have to choose to do this for yourself. You are risking much, maybe everything. It might cost you your legs." He patted his thigh. "Or more. And you have to be willing to pay it." He gestured to me and wheeled over to the wall. "Ballista found this in storage."

It was a collection of faded newspapers all around a picture of five men.

"Each of these articles is the good that I did as Red Knight." It was too high for him to reach so he pointed at it. "The good we did as the Guard."

I looked at a few of the headlines. Terrorist thwarted, people saved, criminals brought to justice.

"Lives saved," he said. "My time with the team was brief, but I am so grateful for those moments."

I looked at the articles. Some gave credit to the Guard, some did not. But Red Knight knew the truth.

My eyes went to the picture of the five men. "Who is this?"

"The Guard, when we first formed. I was against taking the picture. I wanted to make sure we protected our secret IDs, but Imp was a bit of a romantic." He laughed at that.

I recognized a very stern-looking Red Knight, and a smiling almost boyish grin on Archibald Valtire's face. I felt my jaw grind, and my hands tightened into fists. I forced myself to look at the next person in the picture. Anything to avoid thinking about Raptor right now. The tall guy to Archie's left I didn't recognize. He looked younger than I was. "Who?"

"Landslide."

"And this was Imp." His skin was darker, a kind of weird tan, and he had the biggest grin of them all. "Who took the picture?"

Red Knight thought for a second. "It must have been Julia." Then memory caught up with him. "No, it was Wraith. He didn't want people to realize there was more than one of him."

I looked at the last face. He was shorter than the rest, but stood tall and had a pleasant smile. "Huh."

"What?" Red Knight asked. "I usually get more of a reaction out of people when I use the 'more than one' line," Red Knight said.

"Sorry. I was told about... him... by..." I ripped the picture off the wall and looked harder at the image. "This guy is Wraith?"

"Yea, possibly the last photo ever taken. That was a couple years before his death."

"No, it wasn't." I shook my head. "I just talked to this asshole." It wasn't obvious. I had to add twenty years, spectacles, and a gallon of crazy. This guy was the Worm.

"That's not possible." Red Knight shook his head.

I couldn't tear my eyes from the picture. "What were Wraith's specialties, his powers?"

"Besides having three bodies?" Red Knight thought that was enough.

"Four." I was willing to believe the Worm on this point.

"No, he had three." Red had known Wraith.

"Who, What, Where, and Why?" I repeated the information that Worm had told me.

"There was no Mr. Why." He leaned back. "At least none that I knew about." He laughed. "Raptor, you cagey bastard. He kept one in reserve. Or maybe Wraith did. There wasn't a Mr. Why in Section 5. Maybe Wraith hid his fourth self from everyone. And when the rest of his selves were killed, he came out. At least he came out to Raptor."

"So he, Mr. Why I mean, might still be working with Raptor?" I spun and left the bunk room.

Red Knight had to push to keep up with me, but I heard the click of his wheels right behind me.

"Fly, can you run facial recognition for me?" I entered

the main room and interrupted an intense conversation between Flare and Butterfly.

They both clammed up and stepped away from each other like they'd been caught with their hands in the cookie jar.

"Am I interrupting something?" I waved my question away. "Sorry, let's put a pin in that." I handed Butterfly the picture. "Could you find out if this guy shows up as an employee of Bio-Globe or anything connected to the Valtiers?"

She took the picture, and I pointed to Wraith.

"Sure, that's John Quare." She handed me back the picture. "Why is he in a picture with you?" she asked Red Knight.

"I think that could be Mr. Why," I said.

I thought maybe she sneezed, but I realized it was a laugh. "Funny," she said.

"Why?"

She laughed a little harder.

Oh my God, life was passing me by and I was stuck in an Abbott and Costello skit. "What would be humorous?"

"Quare," she said as if that should explain it. "Latin for Why."

Of course it was. I rolled my eyes. "How do you know this guy?"

"I've spent all night researching Bio-Globe. He shows up in a few pictures. He's on my list of employees I couldn't get a title for. There are about eighty on that list, so I didn't think he was anything special."

"Can you get an address?" If this was the actual Mr. Why, then Caesar hadn't killed them all. But his life was in danger now.

"Sure." And since she is a human computer, she told it to me.

"That's too far. Where's Peregrine? Can he get there ahead of us?" My heart beat picked up the pace. I didn't know what the Confessor had, but if Imp knew there was another Wraith out there, they could be looking for him and be hours ahead of us.

"I'll call him," Butterfly said.

I turned to Flare. "How fast could you get out there?"

"I don't know. Five minutes on a straight shot, but I can't do straight shots, not with the SSA everywhere. So twenty, maybe fifteen if I push it and I'm not overly cautious."

I looked at Red Knight.

"Be cautious," he said. "It doesn't do to protect your identity if you're in an SSA prison."

Fair point. "Can you do it?"

She nodded. "Get Peregrine there, too. I'll need support if the Headsmen are there." She took off at a run to the exit.

I heard Peregrine pick up on the party line. I think he was catching a nap in his nest or something. He seemed out of it, but I was only half listening to the conversation.

"Red Knight, what could Wraith do?"

"It depended on the body. One could walk through walls, one could astral project, and one could project a white kind of energy. If they were all touching, they could all become transparent and shoot that energy ray." He thought about it more. "And he was great at following a subject and all means of surveillance. He was a pretty good martial artist, too."

"So we have no idea what Mr. Why could do or which one is the Worm." I thought for a second. "Flush out the astral projection thing."

"He would send his consciousness out of his body and eavesdrop or explore areas. He was just amazing at getting information."

"That would be handy." I'd bet that was what the Worm could do. After Caesar brainwashed or brain bleached him, he put him to work. "I need to find the Worm. He knows more than I thought." And he could see around corners. "Last time I talked to him he siced the SSA on me." He'd said he called the Feds when I was twenty feet away. That would line up with this astral projection, or at least some kind of clairsentience.

"No, I'll go," Red Knight said. "He'll talk to me."

"He hated everything Guard." I didn't think the good old days would get through that tight of crazy pants.

Red Knight shook his head. "He will talk to me. We owe each other that much."

I wrote the address on a post-it and handed it to him. "Maybe I should come and just be in the area."

"And if he sees you coming, even loitering, you have another race with the SSA." Red Knight read the address, as if committing it to memory, then folded the post-it and put it in his pocket.

"I could go out of uniform." BAD idea. Raven, you are coming up with bad ideas.

"That is a bad idea," Butterfly said.

"Yea, I knew it was bad when I said it." I deflated.

"I'll be fine. I can handle Wraith. I'll bring him in." He seemed to be handling his friend coming back from the dead pretty well. "You two hold down the fort." He looked at the address as he spun around and went towards his van.

And then it was just me and Butterfly.

We waited.

And waited.

Time ticked by. Seconds turned into minutes. Minutes into forever, nations rose and fell, glaciers did laps around continents. Bell bottoms came in style again, twice.

"How long has it been?" I asked.

"Fifteen minutes," Butterfly said.

I banged my helmet on the wall. "How do you handle this?"

She turned from whatever she was doing. "Getting a little stir crazy, not moving for a half hour?"

"Your words are sympathetic, but your tone - no sympathy," I noted.

"I have some research on Bio-Globe I could use help with."

"And you're coming to me with this? Hi, have we met?" I held out my hand in a fake handshake.

She laughed a little and turned back to her computer.

"So what is going on with Flare?" I asked.

She froze as if caught past curfew. "Nothing."

I walked around the table and took the seat right next to her. "Your words say nothing, but your tone says 'a lot.'"

"Nothing I can talk about. She just wanted help with a project."

"What project?"

Her shoulders flattened. "I can't tell. It's not our business."

I had a whole plan of attack, stuff about how if it affects one person on a team in affects all of us, but, "Yea, I don't care all that much." I stood up and gave the room a good pacing. "Is it about her boyfriend?"

"You know about him?" She was accusing a little.

"Ha!" I pointed. "It is about her boyfriend." She'd let it slip last week, a lifetime ago, that she had a boyfriend.

"I'm not talking about this."

"But the project is about her boyfriend."

"Not exactly. Yes, kinda." She shuddered. "I promised not to talk about it."

I thought about pressing, but I kinda already knew. Flare had gotten caught in a lie, probably in the line of duty, and needed help to cover her tracks. Why didn't I think of that? Could I get Butterfly to do my homework? It would take her about half a minute to do enough work to get a C-. She could probably copy my handwriting and syntax, too. "Say, Butterfly, I was thinking--"

"I'm not doing your homework." A flat refusal.

"Fair enough." Another round of pacing. "I have got to get out of here. This is driving me nuts!"

"We should sit tight," Butterfly said.

"You know, you've been pretty human for the last hour or so," I pointed out.

"Thanks." Again with words not saying the same thing as the tone.

"It's just..." How to say it? "Are you really trying?"

"What do you mean?" Even through her vocal distortion she sounded guilty.

"Forget Flare. What are you hiding?"

"Nothing." More believable, but that ship had already sailed.

"That's what you would say if you were hiding something." It was also what she would say if she wasn't hiding something.

"I'm done," she said.

"Done?"

"I've done all I can. I've put a bunch of attacks out there but it takes tons of time and luck. It's more like hunting than breaking down a wall. And the system is tight."

"Something about that bothers you?" I asked because something about that was bothering her.

"Well, if the Phoenix is a backup, it should either be in the Bio-Globe system or connected to it. If it's in the system, why all the running around? And Raptor wouldn't put anything that important where it could be subpoenaed someday. But if it's a backup of everything, it would be connected to the main system. And there just isn't any sign of that. It doesn't mean anything, I could be missing it. But it's weird."

I let what she'd said sink in, but it didn't. "Yeah, I don't know what any of that meant. I'm going back to the Golden View."

"Why?" Butterfly flailed me with her razor sharp logic.

"Just about every lead we have is from the Golden View. It's the only place we have a connection to the Confessor. We should at least keep it under observation." At least I could tell myself I was doing something useful.

"Didn't you almost get killed last time you were there?" She was not crazy about this plan.

"That was hours ago. I'm sure things have mellowed out by now." I waved away her concern. "In fact, I think you should come."

"No." Word and tone said the same thing and said it for sure.

"Come on. I'm not good at all the internal espionage crap. You could get us in and out with no one the wiser." I'd seen her do it. It was scary, but it was like walking through a choreographed dance number. "It will be just like old times. Well, last week anyway."

"I can't. I'm not ready to... get back into the field." She looked at the computer.

"Time to get back on the horse." I made a giddy-up drum beat on the table.

"And if this 'horse' decides you are not worth saving or a reasonable casualty of war, I could kill you. You don't know what it was like." She shook her head.

"I know exactly what it was like. I was there. You kept her, or it, or whatever, under control and saved all our asses." Not exaggerating here. I would have been paste without her quick thinking. "Plus, I need someone who can pick a lock. I'm crap at that."

The vocal distortion hissed as she exhaled. "And how do I get there? I'm not going on a parkour run and my usual taxi is flying to another lead."

"That's a good question. How do you and Clockwork get anywhere?"

"He drove me in a vehicle that he cleaned of any identifiable markers."

We stole a van last week and got around in that, but Silhouette broke the heck out of it.

"Well, you could take the metro in your civies. I'll pack in your uniform and you can change when we get there." I already knew her face, so she had nothing else to give up.

She said in a small voice, "I can't go into the field. Not now." She inhaled. "I can't, okay? I'm just, I can't!" She looked at me, then back to her computer. "You don't know what it's like."

She kept coming back to that.

"I'm not like you, okay? I'm just not. I don't love it like you do." She said it quickly, in a whisper.

Okay, that was two. "What do you and Flare think I am? I don't love this. I was serious. I was quitting."

"You just happen to be in the area and in uniform when

Peregrine needed help?" she asked, but she wasn't really asking.

"Well, yes. More or less." I put my hands up.

"It doesn't matter. It isn't about that." She looked a little uncomfortable. "You saw Clockwork... at the end." She replaced what she was going to say with something easier to think about.

"Yeah." It was awful, I tried not to think about it. He was scared. He'd killed himself rather than let his cold logical power take control again.

"Well, that could be me. Clockwork was the most moral, caring man I ever knew."

That was an act. Simon was a full-fledged bastard, and if Jackal was to be believed, the man who really killed Hawk. And I did not bring that up.

"And he got lost in his power, a puppet to his power." She shivered.

"Clockwork was a spy in the Guard and a plant. He was just pretending to--"

Butterfly stopped me by holding up her hand, "Maybe he was, but that just meant he lost himself to the power before he joined the Guard. Even Jackal said you can't trust me." She cut me off, and I was thankful. Clockwork was the one adult she thought cared about her. I didn't want to say that was an act. I knew how that felt.

An aside, Raptor, you suck.

"Jackal is an ass." A very smart ass, not really wrong about things exactly. "He was trying to manipulate us. He just wanted his new trial."

She almost whispered. "I can't go into the field. Not now."

Worst halftime pep talk ever. Good work, coach Raven.

Maybe I should stay? She might want to talk more. God

knows I needed to talk about what was going on in my head. Butterfly was the one person who would understand and willingly listen.

Or maybe I wasn't ready. "Okay, I'll give you a call once I get to the hotel."

TWENTY-NINE

I t was a hard run to get to the Golden View, but in a way that cleared my head and got my blood pumping. I could almost do it with my eyes closed, I'd been back and forth so many times from so many directions.

I made good time, but I also let my mind wander. Everybody seemed to be hitting me with the "I'm not like you" comment, like I was some kind of glutton for punishment. It had been all fun and games when I'd just been training. I'd known Raptor would make sure nothing went wrong. And he'd always been my compass. But now he wasn't here and nothing he'd taught me could be my compass.

"Fly, you on?" I took a seat on the top of the same building I'd used last time to scout out the Golden View..

"Hello, Raven." I couldn't tell if she was a little more Robot-Butterfly, or if she was just trying to be professional since our last conversation was kind of awkward.

"I'm at the hotel." Step one complete.

"What is your next move?"

"Wait for the Confessor to take a smoke break and

deliver some serious justice." Crap, what was I going to do next?

"Or you could go to the room he had his things moved to," Butterfly said, not in an "I work with morons" voice. I totally had that coming, so if would have been fair if she had, but she didn't.

"Well, I could do that. Do you have a room number?"

"Not exactly. I still have access to their reservation system with Clockwork's back door. But there is no one under Kranstan."

"Can't blame them. They were attacked."

"So I doubt they're even staying in the building."

That was a reasonable point, I had thought about that too, I just didn't have anywhere else to go.

"If they are still in the building, but trying to keep a low profile, it is working. I do not know where to start." She said.

I decided to make sure my smoke break plan was a bust, so I ran the perimeter. Pretty easy to do in the dark at three in the morning. Scratch that, it was now into the four AM.

This was stupid. "Did Red Knight turn up anything?"

"The area is under heavy SSA patrols. He is driving around the outskirts of their search area, but it doesn't look good."

"What about Peregrine and Flare?"

"They chose to meet up and progress as a team. It slowed them down."

Understandable. Made tactical sense. But I felt that we were already late on this and we were spinning our wheels. "Did you look at room service bills? If they're lying low they aren't eating at restaurants."

"I did, and no meals were sent to rooms that did not have guests. Assuming they are paying in cash, which they would, that still doesn't narrow the field enough."

To make the jump to the next building I had to get up a good run, jump, spin a couple of times in the air, land, and roll. The other side of the new building gave me a good view of the west wall.

"Of your possibilities, you got any on the tenth floor, west building?"

"Sure, why?"

In one of the windows, someone had hung a towel with a rough black raven emblem drawn on it that matched the one on my uniform.

"I think I have an invitation." I explained what I was seeing to Butterfly.

"Who besides the Confessor would know your emblem? It could be a trap."

"Too obvious for a trap. I think it's Sofia. She wants to talk." Hey, maybe we'd finally caught a break.

"Sofia." I heard her tapping on her computer. "That is the..." I think a computer image loaded. "Pretty blond girl you rescued." A little accusation and a lot less enthusiasm crept into her voice.

"It's not like that. Our relationship is purely professional rescuer-rescuee." And she kind of flirted with me when I met her in my civies.

"Sure." Not convinced. "You weren't in your uniform."

"Well, no..."

"Then how did you identify yourself as Raven when you rescued her?" she asked slowly.

"Long story, but she didn't see my face. Look, I'm going to go talk to her."

"Did you bring flowers? Girls like flowers." Sarcasm came through the vocal distortion. She was so not thrilled with this plan.

"Rescuer-rescuee, that's it." I made sure no one was

observing me as I reached ground level. I got across the main street with a quick run. Traffic was low, and I was to the wall in seconds.

The decorative block wasn't exactly like a ladder, but for a guy like me it was pretty close.

The light was off in the room with the towel. It was four in the morning, after all. I tapped on the glass.

"Well?" Butterfly asked.

"Nothing." I tapped again.

The towel was ripped down. Sofia's face was red and puffy, like she'd been crying. Or maybe sleeping.

Her face lit up with hope when she saw me. She looked around for a way to open the window and forced it open. There was a screen between her and me, but we could talk.

"Is it you?" she asked. "The guy with the ninja t-shirt?"

"With the what?" Butterfly said.

"Yeah, you want to talk?" I did not want to relive my makeshift ninja moment.

She seemed to consider her options and decided to hedge her bets. "What did you tell me about my dad?"

As proof goes, that was pretty reasonable. "He's a parahuman, and mind reader. He works for Jack Midas."

She chewed her lower lip. "You're right."

"That's a change from last time we talked." I tried to scan the room behind her. I didn't see anyone else, but I couldn't be sure. If this was a trap, I was just dangling out there.

"I didn't want to believe you, but big scary parahuman ninjas don't happen to business consultants' families."

So she agreed with the point I'd made. "My cogent argument and persuasion skills weren't the only thing that convinced you." It was one thing to be almost certain and another to try to get your father's enemy's attention.

"My dad is in trouble. In danger." She bit down on her lip again.

That's what the Worm had said. "He's not in danger from me." More's the pity.

"I know. I did a lot of research on the Guard." She made a slight head bob toward her bed. Maybe that was where her computer was? "I know you guys don't kill people. It's the biggest reason the SSA haven't busted you up a long time ago."

And I guess Raptor had some kind of blackmail information on them, but hey, I wasn't going to get into the weeds. The faith-in-the-world-crushing weeds.

"I even found your logo." She laughed at her work on the towel. "On one of your fan sites."

I have a fan site?

"I don't know who else to turn to. I was hoping you'd be patrolling or whatever since you were here to save me the first time." She sounded desperate and bounced a little on the balls of her feet. "Please, I need your help. I need you to save my father's life."

Wow, so conflicted here. I mean, he'd had Yaltin killed. Well no, I guess Heavy Metal Ninja was working for a different carpool. And he'd left Imp alive. I'd rescued Julia before her life was endangered, but come on, he works for Midas. Midas kills people by the dozen. Bakers' dozens.

On the other side, Raptor had always said we weren't police or judges. "I don't solve crimes or punish criminals, I just stop them." That was his rule, the prime directive. "Your father has done a lot of crimes he should go to prison for."

She took a step back.

"But that's not my job. I don't enforce the law, I don't judge the criminal. I just try to save people. I will do what I can for your father." I believed it. All of it. People needed police and judges and prisons in the long term. But in the short term, they needed someone to just be there and do something.

She looked at me hard, willing for me to be the answer for some kind of prayer.

"What are your instincts telling you?" I said *instinct* instead of *powers*.

"That a mentor figure wasn't who you thought he was, and betrayed everything you care about. You have a super scary cat." She seemed confused at that one. "And if I don't help you, my father won't live the night."

Okay, that was kind of creepy. "I wouldn't say *super* scary. Just normal scary for the cat thing." I hadn't seen Feral since the fight with Heavy Metal. I hoped he was all right.

"No, he is super scary." She stuck to her guns. "And he's pissed. He took the whole ninja battle pretty personally."

"Can we keep on task?" Butterfly said.

"Okay, do you know where my cat is?" I asked.

She shook her head. "He's stopped in a couple times to make sure I was okay, but then left in pretty impossible ways."

Wow, he must like her. "Good. I mean I haven't seen him since the fight." I wasn't really nervous that something had happened to him, but the knot in my stomach relaxed. Unlike my arms, that were starting to burn a little. Climbing is one thing, but I'd had to keep the same grip for a while and I was starting to get a cramp.

"Raven! Focus," Butterfly demanded.

"If your father's in trouble, I want to help. What do you know?" Now that she'd confirmed Feral was okay, I could start getting down to business.

"I don't know much, I just got an impression. Like I did with the cat and your mentor. My father has hurt people, gotten into their minds and hurt them. He did it to a woman and to a man. The man was hard, and it hurt him to do it, but he got what he wanted. And something hungry is playing him like a puppet." She shivered again.

"I was there for the woman. Julia, the widow of Archibald Valtire." Why tell her? I don't know. But I did.

Her eyes grew big.

"Who is the man?" I asked.

She shook her head. "Nothing that made sense. He was one of four and four of one." Her mouth said the words like they confused her more to say.

Damn it. He had Quare.

"I need to know where they went." That was the only thing that mattered. Now I was sure they were way ahead of us, but I didn't have any other information.

"I don't know. Somewhere in the Kages." She shook her head.

That narrowed it down from *super* unhelpful to just unhelpful.

"The man, the one of four guy, thought of it as the Book House. He needed to go there to read a letter." She shrugged. She knew it didn't make any sense. "If I'm a parahuman, my power sucks. It doesn't help to know something is coming if you can't do anything about it. Or don't know enough to actually do something."

"Do you know when this guy got the letter?" Wortha shot to ask.

She shook her head. "That's all the information my 'power' gave me." She used finger quotes.

"That seems like a lot." Not super helpful... or the answer to everything. "Okay, good. I'll talk to you later.

Well probably not, but it was good meeting you. Great Raven doodle thing." I nodded at the towel.

I started down, then backtracked up to the window.

"Sofia?"

She had started to close the window, but froze in mid-motion. "Yes?"

"I have a fan site? Seriously?"

"What?" Took her a heart beat to track my question. "Yes. It lit up when I posted I saw you shirtless."

"She saw you what?" Butterfly asked, somehow colder than when she was Robo-Butterfly but not Robo-Butterfly.

"Okay, good." So, so glad to be wearing a full face mask. I was beet red. "Um, I'll go now."

Getting down is always faster, not easier, but I was running in a few seconds. "Fly, call Peregrine and Flare. The Confessor has Quare and we need them back. I'm going to where I think they took Quare."

"What are you talking about? The Book Room?" Butterfly was not convinced my chat with Sofia had gave me any information, but she was still making the calls. "What was that supposed to mean?"

"Where Raptor wanted me to go from the start." I pulled out the letters I had in my pouch and jammed the Jackal one back in. I read the address off the post-it note. "I was supposed to get this letter at that address. Julia just gave it to me when I rescued her. I never went there."

"That's a long shot."

"If this location is the Book Room, then the key to decoding his letter could be one of those books." If this letter was, *oh yeah, you should take care of this Phoenix thing, here's where it is and stuff*, I will freak.

"What did you discover, Raven?" Red Knight was on the party line now.

I told him.

"It's worth checking out," he agreed. "Though the Confessor's daughter could be just trying to throw you off the trail."

That didn't sound right. She was scared, not working a plan. "We weren't exactly on a trail before."

"Wait for us before you enter the building." Peregrine was now on the party line too, so the party could really get started.

"You realize I'm walking here. You wait for *me* before entering." Flyers. They think everybody can just hop around town.

THIRTY

As I approached, I saw Red Knight's van parked a
little down the alley. I did a quick circle, but didn't
see any activity. It was just a boarded-up building. I see this
type of building all the time. It was perfect camouflage in
this town.

"I'm at the location," I said on the party line.

"We're three minutes out," Peregrine replied. Which
meant he could get here faster, but was waiting for Flare.

"Meet me at the van," Red Knight said.

"I'll be there in just a second." I'd noticed an easy way
up on a taller building. Before the flyers got there, I could
check the roof and have a full picture of the exterior.

I scrambled up a collection of rusty pipes, bricks, and
window ledges.

"Guys! I need you to get here faster!" I screamed.

Heavy Metal Ninja was walking out of the roof access
with a body slung over his shoulder.

"I can be there soon!" Peregrine replied.

"What's going on?" Red Knight sounded a little
desperate.

"Heavy Metal Ninja is exiting the building. Carrying a body."

"He will kill you in a fight. Follow him. Do not engage," Red Knight said.

Good advice, but... "I'll lose him. He's too fast." The super jump thing he has going on would leave me in the dust. I didn't know who he was carrying, but they were probably still alive. "Peregrine, get here now!" My vantage overlooked the warehouse by about three floors and an alleyway. This was a little beyond my comfort level.

I ran as far back as I could.

"Raven, what are you doing?" Red Knight asked, but he knew what I was doing.

"Fighting crime," I whispered. I blew out a couple times and ran as fast as I could. I got to the edge and jumped, tucked in and rolled in the air, then stretched and caught the edge of the warehouse roof. I felt the familiar slap of my body on brick. Whew. I'd made it.

And the brick I was holding onto slipped its mortar in my hand.

Come on!

I scrambled hand over hand as all the bricks I was hanging onto started to slip. it was like all the mortar had clocked out and the bricks were staying in place by force of habit.

I finally found something that could hold my weight for a second and kicked my leg over the edge onto the roof.

Plus five points for not dying, minus several hundred on stealth.

"You again," Heavy Metal said.

We were about twenty feet apart. He was probably going to the same corner of the building to jump. If I'd stayed where I was he would have come to me.

"I was just thinking the same thing about you." I couldn't let him jump. I had to keep the pressure on just long enough for Peregrine to get there. Not only was Peregrine a better fighter than me -- tell him I said that and I will deny it -- but it would take more than a super leap to get away. Then Flare could come and finish this asshole off in a shower of green light and attitude.

Good, I had a plan.

I got me feet under me and fly-tackled the SOB.

He pivoted on his hip and I sailed by.

But I had expected that. I landed on my hands and sprung back, connecting with a kick to his chest.

He wasn't ready for it so he didn't go all indestructible and solid.

I jumped up and started applying pressure, mostly crazy flashy kicks to the head, just trying to keep him distracted and backing away from the building ledge.

He blocked my first strike and the second, then dropped whoever he was carrying.

I didn't even have time to confirm who the victim was. Now unencumbered, he started his offensive.

I didn't bother blocking his shot, I just dodged.

Silhouette and Shale had given me a lot of practice dodging for my life. I wouldn't call myself an expert, but I had skills.

"What do you think you're doing?" Heavy Metal asked.

"Kung Fu, bitch." I faked him out with a punch and followed it up with a double front kick right to the chin.

He stepped backwards, tripping over his victim.

I risked a look. It could be Quare. It was dark, and someone had messed up his face good.

I ran up on Heavy Metal and delivered an axe kick to the stomach. Or tried.

I was kicking with the intention of keeping him down.

I did not keep him down.

His hand shot up and caught my ankle. For a split second it felt like an ordinary ankle grab. Oh, the good old days when my opponent just moved at lighting speed and caught my ankle. I look back on that as a time of innocence.

Less than a second later, it felt like I'd jammed my ankle into a vice and had started turning the screws.

"I tried to be nice," Heavy Metal said. "You can't beat me. I tried to teach you that. But maybe you can't be taught." He stood up, and I slipped backwards. Connecting with the roof would have hurt if I hadn't been wearing my helmet.

He had me upside down by one leg, not my best moment.

Heavy Metal was drawing on his power and cracking the concrete of the roof.

"So what's your deal? Who do you work for?" I was in control of this situation. No reason to get off mission.

"Is now the time I tell you my plan? Before I kill you?" His voice thought that was ridiculous.

"Hey, who said anything about killing me?" I kicked him in the face with my free foot. He was carved out of iron.

Come on.

Another kick that hurt me way more than it hurt him.

"Are you done?"

I kicked him again. Ouch! "Now I'm done." I kicked him again. Damn it. "Okay, now for real." My foot was starting to hurt.

"In a way, this will be a favor to you." The tension around my ankle started to crush bones. "When you're old, and have grandchildren, you might look back at this time as the moment that saved your life. The moment you only lost your leg instead of your future. If I don't do this, eventually you will go up against someone who outclasses you and they won't be merciful."

Oh, that hurt a lot. Yes, my ankle, but also my emotional scars. "So, you can control your bodied weight?" I asked through the pain.

"Density," he corrected.

"That's cool." Oh, this hurt. "Why do you want him?" I motioned to the body that hadn't moved yet.

"Still the good little hero, trying to unravel my plans. You're a fool. Not as big of one as me, but still a fool." He applied more pressure. "Or are you trying to keep me talking, waiting for your friend to arrive?" He hissed the word "friend," like it disgusted him.

"He's more of an associate," I gritted out. Then I screamed in pain.

"You can't keep me so distracted I would risk fighting both of you at the same time."

"I wasn't trying to. I was trying to keep you from looking down."

He looked down.

His added density was a little much for this crappy old building. The cracks had increased, and he was close to breaking through.

I didn't want him to break through. He would survive the fall if he kept solid, I would be mangled.

But he reacted by quickly decreasing his density to stop the damage.

Boot to the head, Bitch.

He collapsed and so did I. My ankle was free and throbbing. I said a silent prayer that nothing was too damaged.

And started to put on the pressure like my life

depended on it. I couldn't let him focus for a second or we would be back where we'd begun.

I think I got a really good punch into his kidneys and flipped him around then down on the roof. He solidified as he fell so the impact was more than it would have been. It left a huge dent.

He swung at me, but I sidestepped. If he got his hands on me again, I was done.

When he didn't connect, he used the motion to roll himself out of his crater and onto all fours.

By the time I kicked he was standing and started delivering blows that were too fast and too furious for me to block.

Pound.

He got me right in the chest and I flew six feet before hitting the roof and skidding another ten.

I was so winded I couldn't move, helpless as I watched the building's edge approach. Usually there would be some kind of safety lip, but I had pulled that apart on my leap here.

I stopped with my head over nothing.

Whew.

He started coming, each footfall leaving an indentation in the roof. "I have had enough!"

"Then fight someone your own size," boomed a voice.

I looked.

Red Knight stood on the ledge. It was not the old man in a wheelchair who had seconds of juice before he passed out. This was the Red Knight with red glowing armor, sword in one hand and a shield in the other, the one from the press release and old newspaper. He pointed his sword in the air. "These people are under my protection."

Heavy Metal looked at Red Knight, me, then the person

he was abducting. "Fine." He pointed at me. "I'm sure I'll see you later."

He jumped backwards -- like forty feet in the air -- and I lost him in the light-polluted sky.

I looked at Red Knight. "Holly Hannah, you've got some game."

"Is he gone?" Red Knight asked through our party line, panting.

"Yes."

The armor broke apart and vanished.

I looked over the edge to where Red Knight sat in his wheelchair, one hand still pointing at the space his old form had appeared.

So not all suited up and ready for a fight. More just an energy construct that would disappear if a big gust of wind came by. That works, too.

I gave him a thumbs up. "That was awesome, RK!"

"What was awesome?" Peregrine landed just behind me.

"Peregrine. Better late than never I guess." It was nice to get anywhere first for once. "You missed it."

He looked around at what was left of the building. "I guess I missed a lot."

I'd recovered mostly, but I also felt the adrenaline fatigue start to creep in. I could not... would not... fall asleep now.

I started running in place, then stopped. My ankle still wasn't one-hundred percent. I hopped on my good leg and rotated my head.

Peregrine didn't say anything about the calisthenics. "Who is he?" He hovered quickly to the prone man's side. "He's alive."

Thank God. "Is it Quare?"

"How would I know?" He hadn't seen the picture from the bunk room.

Fair enough. I had to bend close to make his features out in the dark. He was beaten all to hell, but it was him. Because I knew what to look for, I could see twin burns, bright red, the size of the Confessor's thumbs.

"It's Quare," I said. "Mr. Quare?" I shook him a little. "Mr. Why?" I tried.

His eyes fluttered, and he looked up at me. "Hawk?"

The only thing different about my helmet and Hawk's was the color. I'd inherited his old armor. "No, I'm Ra--"

"Raven, of course. Of course." He tried to sit up, but that was a bad idea. He got a good look at Peregrine. "And Peregrine, too. Good. Good." He almost drifted back to coma land.

"Mr. Quare. Wraith!"

That last got his eyes open. "Wraith? I haven't been Wraith for years. Since Caesar killed the rest of me."

"He didn't. One of you is alive."

That confused him. "No, I'd know."

He didn't know *you* were still alive.

"We've got to get him to the hospital." Peregrine was eyeballing Quare's weight. Probably figuring if he could fly him all the way to Darhaven General.

"No." Quare reached out and grabbed my shoulder. His hand couldn't find purchase on my uniform and fell away. "You've got to stop them. They're trying to find..."

"The Phoenix," I supplied.

He nodded. "Right, you know. Good." He went limp again then forced his eyes open. "They got the location from me." He shook his head. "I didn't want to tell them, but they pulled it out of my mind. I'm out of practice. When I was young the Confessor never could have beaten me."

If Sofia was right, he'd put up one hell of a fight and had hurt the Confessor back.

"Where is the Confessor going?" I had to know before we got him to the hospital.

"I wrote it down. I told the third one, the other one, too. I couldn't fight anymore." He was probably talking about Heavy Metal Ninja.

I wasn't sure why the Confessor hadn't just killed Quare before Heavy Metal got there, but thank god for small mercies.

He started twitching, trying to get something from his coat pocket. "I made a copy, a copy before the Confessor."

I pulled the slip of paper out. It was a photocopy of a string of numbers, numbers that looked just like Raptor's code for me.

"I always make a copy. Always mess up the first time I try to decode them..."

I showed it to Peregrine.

He nodded. "Where's the book?"

Quare pointed at the stairwell. "In the Book Room."

Again, fair enough.

"I've got to get him to the hospital," Peregrine said.

"Go. I'll see if I can find the book."

Peregrine nodded again.

I helped him lift the retired Guard. Peregrine made sure he was supporting him the best he could, and he was airborne.

At least Quare was on the small side.

I went down the stairs.

Heavy Metal had left the lights on. Typical. I didn't have a clue where to start looking for the Book Room but luckily it wasn't hard.

I just followed the trail of Quare's blood down a set of stairs. "Found the Book Room," I reported.

"Are you sure?" Butterfly asked.

"Yep."

From floor to ceiling of a two-story room, shelves were crammed with books. Most were in ordered stacks spine out, but some were just in three-foot piles here and there.

Ever start a fifty-yard dash and realize you signed on for a triathlon? That's what my soul felt like. "I found books. A lot of books."

THIRTY-ONE

Butterfly might have been able to sort all these, but how was I going to find the right book before the next millennium?

I looked at Quare's coded letter for the ISBN fragment. I knew what they were if Quare's code was the same as mine, but Peregrine had said his was different. There was no way Raptor would use the same code for Quare.

Damn it!

"Can you decode it?" Red Knight wheeled himself into the Book Room. "Oh, Archie, you bastard." He was as overwhelmed with all the books as I'd been.

"I don't know which one of these million books we need!"

"Try to figure out how the books were stacked." Red Knight rolled over to the nearest wall of books.

"It doesn't matter unless it's by ISBN, starting with the second digit." Raptor couldn't use the actual ISBN -- that could be looked up. It was always missing the first digit, so it didn't look like an ISBN. Then you subtracted the number of letters in the title until the first vowel in the title. Unless the first letter was a vowel, then you... Yeah you get the idea. Only annoying if you had six books to pull from. Soul crushing if you had a million zillions.

"The books seem to be loosely organized by content." Red Knight's disappointment was plain.

"We need Butterfly here." It might not solve the problem. By the time she got here it could be too late. But she was the only one who could process this kind of data if we wanted it done this week.

"Well, she's not," Red Knight said. "What number am I looking for?"

I told him. He started flipping through the books he could reach.

"This won't work." I was panicking. If the Phoenix got into the Confessor's hands we were screwed. Mom, Dad, my half-sister and half-brother, all screwed. Damn it. "Think, think. What would Jackal do?"

"I can't believe you said that." Butterfly was still on the party line.

Me, neither. "He would have some direction, something I didn't think of," I defended my thinking out loud.

"Well, he is certainly not here." Red Knight counted that among our blessings.

What would Jackal say? I thought this time. What would Jackal say?

"Raven?" His voice wasn't clear. It was muted and fading in and out. But it was there. Or was it? Did I imagine it?

"Jackal?" I was so surprised I said it out loud.

"What about him?" Butterfly asked.

Red Knight gave me a look. I wasn't doing a lot to help with the search.

I turned off my communicator. "Jackal? How?" I made

sure I didn't have the idol in my pouch. I knew I'd thrown the thing.

"How? That was *my* question," he replied. "You're not using the idol. I can barely hear you." He was as surprised as I was. "I was just thinking of you, and I heard you in my head. It's never worked like that before."

Okay, this day just got worse.

"Wait, are you still carrying that letter I sent you?" Jackal asked.

My hand went to that pouch. "Yes." I'd had a vague idea of filing it for a handwriting sample, but hadn't known where we would file it.

"Then that's it. I tried to imbue the drawing, but I didn't think it had worked. Funny old world. It probably wouldn't have if we hadn't been so connected lately."

And eww.

"Have you been watching the news?" Jackal asked.

"No." My attention went to Red Knight, who was looking at me a little oddly. "I'll check out over here." I went to the opposite side of the Book Room.

"You're all over it."

"What are you talking about?"

"Raven, a suspected member of the Guard, escaped SSA custody in transit." He seemed to be reading one of those tickers under the news screen.

"How did you get a television?" I thought he was in prison.

"Life is a lot different for me without Caesar orchestrating my torture." He seemed very happy about that. "But I didn't get to the punch line. A combat duty SSA operative was killed in the escape."

"What? I didn't kill anyone."

"I know. I was there. Totally will testify for you if it comes to that."

Well, that made me feel better. "Was it in the explosion?" I'd felt that distraction was a little hard core for an SSA operative just doing a good deed.

"Doesn't say. They're not releasing the name of the agent, either. But it's Robinson."

"The guy who let me go? They killed him?" That was crazy, but the more I heard about SSA and its Section 5 stuff, the more I was ready to believe it.

"No. It bugged me at the time, but that guy was really informed about what went on in Section 5," Jackal said.

"Maybe, but I've got bigger problems." If I'd had a moment to reflect, I would have asked myself why I was so glad to hear the voice of a truly epic, epic criminal. "I need to find this database, the Phoenix. It has all our real IDs on it."

"And what else?" Jackal prodded. "No way would all these resources be used to unmask a couple of kids."

"It also has the Bio-Globe formula for their parahuman test or whatever." Ever walk outside and realize you aren't wearing pants? Because that's what I'd just done. I totally exposed something to Jackal that I did not want exposed. I tried to speak over what I'd said. "At least that's what the Confessor thinks." It was 4am and the lack of sleep was getting to me. This, of course, was why everyone had told me not to deal with Jackal.

Damn it.

"I see." It was 4am for him too, so apparently he didn't make the connection between Bio-Globe and the guard. "Look, you've got to get me up to speed on this." His voice was getting stronger. Not sure that was a good thing.

I was a little hesitant about exposing more information. "I need to find a book." I explained the situation.

"You're never going to find where the book is in time. Look for where the book is not."

"Thank you, Zen master."

"No. I doubt they put the book back. Look for an empty place on a shelf."

Of course. It wouldn't give us a title, but it would give us a topic or category, maybe. I started scanning all the shelves. The books were jammed together as much as they could be. There wasn't a lot of empty room. So it only took me a few seconds to find a gap. It was even better since the book that was missing was book three of a five-book series.

I looked around on the floor and stacks for a book with the same blue gold binding.

"We're looking for *The Rise of Byzantium, Volume Three,*" I told Red Knight after turning on my communications. "Maybe."

"Are you sure?" He didn't seem convinced, but he looked around for it.

Time sped by, pouring through my fingers. I tossed books around on the floor. Come on, it had to be here. Didn't it? What if the Confessor had taken it with him? What if volume three of *Byzantium* wasn't the book, and it had just caught the Confessor's eye while the real book was one I'd already thrown on the floor? I saw the corner of a book poking out from underneath the bookcase. "Here!"

There was even some blood on the dust jacket. This had to be the one.

I pulled a pen from my gear -- first time I'd actually used it -- and started decoding the letter.

It would have gone a lot faster if I hadn't been exhausted, and if Raptor had led with the important stuff.

Flare arrived during my decoding.

Once the page was decoded I went back to the top and started reading out loud. "John." Strange. I thought of Quare as Quare, Mr. Why, or Wraith. I'd forgotten his first name was John. "It's been a good run, but if you're reading this, it's too late for me. Cover my tracks as best you can, then disappear. The apprentices are ordered to do the same. You've been a good friend from the start. I couldn't have done it without you. I have just one more request. Expose the Phoenix for what it is. Expose it to the world. Not the formula -- that's too dangerous -- but tell the world all of it, what we did. What we were ordered to do. Bring down Section 5. I wish I'd had the courage to do this while I was alive. I moved it. It's at--" And I read the address.

It meant nothing to me. Conveniently, it was still in the Kages.

"Why did you read the whole thing? The address was all we cared about," Flare said.

A point. "Context is important with these Last Will and Testament things." I said it as a joke, but it hit me. This could be the last thing Raptor ever did.

Then I thought of my letter. I pulled it out, but the number was not the same. "How important is what's in this letter?" I asked Red Knight and Flare. "It could have need-to-know information, but finding out would mean trying to find a different book."

"We have the address. That will have to be good enough," Flare said.

Red Knight didn't seem as convinced, but he nodded. "I'm nervous going into a situation without all the data, but we just don't have the time."

"Then let's move!"

THIRTY-TWO

Of course, it wasn't as simple as "Let's move."

There was a slight debate as to how. In the end we all piled in the back of Red Knight's van again.

We agreed to meet Peregrine at a rally point just south of the address. Butterfly told us that it was a large factory that was already defunct when Gen X was thinking about the crappy job future and grunge music.

The chain of ownership was long and convoluted, but lead back to Bio-Globe. So there you go.

The van ride there sucked. Not just because Red Knight took us through the back streets. The regular roads in the Kages are potholes pretending to be roads. These were worse, and I felt every bump. The route took longer, too, so I got to experience it repeatedly. Why the back roads you might ask? I know I did. When Red Knight had driven around looking for the Worm, he'd noted dozens of SSA check points. RK was probably their second most wanted, right under me, if Jackal's news report was to be believed. Butterfly had found the story and cross-checked it. You know, trust but verify.

But the van ride really blew because Flare was giving me the cold shoulder. I didn't really want to get into it... you know, ever... but especially with Jackal listening in. I just didn't know why she would be pissed at me. Regardless, she needed to know Jackal was on the party line. She would be pissed, but she might not force me to fry the paper. Red Knight might flip out. Best to just tell Flare, first.

"Flare." I tapped her on the shoulder and reached for the envelope.

She quickly turned at my touch. "David wants to be just like you," she blurted, like she'd been keeping that in, but she'd already told me that.

"What?" It was a confusing side track from what I wanted to talk about.

"David -- you know, Ballista -- wants to be just like you," Jackal clarified.

Which brought me to my main point: I did not want to talk about THIS stuff now. Jackal had talked Ballista through his first surge. He might have saved David's life. And since I was standing there, mine, too. Ballista is the most powerful parahuman I know. If he'd lost control of the surge, he would probably have blown out the top three floors of the building we were in. During that process, he gave us his first name. Unfortunately, 'us' included Jackal.

"I almost had him putting all this crap behind him." She illustrated all of this with a finger at her mask. "Now all he talks about is being part of the New Guard."

"New Guard?" That was the first I'd heard about it. "Listen, I have to tell you something first." I pulled both letters out of my pouch.

"I like the sound of that," Jackal added.

"It's what he's calling it." She did *not* like the sound of it.

I shrugged. "I haven't exchanged three words with Ballista since we all quit two days ago. Listen, something happened. I--"

"Quit," she snorted. "Peregrine went out that night trying to find Red Knight, and you went on a rescue mission to save Raptor's wife."

"Ah--" *Don't talk about that.*

"You did? Was that the call you got?" Jackal asked. I knew enough about Jackal to understand he wouldn't need many more coordinate points to put it all together.

"Stop talking. Before you say anything else, listen." I held up my hand. I would have put it over her mouth if she wasn't wearing a face mask.

"How did she know to call you?" Jackal asked. "Who is she talking about?"

Flare did not stop talking. "I'm glad you saved Julia Valtaire, I am."

I dropped my hands

Jackal said nothing.

Well, nuts. My hands, letters, and all went into my lap. I could still tell her about my connection with Jackal now, but it didn't matter. "Listen, I'm with you. We should all get out of this business. As soon as we deal with the Phoenix and destroy it, we can move on with our normal lives."

She did not respond.

"I'll talk to Ballista and have him put all this 'New Guard' stuff out of his mind," I said.

"Really? Because now that Red Knight is back, he could start teaching us and guiding us again. Isn't that why you and Peregrine went looking for him? So you could keep going?"

"Hey, that was Peregrine's thing. You'll have to talk to him about his plans for the future."

If Red Knight could hear us, he didn't weigh in. We were talking in low whispers in the back of a rattling van, so if he didn't have super hearing, he might not even have known we were talking.

She looked at me. "Okay, after this, you tell him you're quitting." She didn't believe me. "And actually quit."

I wiped my hands as if getting the dirt off. "Done and done."

"Okay." That seemed to make her feel better.

"Get Butterfly to find out who was killed in your escape attempt," Jackal said. "And how he was killed."

"What?"

"I said okay. I believe you." Flare made it a little more believable.

"Do it!" Jackal sounded a little panicked. "This isn't making any sense."

He'd just told me he was sure it was Robinson. Why the panicked request now? But as my granddaddy always said: No point in giving a confirmed sociopathic killer access to your mind and endangering your friends if you're not going to use him. "I just thought of something." I turned on the party line. "Butterfly, you on the line?"

"Yes." She dropped whatever she was doing. "What do you need?"

"The SSA agent that died in my escape. Could you get his name and cause of death?"

"Raven, don't do that," Flare said. "You shouldn't torture yourself."

That was an avenue of self-flagellation that I hadn't thought of until now. After eight hours of sleep I would have gotten there on my own, but I was there now.

"She's right." Red Knight heard that since we weren't talking in whispers anymore. "It wasn't your fault."

"The agent wouldn't have died if I hadn't escaped. So it is on me." *Why didn't I see that before? I was just too tired, and I didn't want to.* Now I didn't care why Jackal wanted the information. I had to know. "Who died, Fly?"

"Raven are you sure? The others are right." Butterfly didn't want to cause me any more pain.

"Just tell me." I appreciated it, but I had to know.

"I don't have the cause of death. His name was Damian Robinson. Been with the SSA for two years. Before that he was in the army military police." *She already had the information.*

Jackal had been right. Robinson was the guy who'd saved me and for that he was killed.

"Raven." Red Knight's voice held a warning. "You can't contact the family or anything like that. They'd just use it as a way to track to you."

"I know, I know." *He was right, I just needed to know.* "Please, Butterfly."

"It will take me a second," Butterfly answered me.

"We're here." Red Knight stopped the van and I heard Peregrine land on the top.

Flare looked at me. Whatever she was trying to convey, she didn't. She walked over to the van's back door and opened it with a roll and a thunk. "We can't worry about this now. Get your head in the game." She glanced back at me.

I nodded -- *total lie* -- but I nodded.

She jumped out of the van.

"She's right, Raven." Red Knight's head was craned over his shoulder, trying to get a look at me. "Whoever Robinson was, you can't do anything for him right now. You can't do anything for his family. But you can do something for your family -- keep your identity secret. You can do something for countless parahumans and destroy the test. You have to focus on the mission."

He was right, too. I nodded with a little more truth this time, then again with a lot more truth. "Focus on the mission," I agreed.

"That's the way." Red Knight's eyes willed me to learn my lesson. "Leave your feelings in the van." He pointed toward Flare. "Go out there and do the work."

I exited the van, and did my best to let Robinson go.

THIRTY-THREE

"What took you so long?" Peregrine asked.

I laughed.

"What?" Flare was not in a laughing mood.

"I'm not the only one getting the 'why are you late' thing." I impersonated Peregrine's angry voice. "Feels good to have company."

"Get Robinson's hometown." Jackal urged, but come on, other things were going on.

"Peregrine, what do we have?" Red Knight said loud enough for us to hear on the other side of the van.

By silent consent we all moved to Red Knight's side of the van.

"They're in there." Peregrine pulled a small tablet out of his belt and showed us aerial photos of the factory.

"Where did you get these?" I didn't know he had a tablet.

"Recon photos I took while I was waiting for you to arrive." Even when he was trying to be all professional, he sounded pissed off, and a little put out that he'd had to do all the heavy picture taking by himself.

"Well, good for you," I told him. "Way to recon like a boss."

He gave me a look. I couldn't see it, but I like to think it was all scowly.

"Yeah, is scowly a word?" I just wanted to know.

No one answered. If Butterfly were here, she would have told me.

"The photos," Red Knight said.

We all huddled around. The camera he had for recon was way better than anything in my gear. I have a jackknife, a few ball bearings, and one more vial of scent-tracker-be-gone. I didn't get a high resolution camera tablet. I could take pictures. I climb tall places and stuff.

"Do you have a camera tablet?" I asked Flare.

"Of course. Pay attention."

Was this a flyer vs pedestrian bias thing? Ugly.

"I got here after them," Peregrine said. "They parked here." He pointed to a bunch of motorcycles of the Harley-Davidson kind as opposed to the Japanese style. And that exhausted my knowledge of motorcycles. One of the vehicles was a sedan, probably the Confessor's ride.

"There are seven motorcycles," Peregrine said.

"Good eye. You must have super counting vision." Cheap shot? Maybe, but there was something about giving Peregrine the business that calmed me. Especially right before a fight.

Red Knight was not accustomed to my brand of pre-fight jitters. He gave me a look to settle down.

Fair enough.

"So seven Headsmen, the Confessor, and whoever he drove with." I tried to be all about the business.

"Each bike could have brought two combatants." Flare beat the stuffing out of my being about the business..

I looked at Peregrine and Red Knight. Then at Flare. "Yeah, I don't see Headsmen doubling up."

"Me, neither," Peregrine agreed with me.

"But it is possible." Red Knight nodded. "So the minimum is seven plus the Confessor. The max fourteen plus five in the sedan. Let's assume we are not clear until we account for all twenty-one."

"Assuming they don't have any flyers that just got here on their own," I pointed out.

Red Knight nodded. "That is true."

"Seven or three-hundred and seven, there are more than three. We're very outnumbered." Just putting a little Raven perspective on things. "I bet Arc will be there. He can shoot electric arcs and has a force field thing. So what I'm saying is Flare, yours."

"Got him." Flare nodded.

"The Confessor doesn't seem to have any ranged powers," I continued with my share of recon, "but if he touches you, he will mess up your stuffing back six generations."

"Keep in mind the Confessor can read your mind if he touches you," Red Knight said. "He is not to be underestimated."

"Circling back to the range thing." I had to state the obvious. "He could have a gun. And the bugger is quick. The only other powered Headsmen I saw took a bullet wasn't that super, so I don't know what else they got. Except guns." I brought up the guns again. "They have guns. Lots of guns. And their trademark axes, but that goes without saying."

"They might be able to call in reinforcements as well," Red Knight said. "So neutralizing all hostiles is not an option. Assume Arc and the Confessor are not the only parahumans in theater."

In theater, I liked that one. If I wasn't quitting, I would keep that in my repertoire.

"Our objective is to destroy the Phoenix," Flare said. "We do that, then we get out."

"Right," Red Knight agreed. "I'll stay with the van." I could see how much it pained him to say that. "Stay on the coms at all times and keep communication going. Don't split up," he warned. "Watch each other's backs."

"And keep an eye out for Heavy Metal Ninja," I said. "The guy has been one step ahead of us this entire time."

"Good point," Red Knight agreed. "We don't know how powerful he is. Do not engage if it can be avoided."

We put our heads together and decided to go in from the north. I wouldn't have a problem getting in the guts of this place. It would shield our approach from any Headsmen guarding the bikes on the south wall. Peregrine and I could be super sneaky, but Flare's glow needed to be concealed.

"Give me the word and I will come and get you," Red Knight said. "Good luck."

With that we were off.

Peregrine and Flare flew together, and I started my run. It was dark, but my helmet had night vision so everything looked like an old black-and-white TV with the odd flare here and there.

If we weren't about to risk our lives in a last ditch effort to save our real identities and possibly the balance of power in the global political sphere, it would have been a fun parkour run.

To be honest, it was still a fun parkour run.

I jumped from pipes to pipes, vaulted over old air conditioner units, and climbed right up the wall, boarded-up window ledge to boarded-up window ledge.

"Find out about Robinson's hometown," Jackal said.

Five minutes in and I was already breaking protocol. I turned off the party line, or as I like to think of it now, coms. "Why? I already know. He told us. He was from Darhaven. He even sounded like he was from Darhaven."

"Are you sure?"

"I happen to know what someone from Darhaven sounds like."

"Just find out." Jackal sounded nervous. When he got like that, things got ugly.

Fine. I turned on my coms. "Butterfly, any progress on the Robinson information?"

"You should really keep focused on the mission," Red Knight said.

Yes, I should. "I just need to know. It'll help."

"If it will get it off your mind," Butterfly said, "I will tell you. He is from Hazelbrook, Georgia. He was strangled." She read the last sentence and stopped in the middle of strangled, as if she needed to reread the sentence.

I ran the length of a railing, then stopped. "Are you sure?"

"That is the information I have."

"Thanks, Fly."

"I need a second of your time." Now Jackal sounded a little afraid.

I turned off the group chat. "Georgia doesn't make sense. And strangled?"

"You never talked to Robinson." Jackal predicted my next objection. "You talked to a guy in Robinson's uniform."

"But who?"

"Who knew you were there?" Jackal asked.

I hate it when he goes all Yoda on me. "Just tell me your theory."

"Who knew?" he persisted.

"Fine. Butterfly figured it out." The gang had been about to head off to my rescue.

"I'm impressed." He sounded impressed. "But Butterfly has put the SSA under a lot of scrutiny and knew what to look for."

"She also didn't know *where* I was." The team hadn't known where to jump into action.

"So who knew where you were?" Jackal didn't really need to know, he was doing the Yoda thing.

"I hate your Yoda thing." Let's just be honest with each other. "Just the SSA. They didn't want to blow my cover if I turned out to be Section 5."

"Wrong. They also told Section 5."

"Okay, yes." My exhausted mind was starting to turn over. I could almost see where he was going with this. "But they couldn't get in touch with the guy in charge."

"Section 5 didn't want you caught. That's why they sent someone to spring you." Jackal didn't really have the patience of Yoda.

"Who?" That was just a general who, a who open to the panel. "And why would Section 5 not want me caught?" If anything, there seemed like bad blood between Section 5 and Raptor. Why would I have a favor stored up?

"So far we know of three groups that want the Phoenix." Jackal seemed jazzed, almost electric.

"Sure, the Confessor, the Heavy Metal Ninja, and us."

"Why does the Confessor want it?" he asked.

"Because it has the secrets to the parahuman test." I

needed to get going. I leapt to a broken light fixture, swung to a ledge, and pulled myself up.

"Why do you think that?"

"Why else would they want the data backup of Bio-Globe? Like you said, they don't want our identities."

"So I've pieced it together. Raptor was Archibald Valtire."

Of course he did, he could hear stuff. "What? That's crazy." A little bit of subterfuge to throw him off the scent. I got my feet under me and repeated to the next window ledge and up.

"If that's true, then the Confessor will not find what he's looking for," Jackal said.

"We'll stop him." Next window ledge. Only two more to go.

"No, there is no test to find," Jackal said.

"Then how did Bio-Globe become the powerhouse it is today?" I had to hand over hand it and swing my legs onto another ledge.

"I told you. Raptor could *see* parahumans. He probably just walked into the blood sample room once a month and picked out any vials that glowed."

Huh, that tracked. Everyone knew Bio-Globe was a nothing until Raptor took over. A minute and a half later they go public with the only foolproof parahuman test.

"Raptor used Bio-Globe to fund the Guard." Drawing the dots as to why he did it was obvious. "Then what was the formula he was talking about in the letter to Quare?" I had just assumed Raptor didn't want the test to fall into the wrong hands.

"That's what Section 5 wants. Whatever that formula is. The Confessor might think he's getting the test, but Section 5 has got to know the truth. Raptor was Section 5."

"So by process of elimination, Heavy Metal has to be Section 5," I said. "And he killed Robinson."

"Oh, it's far worse than that kid." Jackal had bad news he didn't want to share.

"What?" Now was the time for honesty.

"If Section 5 wanted something in Darhaven, they would be tearing this place apart," Jackal continued. "One parahuman operative wouldn't be wandering around."

"But you just said it was Section 5." Maybe if I wasn't trying to scale a wall I could make more sense out of what he was saying.

"Worm said that Raptor had blackmail on Section 5." I could feel Jackal pacing around his cage.

"Sure." If you could believe anything that fruit loop said.

"You can't blackmail organizations, you blackmail people."

"That's semantics. If you blackmail the people in an organization it's the same thing." I needed a second to find the next good hand hold.

"I disagree." Jackal is such a crappy Yoda. "If Raptor was blackmailing one person, then that person could not use Section 5 resources. It would risk exposure."

"So Heavy Metal Ninja is working on his own, because he doesn't want the rest of Section 5 to know about the Phoenix." Fine, didn't really help us.

"Heavy Metal Ninja is the only operative who knows he's working for Section 5," Jackal said.

I prepared for another jump. "These other operatives would be looking for the Phoenix too, but they wouldn't need to know they were working for Section 5?" Sure, why not.

"Agreed," Jackal said.

"They might not even know what they're looking for."
The Confessor didn't really know what he was looking for,
so there might be more patsies out there.

"Agreed."

"Section 5 has been a step ahead of us this whole time,
so that team must be here, too." Great, now we had a whole
other team in this cesspool. I should tell *my* team.

"Agreed."

I almost went on the group channel. "But the only
people here are the Confessor's crew and us." Assuming the
patsies didn't just walk here.

"Agreed."

"Agreed? Agreed with what? If this off book Section 5
patsy team is looking for the Phoenix than they should be
here. But the only people who are here are the Confessor
and us." So what was the point of this line of reasoning?

"The Confessor and us," he repeated.

"The Confessor." He'd switched back into annoying
Yoda again so my response was a little snippy. "And..." The
air went out of my sails. "Us," I repeated.

Oh, crap.

Oh, crap.

"No, no, no." It all started to fall together. "The
Confessor never went after Yaltin, because he knew it was
Mr. Why not Mr. Y."

"Don't know what you're talking about, but run with it."

"Heavy Metal Ninja killed Mr. Y after he realized he
wasn't the man he was looking for. But he got Yaltin's name
from us. From me." Oh no, no, no. "After I figured out the
Confessor's real name, his family became a target. Section 5
wanted to use his family as leverage on the Confessor."

"So how would Heavy Metal Ninja get that

information?" Jackal asked like he was teaching his star pupil.

"I'm already there, J." The Worm had said the original Guard were all part of Section 5 except one. That one was *not* Red Knight.

Like I said, getting down is faster. Just not easier.

THIRTY-FOUR

W hat needs to be my next move here? I mean, what? Good news is our secret identities are safe. The Phoenix isn't a data backup, it has "The Formula" -- whatever that is -- and the blackmail proof Section 5 was so scared of getting out that they stayed out of Raptor's playground until they'd heard he died.

"It wasn't like Red Knight found us." I had to be wrong. "Peregrine went looking for him."

"Really?" That was new information to Jackal, but he didn't seem impressed. "Let me guess. He did something heroic that got a little news coverage. Then maybe you had to save him? At least, that's is how I would do it. Invest you in my safety right away. Oh, did he drop money or resources on you? Now the debt goes both ways."

He had led us to a new base. A new-old base anyway. "No. He was one of the founding members of the Guard."

"The Worm told us the Guard was founded by Section 5. If he was a founding member, he was part of Section 5."

"So Section 5 has two operatives in the field, Heavy Metal Ninja and Red Knight?"

"No, Red Knight is the guy running this op, and it's off book or they wouldn't need you at all."

I shook my head. "Doesn't change a thing right now." That was overstating it. It changed everything, but... "I have to support my team. They're going into a fight."

"It isn't your fight," Jackal pointed out. "Call everyone off and get some answers from Red Knight on your way out."

"No. Raptor didn't want anyone to have access to this 'formula.' We still have to stop the Confessor from getting it." Right, mission set. I couldn't tell the rest of the team what I suspected. I couldn't use the radio or Red Knight would overhear.

I turned the radio back on.

"Raven!" Peregrine was yelling. "Raven, where the hell are you?"

"Tech issues. Report." I started climbing and climbing fast.

"We're in a fight! Get your ass up here!"

Damn it. That shouldn't have happened so soon. Maybe there was another team of villains here. If so, Red Knight might be in the clear. Other Section 5 resources might be here.

"A couple of powered Headsmen were watching the roof."

Okay, still Headsmen, so not Section 5.

"Raven, this is Red Knight." His voice seemed a lot more sinister now. "Why did you go radio silent?"

"I ran into a tech issue. It just cut out. It seems to be working now," I lied. I'm not a good liar.

"Peregrine, Flare, break off the engagement. Raven, you need to get into the building and find the Phoenix." Red Knight sounded harsh. Was that because he was harsher or were my doubts coloring what I was hearing?

"Are you able to break off?" I asked Flare and Peregrine.

I saw a glow of green and the light faded. "Yes, no flyers," Flare said.

"Incorrect, you picked up something on your six," Peregrine yelled. "Cut right."

I wanted to shout, I wanted to know what was going on, but I couldn't help and it would just clog the radio. Flare and Peregrine would need it clear to work together.

"What is it?" Flare yelled.

"It's a super, he can fly."

"Raven, continue with the mission," Red Knight ordered. "You can't do anything to help them. While they're distracting the Headsmen's supers you need to get the Phoenix."

"Do it, Raven!" Flare yelled. She was telling me to save her secret ID, not get some blackmail file for Red Knight. She didn't know we were looking for something else. She whipped around my side of the building and I saw the briefest of images.

The flyer was just behind here and looked encased in a grey heat shimmer.

Maybe with that description Butterfly would know who it was, but I didn't want to confuse the radio waves if Peregrine needed to talk.

"I'm going in." I kicked in the nearest boarded-up window and landed in a hall. The walls were exposed cinder block shellacked in graffiti, no carpet or tile on the floor, just more exposed concrete. The detritus of beer cans and empty food wrappers littered the floor.

The hall followed the edge of the building but I could see many walls that branched off deeper into the building.

This place was a maze. I'm not sure I could find a bathroom, never mind locating people doing crime?

Peregrine gave more instructions to Flare. They were in full combat in the sky. I couldn't follow all of it but the bad guy had a ranged attack. Every time he fired his speed slowed.

Peregrine was faster than Flare and Flare was faster than the Headsman. They didn't need me. They didn't. I kept telling myself that. But if Flare got hurt, I would never forgive myself. If Peregrine got hurt, I'd feel bad for like hours. It could ruin my weekend.

I started down the hall. I could search this place for the rest of the night and I wouldn't be any wiser. I listened for anything like movement. Nothing.

A couple rats and a lot of cockroaches, but nothing else.

I picked up my pace, trying to ignore the conflict going on outside.

"Now!" Peregrine yelled.

I stopped breathing.

"Hold him, I'm coming around," Flare yelled. "Away.Tango down." She was laughing into her mic. "I got him."

"Yes!" I shouted. "Good work team."

And somebody started shooting at me. Rude.

They weren't crack shots, but how good do you have to be? The concrete sparked in front of me as bullets ricocheted around the hall. I didn't bother looking where the shots were coming from. I went through the first door I came to. There was another door out the other side. I ran for it. Bullets and concrete exploded behind me.

I didn't even feel it at the time, but later I found a big crease in my helmet I think I picked up from some flying concrete.

I didn't bother opening the door, I just jumped through what was left of the broken glass at the upper half and rolled up.

It surprised the hell out of the guy coming from the other end to trap me.

I reacted just a second faster, jumping off the wall opposite him and landing a hard cross with my boot across his face.

I didn't recognize him, but he was definitely a Headsman. If the crossed axes over a skull patch didn't clue me in, the axe on his belt did.

The other gunmen -- I'm sure if it was more than one -- stopped the indiscriminate shooting.

"Thanks," I told the guy. I should have done something to wreck the gun, but I didn't have time. Instead, I snatched up his gun and started running. Lucky this guy hadn't fired it yet, so it wasn't hot. Something I thought about just after picking it up. Oh, well. If anyone asks, I knew the barrel was cold.

A man stepped out into the hallway fifteen feet ahead of me. He wasn't that big, but athletic. He was covered in tattoos and sporting a big gold earring with some crazy dreads. His eyes glowed in my IR like everyone else's, but his glowed more.

Well, we were in pitch back, so the odds were he couldn't see me.

"You!" He pointed at me.

Ryan Blackwater, beating the odds since 2016.

"You killed my brother!" Glowing Eyes accused me.

Not sure who he was talking about, but he seemed really sure of it. "Who?" I hadn't really done a lot of these grief counselling through combat things, but in retrospect, I'd just implied his brother wasn't important enough to remember.

His eyes flared brighter.

I dropped to the floor. When you're fighting in this line of work, you have no idea what's going to get thrown at you. Sometimes a face of anguished concentration is unfortunate incontinence. But sometimes they're calling forward vast energy for science-defying destruction. You don't know until it happens.

This guy was of the science-defying kind. To be fair, he could have been a little from column A too, but I can't speak to that.

My infrared whited out as whatever he tried to fry me with zipped down the hall.

"He was guarding that rich bitch, and you blew his head off!"

My feet were underneath me and I rolled into another door. It didn't open, or even give a little. Actually, it hurt.

"Oh, big guy with an axe. Sure, I remember him." Not the thing to say, apparently.

I rolled away from the door and he blasted it open. Decent of him.

So good news, the door I was going for was now open. Bad news, it was just an empty supply closet.

"I didn't kill him." It wasn't like I was super sad he was gone, but this is the kind of thing you run into if you go around killing people. They always have someone who is willing to return the favor.

He did not believe me. But it wasn't like I was going to throw Julia under the bus, so there you have it.

The bricks behind me were scored with a white line. Not as intense as the first two, so maybe he was tiring out.

I tossed my last ball bearing.

Either he was too blinded by rage, or couldn't really see

me that well. He didn't see it coming and it doubled him over with a blow to his stomach.

I only had a few seconds to close the twenty feet. It wasn't enough.

He was still curled over in pain but looked up and sent a beam of angry right at me.

I dropped to my knees and kept sliding, bending over as low as I could.

Heat off the death ray warmed my chest as I passed under it. I popped up and delivered an uppercut to his chin. I kept moving, going over him and down the hall.

The shooters from before were looking right at me, but apparently they couldn't see in the dark. Thank you all that is holy.

"Karl, did you get 'em?" one shouted, moving his head as he tried to make out shapes in the dark.

There was a chance that I could just run away down the corridor, but if they started opening up, I didn't think poor Karl would make it.

I ran for them.

One brought up a flashlight.

Damn it! *I tried, Karl.* I jumped off one wall, kicked off the other side of the hall, and did a dive roll to make up the rest of the distance.

They tried to track me, but they couldn't with their flashlight and their guns. They got off a couple of rounds but they were more a danger to each other.

I dropped a kick into the one on the left and landed a punch into the other guy's neck.

It was enough to give them other things to worry about than shooting me or Karl. I followed it up by kicking the right guy's leg out from underneath him and taking an elbow to the left guy's collar bone.

They dropped by the numbers. A job well done for Team Raven.

"Did you leave any for questioning?" Jackal asked. "We still don't know where to go in this compound."

I looked around. "I'm sure they'll be awake in a minute or ten." Alright, a job done okay by Team Raven.

"They came from this way." I pointed.

"Doesn't help me, but let's try it." Jackal, allegedly, couldn't see the direction I was pointing.

I quickly zip-tied them. Might as well try to slow them down, especially the parahuman with the eye beams. Him I dragged into the utility closet. Not sure if that would slow him down or not.

"Look for a radio," Jackal said.

I patted them down for a radio. I found a cell phone.

So they were using cell phones. Lo-tech, but I suppose.

"You think they're getting reception down here?" Jackal asked.

"Not really." Not deeper in the facility, anyway.

"Look for earwig things. I saw them in a movie."

"I can't tell in the dark. Oh, yep." I plucked the receiver out of one of the guy's ears, totally covered in earwax of course. I dropped it.

"Put it in. We could hear their communication."

I stepped on it. "Gross. Besides, I'm not taking off my helmet in the field." That was a great way for your ID to get burned.

"Really, you're too sensitive to take a huge tactical advantage?"

Yes, I sure was. That was icky. "I'm just following protocol." I dropped the phone, too. I have this recurring dream that I'm about to sneak up on some criminal element and my cell phone goes off. At that point I realize I'm also in my underwear.

I started down the hall. Windows let slivers of light from the exterior into this area. I found a stairwell and a light source down below.

Made a quick look around and found the elevator. Maybe I could force it open, but it wouldn't be quiet.

I went down the stairs.

I didn't hear movement, except the steady drip of some liquid. I took a quick look around the corner and then back into cover.

"I found another Headsman," I whispered to Jackal.

"Does he look superpowered?"

"No, he looks dead."

I looked again, slower. I remembered how Flare had described Yaltin. This guy was about the same. "I think Heavy Metal is here."

I stepped around the corner and Heavy Metal dropped on me.

So I was right. I'm getting better at this investigative stuff.

Heavy Metal Ninja was doing that whole suspend yourself from the ceiling thing. I could have done that, waiting until I wandered by.

He had me in a monkey death grip in a second, then did his solidification trick. "Ryan, if you say one word to warn your friends, I will crush you."

And my real recurring nightmare had just happened. My ID was burned.

"I'm not transmitting."

"I know. But who were you talking to?"

Wasn't sure how much he'd heard. It was now or never. I had to strike and strike hard. This was bad, on a scale of magnitude that I couldn't even wrap my head around level of bad.

"Did he just call you Ryan?" Jackal asked.

Like I was saying, a magnitude of magnitude scale of suck.

I had to go now!

I don't care how strong you are, there are still pressure points where you're the weakest. I focused all the strength of my terror on those points.

And I pushed, I pushed hard!

"Are you trying to escape?" Heavy Metal asked.

Oh, suck. "No, just stretching a little. Something I like to do before I completely capitulate."

"Okay, this changes our strategy," Jackal said as one word. "But the good news is you would be dead if he wanted you dead."

"Yep, good news."

"Are you talking to someone?" He sounded a little confused.

"Nope, that's just the capitulation song I like to sing." I put it to music. "I'm so boned, yep that's good news, just not for me."

"I can kill you--"

"Already there, Heavy Metal. Can I call you Heavy Metal?"

He laughed a little. "As good as any name."

"Like Osprey," Jackal said.

"Like Osprey?" I repeated in shock. But if you're not used to the vocal distortion, you might not be able to tell question tone from statement tone.

"I'm impressed. But I haven't used that name in years." He didn't sound impressed, just kind of pissed. He didn't squeeze me to end my life, so he couldn't have been that pissed. "What else have you been able to figure out?"

Should I hit him with the section 5 stuff or just play dumb?

"Tell him everything we figured out," Jackal said.

Oh great, he has my first name, and he can read my thoughts. Can he read my thoughts?

"What are you doing? Tell him already," Jackal said.

"I figured out that Red Knight isn't coming out of retirement, he's just undercover from Section 5."

"And?"

That wasn't enough? That was some of my best stuff. "And the Phoenix doesn't have my secret identity or the parahuman test."

"And?"

"And... Yaltin wasn't Mr. Why." I threw that out there. "The Worm and Quare are different bodies of Wraith but Caesar or Mindraker figured out how to split them. They're split and they each think the other one is dead."

"And?"

"And... that's it. I don't know how you found out my real name."

"Red Knight wasn't unconscious in the van when you saved him. He was able to use that information to put the pieces together," Heavy Metal or Evil Osprey said.

"I'm thinking of you as Evil Osprey now, just for the record."

He laughed. "I like you, Raven. You remind me of Hawk, and it's not just the uniform. He always faced his fears with a joke." He paused and all the points I'd gained for my Hawk resemblance flushed down the toilet. "You should have already figured out that Raptor wasn't the man, wasn't the hero, he pretended to be."

"Oh, yeah. I figured that out, too," I allowed.

"He was a hypocrite. Telling us how to act, what we were fighting for, and it was nothing."

"Well, I found that very disappointing, too." I twirled my finger, but could barely move it. "Let's get to the point where you tell me why I'm not dead."

"Really?" Jackal asked. "What if he doesn't know?"

That would have been good insight to have before I tried to act all cocky and stuff.

"I need your help," Evil Osprey said.

"Let's just put this on fast forward: 'No I will never help your evilness be evil,' then vague yet still clear threats to my family, and I give in because you've got me tied in knots. Just answer me this one question."

"What question?"

"How can I help?" He had me cold, and my friends were still flying around in danger. I was burned, but maybe I could keep Flare and Peregrine out of this.

He laughed again. "I need you to distract them, so I can get the Phoenix when they open the cell it's in."

"Cell?"

"It's in a secret base thing behind some machinery." He tapped his ear. "That man's earwig has been very useful keeping tabs on the enemy.

"Okay, give *him* my note. I want to work with some professionals," Jackal said.

"The Confessor got some information on what to look for. But he didn't have the code. They found a door, but not how to open it. They're drilling through it."

"Then let's do this." I'm all about the team playing.

He let me go, and that felt better.

THIRTY-FIVE

"How are my friends doing?" I asked.

"They were in conflict with three supers on the top two levels." Evil Osprey led me quickly and silently through the corridors. "They're hurt, but I don't know how badly. I appreciate the distraction. They've tied up four parahuman Headsmen."

"I got one." Shout out to Team Raven.

"Good." He nodded. "The body you found was another."

"How many do they have?" Parahumans aren't *that* common.

"I was going to ask you. This is your area isn't it?"

"Too busy digging into my life to research the real problem?" That was stupid. Let's all think about how much I'm screwed.

"I only know your first name. Mr. Bosin has been doing the *digging*." He held up a hand and stopped my movement.

A second later the bobbing of flashlights came into view.

I knew how to hide. Evil O was better. Two Headsmen passed by without any suspicion.

"Here's the plan," Jackal said.

I couldn't tell him where to stick his plans, so he kept talking.

"You have to kill Red Knight. Ditch this asshole, circle back, and end him in a hurry."

The coast was clear from Headsmen, but I still couldn't talk with Evil O right there.

"So what's your plan? I have to say, any plan that involves killing people, I'm out," I told Evil Osprey and Jackal.

"You work for Section 5 now." There was no victory in Evil Osprey's voice, but maybe some shame. "You do as you're told, or Mr. Bosin will hurt the people you care about." He turned to me. "It gets easier, and Mr. Bosin doesn't order the death of innocent people." He paused. "Often."

There was a line about Yaltin there, but I kept my mouth shut. The only thing Yaltin did wrong was come into town to pick up Raptor's mess.

"I won't work for him. I won't become his thug." Did I believe that? If it was some guy I didn't know or my mom, who would I pick? What if that guy was a killer himself? Where does the line get drawn?

"I'm sorry to hear that. I'm sure your family will be sorry to hear that, too." He didn't believe me.

"I won't kill someone to stop him from killing my family." That was not a bargain I could win, but what would Mom think of me if I made that trade?

"I didn't say kill, I said hurt. He won't kill them. His stable of egoists destroy people from the inside."

He'd talked about them before, He'd had the same level of disgust when he was pretending to be anti-Section 5.

"Who does Red... Bosin have of yours?" It was a shot in the dark, but I scored.

His head bowed and his shoulders slumped. "I hope you make better choices than I did. I couldn't see a way out."

"This makes sense," Jackal said. "Bosin has leverage over Osprey here. That's why he's running him on this op. He needs to get the Phoenix without anyone he can't control knowing it exists."

"Makes sense." Wasn't exactly a non sequitur to Osprey's admission, but whatever. I was also trying to have two conversations.

"This is good." Jackal was speaking quickly in his electrically charged way. "New plan. You have got to get your hands on the Phoenix. Whatever it is gave Raptor leverage to keep Bosin out of this town for almost two decades. You get the Phoenix and you muscle him into leaving you alone."

That was a plan I could work with. I didn't know how to set up something like that, but between Jackal and Butterfly we could rig something.

"Ask him if he knows why the Confessor is looking for the Phoenix." Jackal kinda ordered me.

It was a good question, so I asked it.

"We don't know. Until you told Bosin there was another team in the field, we didn't even know about them. It pissed Mr. Bosin off." He seemed happy about that. "I have something I want to show you."

This area of the abandoned factory was a bit of a mess. If I'd had to get out of here I could've done it by retracing my steps, a perk of my power. If I took off my helmet and was in the dark, I could still retrace my steps. But I didn't know which direction was north.

He pointed in the opposite direction from where the two Headsmen guards had walked.

I followed. Good Raven, can I have a biscuit?

I turned a corner and saw what he was directing us to. It was about the size of a piece of paper and would be invisible in the dark, but with standard Guard gear I could see the image painted in some specific type of paint.

"That's Raptor's sigil." I pointed at the hawk in profile with talons extended.

He nodded.

"Is that where he stashed the Phoenix?" Here's hoping the Confessor is at the wrong place.

He shook his head. "I already checked it, but you might find it interesting. I know I did."

I followed him over the edge of some equipment. He climbed down like he was swimming underwater. I suppose he could reduce his density to aid with the descent.

There were enough bits and pieces so that even though I had to climb the old fashioned way, I could do it.

This had to be a place Raptor wanted someone else to find. Why mark it with a raptor even if the odds of someone seeing it were low?

Another raptor image.

Evil Osprey knew what to look for and he rotated a pump cap to reveal a keypad.

I don't want to tell Raptor his job, but if I had a data backup thing that contained a secret dangerous formula and information that could bring down a government agent, this is where I would have stashed it.

A portal opened about three feet in diameter into a tank slash lair. I recognized the floor plan. The same person had developed my nest. There was a work space, cot, shower, and laundry. What the place lacked in work room to effect repairs it more than made up for in guns.

Guns, guns, and oh I almost forgot, guns.

Lining the walls, the weapons given little hooks to suspend them like the world's tiniest gun show. For the other wall, the decorator had gone with more of a tinfoil hat conspiracy wacka-doo vibe. Pictures and newspaper clippings were tagged on the wall with strings connecting them.

Some pictures had red X's over them.

"This is how your mentor spent his off hours," Osprey said.

"Everyone needs a hobby," I murmured. This looked less like Raptor's nest and more like a cabin in the woods for a unabomber.

"What do you see?" Jackal asked.

He could sit and spin.

"Fine, this looks like the last stop on the crazy town express," I admitted.

"This looks like an assassin's lair." Evil Osprey said it like he was vindicated.

"Assassin's lair? How so?" Jackal asked.

"You have no idea what he was using this place for." He could have been a really passionate Rambo cos player, or tested weapons for duck hunting. Not my thing, but I don't want to judge. Or he could have been... an assassin planning his next target.

I looked at a few of the pictures with X's through them. No one I knew. There were articles connected with string but I didn't have time to read them. I needed to get a digital camera thing as part of my gear. If I could get this wall to

Butterfly, she could probably figure out what the hell was going on.

"Your mentor, *our* mentor, was a hypocrite," Evil O spat.

This was just the last piece of the puzzle for me. "I know." My vocal distortion might have made it inaudible. Osprey didn't act like he'd heard me.

"He told us again and again that we had to hold to a high code, but when it meant actually getting things done, he was the biggest vigilante of the bunch." He pointed at the X's. "These are all people that died. Some mysteriously, some with a bullet in the head." He pointed at the wall of rifles.

"You don't know that."

"We both know that!" I was glad he was wearing a mask because I think I would have gotten spittle on that one. "I tried so hard to be a good little hero. I felt like *I* had let *him* down every time I had to kill for Bosin. But he's the one who let me down. He abandoned me."

He had a point, especially about the whole abandoned thing. How could Raptor just let Bosin walk off with one of his apprentices? Was it part of the deal he'd made that kept Section 5 out of town? If Raptor had leverage on Bosin, why didn't he use it to protect Osprey?

"Give me a description, something. What are you guys talking about?" Jackal sounded like a fan boy missing the post credit stinger clip. Well, maybe not *that* anguished.

"What do you want me to say?" I had nothing.

"A description of the room would be good." I could almost see Jackal rubbing his temples.

Not talking to you.

"Nothing. I just want you to understand that Raptor and the rest of them are not worth your loyalty."

"They're all dead men." I could say that as a fact now and not sound like a scared little kid.

"You sound like a scared little kid," Osprey sneered.

I stand corrected.

He started to pace back and forth in what little room there was. "They all died, and we're the pieces they left behind."

Was he pissed that they'd died? Was this his way of handling grief?

"I know a thing or two about assassin's lairs. Give me some coordinates here," Jackal said.

Fine. As a rule, I don't like giving Jackal information. He's too clever and he can put things together six steps ahead of me. I was always nervous about what he would do with the information.

On the other side of the argument, the only thing he'd done with information so far was arrange for a perfectly legal trial and continually save my ass. Let's sign more of me over to the devil. What could it hurt? "Sure this looks like an assassin's lair, with a wall full of snipperish rifles and another wall of news clipping and target research. But we don't know for sure." I totally knew for sure, especially in light of what Julia had told me.

"Was that so hard?" Jackal asked. "And yeah, that totally sounds like an assassin's den. Do you recognize any of the faces?"

I tried to get a better look, but Osprey was standing in between me and the cork board.

"You can't cling to some dream that your hero was a good man." He pointed at one of the faces with the red X.

"No, I can't." That just slipped out. "It was all crap, all of it. Everything he told me, told us! I get it, I know. His little mission was a con. I sacrificed everything for a man who was conning me. What really pisses me off is I don't know why. Why do any of this? The guy was loaded. His wife wanted him out of it. What was the damn point!" What was the damn point of it?

I don't think he'd expected me to convert so easily. It kind of took the wind out of his sails.

"And now, to protect my family, I have to do this for the likes of Bosin. Fine! Let's do it and stop poking through Raptor's crazy crazy." I waved my hand around the room.

Evil Osprey let me pant it out for a second.

I was pissed. I was pissed at him for working for Bosin, I was pissed at Bosin for bringing my family into this, and I was pissed at Raptor for not telling me what I really had to fear.

"I brought these." He picked up one of two briefcases and offered it to me. I hadn't noticed the briefcases before. If I'd been seeing everything in regular light, I think I would have noticed, but in the black and white of the grainy IR, they just blended into the background.

I took it. It was heavier than I'd thought it would be. "What is it?"

From a little pouch at his belt he handed me an egg timer.

"Oh."

The egg timer had about fifteen minutes left.

"You'll need to place your case where they're drilling, get the Phoenix, and get out."

"I'm not going to kill anyone," I told him. Even if it meant my family was exposed. I wasn't going to be Bosin's hitman.

"Then figure out a way to get everyone out. I don't care. Bosin wants the Confessor alive just long enough to know where he heard about the Phoenix. No one else matters one way or the other."

"Where is the Confessor then?" If I had fifteen minutes to find him, I'd need a little bit of a pointer.

"Climb back up to the walkway and follow it until you come to a main hall. Take a right and follow it until you hear drilling." Osprey picked up the other briefcase.

"What are you doing with that?" How many people did he want to blow up? How many people were left to blow up?

"The same thing you're doing. Fulfilling my debt to Mr. Bosin."

I was going to ask him more questions -- does the evil army have dental? -- but he fluidly ducked out the aperture and dropped.

I looked over the edge and saw him fall in a controlled slow motion sixty feet to the machine shop floor, and dart off.

"Well, Raven, those competing malevolent organization minions aren't going to blow themselves up." I picked up the briefcase.

I retraced my climb and ran down the catwalk we'd used to get to Raptor's little psycho dream house.

"What are you going to do with the bomb?" Jackal asked.

"I don't know," I panted. I was running as fast as I dared. Each footfall was a painful loud echo in the dead building. "First, I'll find the Confessor, then I'll figure out what to do with the bomb."

"That's probably backwards. Stash the bomb. There's got to be some place around here. This is a machine factory."

"Probably." I kept running until I reached the first

hallway. "But what will Bosin do to... my family if I don't follow orders my first time out?"

Jackal didn't say anything.

I reached the main hallway. Now my footfalls were on concrete, a hundred times quieter then the rusty iron, but might as well have been a siren in the deadly silent hallways.

I think I ran a mile, maybe seven hundred and thirty-five, or something in between. I was starting to panic.

Was the drilling finished? Did the Confessor have the Phoenix already? Did I run past them?

I stopped to listen and got my breath back.

I heard something, footfalls on concrete running my way.

I was in a long corridor of concrete walls and floor. I tried the nearest door, but it was locked. I could break it, but they would hear that for sure.

The bouncing shadows of a flashlight preceded around the corner.

Well, if Evil Osprey could do it.

I kicked off one wall, then the other wall and grabbed some overhead pipes. I lodged myself as tight to the ceiling as I could.

The Headsmen, both with big automatic rifles, didn't break their stride and passed directly under me. Wherever they were going, it seemed important.

Should I follow, assuming they were running to the Confessor? Or were they running away from the Confessor to check on people who had not checked in?

Nothing like a 50/50 shot to determine your life's outcome. I backtracked their path. Hopefully I would find some sounds of "drilling" soon.

I did.

It was a lot quieter than I'd thought it would be. They were using a metal drill through concrete and iron machinery. I'd figured I would hear it for miles, but I was almost on top of them before I heard it.

The drill looked fancy, so maybe it was for quiet work.

The Confessor was there. He looked nervous as hell, walking back and forth.

This far down in iron and concrete he probably felt the lack of connection with his sentries.

There was a guy working the drill, not the normal Headsmen model. He was short and thin. He also had special gear on so I wasn't sure if he was covered in tattoos and had the patch. He might have been hired help to work the drill.

Arc was there, a pillar of calm compared to the pacing Confessor. Another super -- the scales and seven feet tall thing gave it away -- was sporting the gang collars. He was leaning up against the wall and chewing on a dead cigar. That guy didn't look familiar.

The other two had handguns and muscles. They could have been vanilla or chocolate. No way to tell until the fighting started.

I looked at my egg timer.

Ten minutes.

What was I supposed to do now?

THIRTY-SIX

Whatwas I supposed to do now? I didn't know if they would be through the door in ten minutes. That would not give me a lot of time to get rid of this bomb and save five guys who wanted to kill me.

Working for the bad guys sucked.

I tried to scope out the area and look for any place I could sneak and get closer. I still had to grab this Phoenix thing on my way out. Hopefully, it was something small and easy to carry, but I also thought of an old massive server or something. There were too many unknowns for ten minutes.

Scratch that, nine minutes.

"I'm open to any ideas," I whispered to Jackal after I described the scene.

"You can't act until they get the door open." Jackal didn't seem to like that idea any better than me. "The code pad might respond to one of your codes, but it's probably broken beyond use right now, anyway."

I looked a little harder, and sure enough, the guts of some kind of keypad had been ripped apart by the drill guy.

Now I had seven minutes to do whatever I wanted.

I was chattering with adrenaline. "If this is the main event, where the hell is Osprey?" I murmured.

"He probably found something better to do than stand around holding a ticking bomb," Jackal pointed out.

Working for the bad guys really sucked.

The thin whine of the drill stopped.

The sudden silence was deafening.

"Well?" The Confessor ran up to Drill Guy. He seemed as stressed as I was.

"That should do it." He stepped back and pulled his equipment with him.

The Confessor motioned to the reptile parahuman, but was too intent to notice that Scales did not move. Instead, he looked at Arc. Arc nodded. Then Scales pushed himself off the wall and walked to the door.

Six minutes! Come on Scales, a sense of urgency, please.

He tried forcing the door. Wasn't as easy as he'd thought it would be, so he positioned his grip and tried again with a grunt. The door rolled back, giving a crack wide enough for the Confessor to enter.

I told Jackal what I was seeing.

"Wait for the Confessor to come out," Jackal warned. "Then move like a bullet."

Like a bullet.

Four minutes.

"Your only hope is to get these guys to follow you," Jackal continued. "If they don't, the explosion will kill them."

"I was just going to yell *BOMB*." I wasn't going to be subtle.

"I like where your head is at," Jackal agreed.

The Confessor came through the door. Now he was carrying a big bulky metal case. It looked like something straight out of an old spy movie.

"Get it?" Arc asked. He didn't seem to care one way or the other.

"Yes." The Confessor turned the case to show a faded image of a bird flying out of flames and a military-looking Top Secret. "There are other files in there. We should--"

For being able to read minds, he could not read a room.

Scales removed his axe from its holster and pulled back.

"Confessor, behind you!" I yelled.

The Confessor actually looked behind him.

I wouldn't have. That sounded like the cheapest trick in the book. I would have looked at the strange mechanical voice talking. But the Confessor actually looked behind him and it saved his life. I mean, it saved his life for now.

He was still in a room with four guys willing and able to kill him. Well, I don't know about Drill Guy. He seemed legit. And if the Headsmen didn't get him, the bomb that would go off in three minutes would probably do the trick.

So he was still screwed, but now I was, too. Yay?

The Confessor reached out his hand and pressed it on Scales' exposed stomach.

Scales wanted everyone to know how much of a badass he was and only wore a sleeveless jean jacket.

The electric white light flashed between the Confessor's hand and Scales.

Scales convulsed and threw the axe he was holding at Arc.

Not well. Even if it had hit Arc, it probably wouldn't have hurt him much, but it forced him to move. He stumbled close to me.

I shot out like a bullet and did considerably more damage to Arc than the axe would have.

I landed on his head, changed my momentum and flipped him over, delivering a crack to the base of his skull. "Bomb!" I yelled as I tossed the briefcase through the door.

Because that would have been cool, sliding the briefcase through the door just in the nick of time.

But a briefcase is not a good throwing thing, and Arc buckled under me. So the briefcase bounced off the edge of the new door and skidded underneath some pipes and machinery-looking stuff.

"Come on!" I yelled.

Arc bucked again and got out from my hold. Not a huge accomplishment because I was letting go. I had a bomb to get where it was supposed to be.

"Shoot him! Shoot them both!" Arc yelled to the two thugs. They were lining up their weapons, but didn't want to fire and risk hitting Arc.

So no, I couldn't just go get the explosive device. I had an errand first.

I rolled, keeping as close to Arc as I could. It worked, they didn't shoot at me. And it didn't work because Arc lashed out with his hand and blue electricity lanced around my body.

I twitched, my momentum stalled, but I had enough to carry me away from Arc's reach.

So I was free, hurray! And now a sitting duck for Thug 1 and Thug 2, boo.

At this point Scales screamed and stomped down on Arc, hard.

The Confessor had worked his way behind Scales and had both hands on his back. The white light was working overtime. Scales was trying to fight it, but the Confessor was controlling him like a puppet.

"Why are you betraying me?" the Confessor asked.

Thug 1 and Thug 2 were distracted. Can't say I blame them. I was distracted. Scales via the Confessor, or was it the other way around, had just messed Arc up.

"Midas wants the Phoenix!" Scales shouted.

"You are supposed to work for me!" The Confessor didn't ask a question, so Scales' lips were shut.

Oh yeah, two gunmen, then bomb.

"Seriously, it's a bomb!" Or at least I had it on good authority.

I got my feet underneath me and leapt. Thug 1 and Thug 2 were standing close enough to both take a boot to the face, and down they went.

Of course now I had those to get out of the blast radius, too.

I looked for Drill Guy, and I would have found him, too, maybe in Ohio. That guy was gone.

Smart Drill Guy, clever Drill Guy.

I wouldn't waste time being careful around Scales/Confessor. I dived for the briefcase and felt around where I'd seen it go under.

"What were you going to do to me?" the Confessor said.

"Midas wanted you dead," Scales answered. "He doesn't want competition as he takes over Darhaven."

I got the tips of my fingers around the bomb and dragged it out.

"You have less than a minute." Jackal had started his own timer, I guess.

"Confessor, can you get Scales to close the door?" I slid the briefcase across the floor. This time I made a goal.

The Confessor saw the bomb skid past.

He made Scales slam the door shut.

Boom!

The explosion went out the back, probably through air vents or something, but still managed to shake the room and knock us all off our feet.

So, not a big deal.

Except the Confessor was no longer touching Scales.

That turned out to be a big deal.

Scales was angry, understandably so, but he had tried to kill the Confessor, so it wasn't like he didn't have it coming. Not that I condone mind control or any kind of compulsion. I'm just saying Scales wasn't innocent as the driven snow here, either.

I launched myself with my patent-pending trademark two boots fly kick right at the guy's nuts.

I've fought the solid muscle types before. You can't be civil, you just can't be.

Now Scales was angrier, and bent over a little. He had one hand over his manhood and swung at me with the other.

I rolled out from under his swing and kiped up.

This situation had come up more times than you would think. Normally when I'm severely outclassed by someone who wants to kill me, I fight until we can all agree that it's useless, then I dodge, and eventually I get hit and dropped like someone else's laundry.

I was going to go a different direction here.

I looked for the Phoenix.

The Confessor had dropped it so he could hit Scales with both hands. It was now by the discarded drill in the center of the floor.

I scooped it up and ran for the same door Drill Guy had

used. I didn't know what was that way, but Drill Guy seemed to know what he was about.

And, whamo! I got hit with a thousand cattle prods to my heel.

Somehow the Confessor had made a mad scramble and connected with my foot.

I skidded out, colliding with the exposed brick wall.

Scales stood, completely recovered from my ball shot. Bummer. It wasn't like the mass of scales and teeth gave a ton of emotional range, but now he looked pissed. He wanted to literally tear us apart.

I tried to get up, but my leg was not cooperating.

The Confessor ran by me, picked up the Phoenix, and kept running.

That's what I got for saving his life.

Scales picked me off the floor and tossed me up. The only thing preventing my brains from splattering on the ceiling was my helmet.

Before I could scream, or even register the impact, Scales out screamed me. With both hands on my neck, he picked me up and squeezed.

I got to say, that stung a lot. I mean a lot a lot.

My left leg was still unresponsive, but I kicked like crazy with my right and tried to deliver a strike with my arms. But I couldn't get any leverage.

I couldn't breathe.

The Confessor had apparently had a change of heart, because he'd circled back around and came up behind Scales. He palmed Scales' head and fired off the brightest flash of light I'd ever seen him give.

Scales dropped in a heap, with me at the bottom of said heap.

Still better than being crushed... I guess.

Before I could get out from under the dead and stinky weight that was Scales, the Confessor made his way around to me and laid a hand on my chest.

Oh boy, now I looked fondly at just being savagely crushed. I mean, those were the good old days. You never appreciate the crazed murderous savage monsters when you have them.

I could have been out for days or minutes, but when I regained consciousness, it was to Jackal screaming in my ear. Or my mind, maybe. "Get up! Raven! Get up!"

I was still under Scales, my left leg was still unresponsive, but that was now the best feeling part of me.

The Confessor was still there, too, yanking on my glove.

"What?" I got right down to business.

"He's trying to get skin-on-skin contact. If he does, you'll be completely exposed!" Jackal yelled.

That sounded bad. Somebody should do something about that before that poor Raven guy got exposed.

Hey! I'm that Raven guy!

I hit him. I didn't have leverage, but I still connected with his face and made him backpedal.

I extracted myself from Scales, rolled away from the Confessor, and stood up. It was like pins and needles in my soul, but I was shaking off the effects.

He came at me again, but I was able to dodge his hands and got close enough to head butt him.

"Who do you work for?" The Confessor was probably going to compel me to answer that question if he'd gotten my glove off.

"It's complicated." I saw the case with the Phoenix and moved for it, but the Confessor got in my way.

"Raven, you have got to get out of there. The patrolling Headsmen must have heard the explosion. They'll be returning to check it out." Jackal, reminding me about the explosion that had happened forever and a half ago.

"I need that," I told the Confessor.

"So do I."

I believed him, there was a lot of desperation in that voice.

"How did you find out about this?" He twitched his head toward the box.

"What is it?" I asked.

"I don't know." He seemed a little confused. "Don't you?"

And I dropped him with a jab to the face. He never saw it coming.

He was fast but not that good of a fighter. I picked up the case and started running.

THIRTY-SEVEN

"What do I do with this thing now?" I asked Jackal. I had nothing. I had a vague sense I could use it to get Bosin off my back, but how? What if it was just the formula, whatever that was? I might have destroyed all the blackmail stuff.

There was a depressing thought.

"You need to get it to Butterfly," Jackal said. "She's the only one that might make it useful."

Good point, but again, how? She still thought Red Knight was one of the good guys.

"Good work, Raven. I'll take that." Osprey stepped out of the shadows and slammed me against concrete.

Working for the bad guys sucks!

I twisted, but he had me in his iron grip.

"Where the hell were you?" I was stalling and stalling badly.

"You can *not* let him take that," Jackal warned.

Osprey's hand moved glacially slow as he took the case's handle. "I was busy."

"Hey, busy. That makes sense, sure." Stalling really badly.

He pulled it out of my hands, still slowly, but I had nothing.

"You detonated the bomb in the vault?" Even his voice was slower.

"Yes. I didn't have a choice or anywhere else to put the bomb." Not happy.

"Control." He wasn't talking to me. I bet Bosin was on the other line. "I have the Phoenix, and the blackmail information is destroyed."

So that's what was in the vault. I'd known it. Even as I'd dropped the bomb, I known. I just hadn't seen any other options in the time I had. Being powerless can feel pretty powerless.

"He wants you to stay here," Osprey told me. "We'll be in touch. And welcome to Section 5." He clicked off the radio. "Sorry, Ryan. He has leverage over me, too. I don't make my own choices. You'll get used to it. And sometimes we do some good."

He let me down.

"Don't hit him!" Jackal said.

I wasn't going to hit him. I wasn't.

"Get him talking," Jackal said. "We are out of plays here. You need to get more information."

"If he has leverage over you, why did you just make me blow up enough leverage to get Bosin off both our backs?" I thought that was a very good question.

"I don't have Raptor's resources and contacts, and neither do you. He would hurt my family before I figured out how to use it. I've tried before. It taught me a valuable lesson."

"What lesson?"

He was still moving slowly, still solidified beyond my ability to hurt him.

"That I work for Bosin now. You'll learn that lesson, too. It'll be awful, but it won't be the worst thing that could happen." He started walking away.

I wasn't sure If I should follow.

"What's worse than being someone's puppet?"

"Seeing your family die." Didn't even pause. "Then he'll have you declared an enemy of the state and the SSA will hunt you down." He stopped. "I've seen him do it to other operatives that tried to get free of him." He started walking again. "This is the only time you'll see Bosin in the field, not surrounded by his parahuman guards. He's never been this desperate. It made him dangerous. Now he's victorious. My family will live."

"And there walks your future." Jackal swore. "Enough kid, you can't do this to yourself. You heard him, this is your only shot. You need to kill this Bosin guy and kill him now! Once he gets back into Section 5, secure that Raptor's blackmail is gone, he'll be one hundred times worse than he is now."

I sat.

"Raven, if you ever took any of my advice, you have got to take *this* advice. You have got to go and kill him. Go back to that gun room. I can talk you through it."

I sat.

"This is going to be a moment you'll regret for the rest of your life. You think Red Knight isn't going to make you a killer? You ask Osprey if he'd had this chance before it all started, what would he have done? All the good that you're capable of will be up in smoke and twisted. Just take this one justifiable action and you'll be free."

I sat.

In a few minutes I'd take out the paper Jackal had sent and rip it up. I just couldn't do it right then. "I lost," I told him. "I tried my best, and I lost. Bosin was pulling my strings from the start. At least now I know it." Was there ever a move? Could I have done something at some point to get out from under?

My heads up display informed me a text was coming in from my mom. One good thing about life and death conflicts, it lets you forget about all the domestic stuff. Now the domestic stuff had to land on me, too. Universe bajillion, Raven zero.

I didn't stop it, so the text came through: *Raven, this is RK. Your associates are interfering with my operative's exit. Stop them.*

"He has my mother," I said.

"What? Why do you think that?" Jackal asked.

I told him about the text message.

"No, he cloned your mother's phone. Still bad, but it's an object lesson. And the type of thing you have to look forward to as a disposable operative for Section 5." Jackal would not give up.

Bosin might not physically have my mom, but this proved he had more than just my first name, if there was any doubt.

I'm not a killer. I'm not even sure I could kill him. Given a week to practice, I bet I could use one of those sniper rifles with the needed accuracy. But not now, this second. I learn fast but I still need to learn. And It wouldn't change the fact that I couldn't pull the trigger. "I'm not a killer," I whispered.

"You think Osprey was his first day at Section 5 summer camp?" Jackal said.

I got up. "Enough. I have to go fight my friends." I

started walking down the hall. "Well, a friend and an associate."

It didn't take me long to find where Flare and Peregrine had Osprey pinned down. This building was two floors higher than the east wing of the same factory.

They'd forced Osprey to become solid to the point of immobility, as Flare streaked down and launched beam attacks. After she flew past then Peregrine would start the pressure with his three-dimensional kung fu.

Osprey could desolidify to the point where he could fight Peregrine, but then he had to solidify quickly to avoid getting blown to hell by a blast from Flare.

This was a kickass level of teamwork. If they were patient, and not unlucky, they could wear him down. It had to take a lot of energy to become that solid.

And they would have gotten away with it, too, if it wasn't for their team member.

"You can help them. Get the Phoenix away from him and then you have leverage," Jackal told me.

"I blew up all the blackmail stuff. You think I won't hand over the case to save my mom?" Or my half-sister, for that matter.

"Then drop Flare." Jackal's voice was as defeated as I felt.

I had already come to that conclusion. I'd sparred enough with Peregrine to know one-on-one Osprey could take him. It wouldn't be automatic, Peregrine had game. But Osprey was the better fighter, with a power that could be pretty deadly and make him impervious to Peregrine's attack. The only thing keeping Osprey from escaping was Flare.

She went in for another shot, and I could hear them over the common channel now.

"Up!" Flare yelled.

Peregrine zipped up, just missing a green ray that connected with Osprey. Osprey used his body to protect the Phoenix, but he bounced off the roof and collided with a big air conditioner unit.

He got up right away, but he was teetering.

"It's working." Peregrine resumed his onslaught.

Osprey was actually feeling some impacts.

I had to time this just right.

Osprey couldn't be the only one running out of juice. Flare's defensive aura was fading in and out. She landed with a stutter step and turned toward Osprey.

I knew this move. She was going to hit him with everything she had and finally drop him.

I leapt, tucked in tight and spun three times, slamming my feet into her back as she fired.

The impact sent the beam wide.

She staggered under the force of the blow and the sudden draining of power.

And the worst moment of my life so far. I ducked under her weak swing and delivered a blow under her armpit, swept her leg, and delivered a blow to the back of her neck.

I gave a two count then jumped and kicked in Peregrine's direction. He was a better fighter than me unless I got him mad. Then he was predictable. I knew he was going to aim at my center of mass, so I made sure my heel was aimed at where my chest was, but a little off to the left.

I caught him right in the shoulder and used his own momentum to deliver my blow.

I was ready for the impact and rolled as Peregrine dropped into part of the air conditioning mechanism.

I closed the distance and wrapped him in a hold before he had a second to get his bearings.

I looked over at Osprey. He gave me a two fingered wave -- dick -- and hopped off the building. More impressive if you realize he needed to arc about thirty feet in the air to clear the east wing and land on the ground out of view.

"Raven! You bastard. What are you doing?" Peregrine started yelling.

"What is going on?" Butterfly demanded.

So nice to be part of the group again.

"He betrayed us! He hit Flare!" I guess that was a bigger deal to him than completely owning him.

"Could it be mind control? We know the Confessor was an egoist," Butterfly said.

"It's not mind control, it's good old-fashioned blackmail. Or extortion," I said. "I'm burnt guys. They got my name, my family, everything."

Peregrine stopped struggling. I'm sure he was wondering if I'd given him up. "The Confessor?"

"No, Red Knight. Bosin is with Section 5. Hell he *is* Section 5."

"Where's Butterfly?" Jackal asked. "Does Bosin know where she is?"

That was a point. "Butterfly, abandon Alpha Base."

She didn't respond. Was I too late?

Her reply came through "Abandoning Alpha location. Ballista and I are falling back to Gamma Charlie."

Good, she was a step ahead of us. And I turned off my group line. If my new boss wanted to talk to me, he could just text me.

"What's going on?" Flare was groggy, but she had her glowing hand pointed right at me.

I let Peregrine go. I didn't care if she shot me or not.

"I don't believe you," Peregrine said. "Why would Red Knight do this? The man's a legend."

I shrugged and made no motion to move. "Maybe they'll cover that in the Section 5 orientation. I guess that's my career path."

"I have to hear his side of it," Peregrine said.

"You moron, this is all your fault!" I yelled at him.

"You got burned."

"Because you brought Red Knight into our group. You couldn't just leave it alone. You couldn't just retire." I stood up and closed the distance. "You still wanted to play hero."

"I wanted to be a Guard! I wanted the Guard to survive," he shot back. "That's all I ever wanted!"

"No! You wanted to avenge Hawk, you wanted to be a big bad superhero like your brother!" In retrospect, saying that was a mistake.

"Brother?" Flare asked.

"Brother?" Jackal asked.

"What do you know about it? You never cared about anything!" If Peregrine had registered I'd ripped some of his cover, he didn't show it.

"I wanted to be a hero for my brother, I wanted to be a hero for Raptor!" he screamed.

"Well you can't! They're dead." I ducked the swing I knew was coming. If I'd had two more seconds to think I wouldn't have said it. If I'd been given one more second, I wouldn't have ducked. "You can't be a hero for Raptor. He wasn't the man we thought he was. He was just another thug."

"Liar!" This time it was a lot harder to block his strikes, but he was furious, so not fighting his best.

"He killed people, and he made deals with the biggest slime in this town." I trapped both his arms. "He was a bigger part of this town's corruption than Jackal!"

I used Jackal's name because I knew it would drive Peregrine crazy.

"Well that hurt," Jackal said.

"No!" He broke my hold, started chops to my head, then went airborne.

I dropped a double front kick into his stomach before he could get off the ground. Then wrapped him up in a hold and slammed him to the ground. "You can't be a hero for Raptor, you can't be a hero for your brother. You can only do this for yourself. That's it. That's the only reason."

He struggled for a little while longer, then stopped.

"That was inspiring," Jackal pointed out. "That whole be a hero for yourself thing. You believe that?"

Yeah, I guess I did.

"You're burnt, but we aren't," Flare said. "I don't want Red Knight to get the Phoenix."

"It doesn't have your IDs in it."

"Good." She didn't miss a beat. "But Raptor said it was too dangerous. So I'm still going to stop him."

"You tried. That case took one of your blasts and didn't even get a scratch," Peregrine said.

"Then I will try harder."

"I can't," I told her.

"I'm not asking you to." She leveled her hand and shot me.

THIRTY-EIGHT

"Come on, Raven. You have got to wake up!"

Jackal again.

"How long?" I finally figured out how to put those words together.

"I'm getting really sick of this." Jackal sounded a little relieved.

"You are?" I felt my uniform's chest. The plates had melted a little, but no holes. The damage would be a bugger repairing if I still had to do that kind of thing. Maybe Section 5 would have minions to handle it for me. "Where is everyone?"

"If you're out, I'm deaf and blind," Jackal said. "If they don't know where Osprey went, they would head to the van."

"To the van then." It took me two attempts, but I got up. "I can't believe she shot me."

"That one surprised me, too."

Whatever. I got my bearings and started toward the van. it was good to move and shake off the effects of Flare's jolt.

"Of course, what are you going to do once you get there?" Jackal asked.

"Make sure my friends don't get hurt."

"Like the time you just hurt them?" Jackal pointed out.

I didn't answer.

"An example... taken at random."

I went up the wall, pulling myself from window ledge to window ledge, then the rest of the way up by a drain pipe, and a quick run across the roof. Things had progressed while I'd been away.

Maybe they'd followed Osprey or maybe they'd gone for the van. Either way, both roads took them to the same place. Osprey was with Red Knight.

Their mistake was thinking they could do anything about it.

Osprey had Peregrine with one arm around his chest, completely pinned in his dense solid state.

Flare was bound to an x of red glowing wood with red glowing chains.

The Phoenix was at Bosin's feet.

Osprey noticed me and said something.

"Come down and join us, Raven," Red Knight bellowed.

"Do I have another play here?" I asked Jackal.

Nothing.

"Jackal?"

"No, I'm thinking. But no," Jackal said. "We don't have another play."

Nice of him to use the "We" and not "You," but we both knew I was in this alone. I got down as fast as I could.

"We don't have much time," Red Knight said. "The Headsmen are regrouping and will find us soon."

Headsmen, right. I'd almost forgotten about them.

"Okay." He had us. So why wasn't he just killing us?

"I want to offer you all jobs," Red Knight started. "I mean, you're rough around the edges, but you have the makings of a quality team. I could use you."

"I thought I already worked for you," I said.

There was something different about Red Knight. His voice was deeper and his shoulders were straighter. He was still in the wheelchair, so I guess he actually didn't have the use of his legs. "Oh sure, I could coerce you. But I want to give you an offer. Like I did with Osprey here," Red Knight said.

Osprey turned his head, but didn't say anything.

"I hired him away from Raptor with one simple offer." I didn't think he was going to tell us, but he did. "I told him he could kill Shadow Hawk with his own hands."

That wasn't the story Osprey had told me, at least not the whole story. "Well, that still hasn't happened," I said. "Silhouette's in an SSA facility." I'd made sure of that when I'd beaten the crap out of him after Butterfly had turned off his powers.

"No, he was killed trying to escape." Osprey's voice was slow.

I see. I was complicit in a murder. One more way Bosin had played me.

"And the world was made that much better for it," Red Knight said. "Now, what can I offer you? Peregrine? Is there some way you would like to make the world better? I can hear it in your voice."

"Uh-oh," Jackal said.

"Some criminal that deserves more than the catch and release crap that Raptor made you play by?" Red Knight asked.

I couldn't see Peregrine's face of course, so I don't know how big a temptation it was. He didn't say anything.

"Or you Flare? Anything I can do for you?"

"Go to hell?" she spat.

"How about an actual opportunity to do what you set out to do. Be heroes. Without Raptor you need funding and resources. I can do that. You can start making this city safe again. You'll have teams of investigators, training, more team members, a salary. You can do this full time and actually be doing something legal."

"And all we would need to do is sell our souls to you," I said.

"Please, I don't ask for your souls. That was Raptor's thing. I want to make you a team that doesn't need to be beholden to the likes of Caesar or Midas to operate. It's time the criminal parahumans learn what it means to use their powers. Raptor lied to you. He wasn't what he pretended to be."

"No, he wasn't," I agreed. "He was just a guy trying to do the right thing for the most people. I don't think he got it right." I didn't. What was he thinking, becoming a slave to Caesar? "But I don't care."

"No?" Red Knight smiled.

"No. Because I'm not a hero for Raptor. I'm a hero for me." I ran and landed both boots into Red Knight's face, shattering his hold on Flare, and she finished him off.

Or at least that would have been cool.

I jumped sure enough.

Red Knight held up his hand and a red glowing ball and chain appeared around my ankle and pulled me down. I did a complete face plant into the concrete.

At that same moment, I heard a scream, more of rage than fear.

The fear was mine. I recognized Scales.

"And I think that's my cue." A small red forklift materialised and carted the Phoenix into the van. Like a cartoon, its wheels extended at the door and it set the case on the passenger side. At the same time, a red chain wrapped itself around Peregrine and lowered him to the ground.

"Peregrine, Flare, the deal will be on the table for one week." He held up a warning finger. "Then I stop playing nice." He dropped his hand. "Evidence will be found that links the Guard to the explosions at Bio-Globe and the death of poor Mr. Yaltin. Soon everyone will realize the Guard are part of the Parahuman First movement." His red light circled his legs, and he stood. "As for you, Raven, your next orders will be placed in your family's cookie jar in three days. I have a few more things I would like blown up." He clapped his hands together. "Good talk." He nodded to Osprey. "Return to the fall back location."

Osprey nodded.

Bosin folded up his wheelchair. "I hope the Headsmen don't kill you." He slid it in the side cargo door. Using his powers didn't seem to wind him like before. "This was fun." He got behind the wheel. "It's been so long since I've been out in the field. Good to see I still have it." He started up the van.

I wanted to hit him. I wanted to wipe that smug grin right off his face. Even though I could never hope to beat Red Knight at his full power, I still would have tried. I managed to stand, but the ball and chain was still around my ankle.

He drove away.

"So that's it? You wanted to kill Silhouette? That's why Raptor didn't free you? You *wanted* in?" I yelled at Osprey.

"I did." He nodded. "But once in, I found it hard to get out."

"Well, it didn't seem like you were trying that hard!"

"I told you, this is the first time I've seen him in the field. He's always heavily protected. I couldn't free myself."

"Well, he wasn't protected now!"

He pointed at my team with a wave. "But still powerful. I needed it to be the perfect time. With the perfect distraction."

"Did he just use past tense?" Jackal asked.

His hand went into his pocket and back out. He flipped me something.

I caught an egg timer.

"While you were getting the Phoenix," he said, "I was busy."

Ding.

Kaboom!

It was far enough away that I wasn't knocked down by the blast, but I felt the wave of heat and dust.

Red Knight's objects vanished at the moment of the explosion.

"He was the only one with your name, Raven. You're free. Keep out of my way." He gave me another two fingered wave and did one of his super jumps into darkness.

THIRTY-NINE

For those keeping track at home, I owed Jackal a favor. I dug up a bag of money under a tree in a park. Ironically, it was the closest I'd ever gotten to getting busted by the police in my life. I guess the city takes its parks pretty seriously.

Just so you know, I didn't drop a duffel bag of large bills to just anyone. Before I even dug up the package I did my research. She was a mother of two, barely getting by. The kids' dad died five years ago in a gang-related shooting, with no convictions or any police action whatsoever reported.

Something that hit a little home with Mindy. My sister's case was just as thoroughly prosecuted.

I snuck in during the middle of the night and left the bag on the kitchen counter. Jackal didn't even want a note. He wasn't sure she would take the money if she thought it came from him.

I'm still crashing at my nest. I haven't had the conversation with my dad. He had to go back upstate to finalize the last stuff with the move. I'm going to need money. Jackal offered, and yuck. Butterfly has helped me out with some walking around cash, so I'm not going to starve yet.

So that all took me three days. Right after dropping the money off, I headed here, to where this should have started. The Book Room in the crappy warehouse. It took me the rest of the day to actually find the right book, so my mind was fuzzy decoding the letter. If the letter said something like "don't trust Red Knight" I was going to flip a nut.

Like I said, my mind was fuzzy. Normally I kind of know what the letter is saying as I decode it. This time it was all I could do to decode one word at a time, so when I finished I read it again from the start.

Raven,

If you're reading this, then I'm dead.

Not really current events. I know it had only been two weeks, but it seemed like so long ago.

There is a traitor in the Guard, but I do not know who.

Again, great info a week ago, chief. It was Clockwork.

I have traced the betrayal since before you and Ballista joined, so I can only trust you with this.

Was this note written before or after you decided to fire me?

There is a threat facing this city that will break it and send shockwaves through the world. You must get this message to the one person who can stop them. Warn Caesar the Legacy has returned and his organization is infected.

I read that line about six or seven times, asking a vulgar question each time.

Protect this city, Raven. Deliver this message! Raptor.

Well, huh?

FORTY

Linda jolted awake. Something was wrong. She tried to keep her breathing slow, listening. Was it just a dream?

She almost rolled over and went back to sleep. But no, she wouldn't find sleep if she wasn't sure. And besides, the last couple of days she'd had this feeling of being watched. She might just be paranoid, but as her old boss used to tell her, it's all paranoia until they're trying to kill you.

She silently slid out of bed, the floor cold on her feet as soon as she got off the rug. The kids were still asleep.

They had bunk beds, but Oliver was sleeping beside Allen with a book under both their heads. Drool now stained the page.

She gingerly lifted the library book about a talking boat out from underneath Oliver's head. He rolled over and smacked his lips.

Allen would never remember his father, even though he was his spitting image. Oliver looked like an even blend of the two of them, except when he was asleep. His father really showed through then.

She smiled.

She closed the door slowly and quietly, although she could have slammed it and not woken up either child. Once out, they were out.

She almost went back to bed, the cold chill of fear ebbing. But the apartment was small and a quick walk through would just take a second.

She didn't bother turning the lights on in the kitchen. She'd already spotted something that made her breath catch.

A black duffle bag sat in the center of the small kitchen table.

She looked at it from every angle, not daring to turn on the light until she was sure no wires connected the bag to her light switch.

It was clean.

Not the bag. The bag looked like it had spent twenty years underground.

She unzipped it.

Stacks of twenties in plastic wrap looked back at her.

She pulled the packs of money out, about ten pounds worth, so around one hundred grand.

She set the money aside and started feeling inside the bag. There had to be more. She felt a lump sewn into the lining.

She retrieved a knife and made a small cut. The lump was wedged in the liner but she worked it out and held it up to the light. In her hand was a small carved statue of an Egyptian god.

"Jackal."

A glow sprang around the idol. "Pixel, it's been too long."

Linda smiled. No one had called her that in ages. "It's good to hear your voice, boss. I thought you were done."

"We'll have time to catch up later. Let's get to business," he said, as he always did when he had work to do.

FORTY-ONE

The freak walked in. Oh, how Malice hated dealing with freaks. Especially this kind of freak. The mind was their domain, and the idea that this freak could enter his kingdom unasked, and without the work needed being done, was disgusting. An affront to his years of study.

This freak wore his ridiculous red robes, a mockery of something religious. Malice didn't much like priests either, but still he hated freaks more. None of that touched his face.

With a wide smile, he turned to the freak. "Confessor, you look--" The Confessor did not look well. Malice changed his tactic. "Awful. What happened?" He stood and slid a chair over.

The Confessor looked at the chair, then at Malice. He refused the chair with a shake of his head.

Malice took his seat again, holding his hands up to show no offense had been taken. "Can I get you something to drink?" The freak did not look well, like he had just gotten the hell kicked out of him.

The case he was carrying looked heavy. There was no

desk or table in the room. The Confessor compromised and set the case on the chair Malice had just offered him.

The logo caught Malice's eye. "Is that IT." Malice steepled his fingers together, lightly tapping them in excitement.

The Confessor didn't answer right away. "I don't know. I don't know if it survived. It was in an explosion."

Malice did a little hop in his chair, making the ancient wood creek. "Oh, my. How exciting." His fingers fluttered together. "This must be quite the experience for you."

The Confessor was silent behind his hood.

"If the case opens, and it is intact, you gain sizable power and money. If it is useless, it will be the last thing you ever see." Malice couldn't help but be excited. He gave a little clap with just his finger tips. "I could arrange a fantastic meal. It could be your celebration feast or your last meal. And we will open the case just after dessert."

The Confessor made no move.

"You don't like the idea." Malice's shoulders slumped. "Well, let's just grab hold of your destiny. I can appreciate that."

"I couldn't get the case open."

"But you still brought it here. I'm impressed." He was. A lesser man would have run, but the Confessor wanted power too much. He would risk his life right here and now. Malice decided that if he had to kill him, he would make it quick. Such courage deserved that at least.

"If I didn't, you warned me you would kill my daughter," he said. "Just open the case."

Malice showed all his teeth. "I hope your daughter appreciates how noble her father is." He looked at the locking mechanism. Shrugged. He'd never had any time for the fancy stuff. He released a little energy and the lock popped open. He moved to lift the lid, then stopped. "Is there any message you want your daughter to have... you know if... this goes poorly?"

"Not from you."

Malice shrugged. "Fair enough." He moved the top of the case an inch then let it drop. "No, let's give this a sense of occasion." He clapped. "Martin."

Martin was a large man, a local freak Malice had hired.

He appeared from the back room, a cleaver in his left hand. In his right hand, he held an envelope.

"Now, here are the rules. If I say right hand, you get the envelope. It has a key to a safe deposit box. In that box you'll find account information, contacts, and all the business opportunities you could want. Plus, I will give Martin here as the first member of your organization. If I say left hand, then all your problems will be over."

"Just open the damn box," the Confessor said through gritted teeth. He didn't even look at the left hand.

"Okay." Malice turned to the box then turned back. "But first tell me, what will you do with your new found power?"

"I will show Midas what happens when he goes back on a deal." That came quickly to his lips.

"Ah, the Headsmen's treachery. Excellent."

He turned back to the case. "Here we go." And he opened it.

Two cylinders of blue goo were broken and oxidized, leaving a sticky goo around the inside of the case. But one cylinder was intact. The notes on paper and the CD were still intact.

It was better than Malice could have hoped for.

"Right hand, Martin." Malice smiled again. "A pleasure doing business."

Malice looked on as the two freaks left. He wasn't sure what the Confessor would do with Martin. But he wished them both the best.

"Come out," he told the last freak in the room.

This freak was timid and broken. He smelled like a homeless person and his name was apt. "Well, is it what I promised?" he said.

"Everything and more." Malice produced a second envelope. "You earned every penny."

The freak did not take the envelope.

"Well, what is this?" Malice was concerned this freak would get greedy, and then dead.

"I want to renegotiate our deal." The freak's eyes did not land on him, but darted away.

"Oh." This was displeasing.

"I don't want money." He seemed disappointed, like the money was something he'd thought he wanted, but now that he had it, he realised it was an empty cup.

So maybe there was hope for him. "What do you want?"

"Vengeance."

Malice could appreciate that. "Vengeance against who?"

"Raptor... Caesar!"

That could be a problem. "I already had them both killed. If I'd known your interest, I would have arranged things." He held out his hands, palms up

The freak shook his head. "No, I know they are dead. But it isn't enough. I want what they cared about to be destroyed."

He weighed that. "Well, Caesar's organization is in pieces and his beloved mindreading freak son is dead. I guess we could look for Raptor's wife, but I'm not sure they were even that close at the end."

"No! I want the one thing they both loved destroyed. I want this city to burn!" The small little man's eyes glowed with hate.

Malice tucked the envelope back in his pocket. "You know, I think we can do business. Tell me more, Worm."

From the author, Arthur Mayor.

I hope you enjoyed my story. Get a FREE SHORT STORY, *Origin,* when you join my newsletter. Origin tells the story of when Ryan's powers first manifested, how he met Raptor, and became Raven. The Dark Shadowy Cabal newsletter will also give you updates and new releases from Dark Shadowy Cabal, cover reveals, deep dives into characters, and other "blu-ray" extras.

Become a member of the Cabal today: https://www. subscribepage.com/b5v7p6

Continue following Raven's thrilling adventures in *Vigilante, Superpower Chronicles book 3.*

For my sister,
You read for me before I could read for myself.
*You read **ALL** my early stories.*
You always encouraged me to write more.
Thank you!

ACKNOWLEDGMENTS

Special thanks to my editor Audrey Sharpe

Cover Design by Nicole Montgomery at Significant Cover
https://significantcover.com/

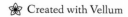 Created with Vellum

Made in the USA
Columbia, SC
13 April 2022

58903056R00202